The Orphans of the Apocalypse

William Vasquez

CONTENTS

CHAPTER 1

The grey clouds moved through the sky without urgency, quite a contrast to what was happening below. Florian breathed heavily and loudly as he was sprinting. The swaying trees moved at a steady pace. He bit on his bottom lip as he ran. Panic and confusion ran through his mind.

These weren't emotions he usually felt. In his panic, he failed to notice the tree root sticking out of the ground and took a tumble. He landed face-first. He felt nothing but adrenaline as he looked ahead. He saw the figure of Ashe sprinting through the forest away from him. Florian got up and rapidly dusted himself off before taking off in a sprint once again. Some mud clung to his face and clothes from the fall.

His lungs burnt as he tried to catch up with Ashe. After five hellish minutes, he had finally caught up with Ashe. Something was amiss though. She had been hunched over on her knees. She had been throwing up. As he walked over to her side, he noticed what she was reacting to. Florian's blood ran ice cold.

The familiar town he knew like the back of his hand, the town he grew up in stood largely unchanged. Tears flowed out of

Florian's eyes while he attempted to fight the bile rising in his throat. The gravel road that stood before them was painted red by the blood of about a dozen corpses that lay on the road. Some of the corpses Florian recognized as the townsfolk within his town. People he engaged regularly with.

The rest of the corpses were men dressed in blue robes. He had heard of these people before from Priest Able. They were known to common folk as Casters. "Alaric...where.." Ashe whispered alongside him. More panic set within him. Fighting his urge to throw up, he walked out onto the gravel road. As he got closer to the corpses he noticed a difference between the corpses of the townsfolk and the corpses of the casters. The townsfolk had some sort of solidified rock protruding from their chest, while the robed men seemed to have their throats slit.

He looked at the cold lifeless faces of the townsfolk. They were in such high spirits earlier. Wooden houses surrounded him as he walked through the town. The gravel road finally forked in two, one path leading straight ahead while the other forking to the left. He could see more corpses laid out on the road straight ahead. Florian chose the path to the left. The large cobblestone building at the end of the road came into sight.

The road towards the cobblestone building however was the worst. There laid about fifty corpses on the road about half of them had been women and children. Florian also noticed that most of the robed men lay lifeless on this road. Florian danced around the corpses in a way to not step on any of them. He now stood in front of the large cobblestone building that he has called his home for the past 20 years.

Florian then saw a figure lying in front of the large wooden doors of his home. The figure had been covered in blood however there had been no rock sticking out of his chest. Florian's face paled. He ran up to the figure. Florian knelt before the bloody man as tears and snot gushed from his eyes and nose respectfully. "Alaric, you cannot die here. I need you...Ashe needs you." Said Florian as he cried in front of his home. Desperate and alone.

Chapter 2

Two Hours Earlier

Florian lay fast asleep on his straw bed when a loud knock broke his slumber. He groggily got off his bed and onto his feet. He rubbed at his light brown eyes, desperately attempting to wipe away his sleepiness. His room was bare. The four cobblestone walls were largely empty save for the one large window where the light shone through.

The only decor within the room was one large chest, where he kept his garments, and a small desk next to his bed. Despite the bleakness of the room, Florian would not exchange it for anything else. More knocking could be heard from his door. The wooden floors creaked as he walked toward the door. Dressed in only his white undertunic and brown breeches he swung open his door revealing the figure on the other side. Alaric stood a good few inches taller than Florian.

Alaric stood frowning at the door refusing to go inside. Florian could sense something was amiss but disregarded it. In many ways, Alaric had been the complete opposite of Florian.

Alaric had short, well-kept black hair in contrast to Florian's unruly and curly brown hair. The differences did not end there however as Alaric's piercing blue eyes contrasted with Florian's soft brown eyes. Alaric had also been very skinny while Florian had been decently muscular. Alaric had worn a white linen shirt with black trousers and leather shoes.

"What have I done now?' Asked Florian

For as long as he knew Alaric, he had always been a very stern person. This was the trait Florian hated the most.

Alaric shook his head as his serious expression turned soft.

Strange.

Alaric finally spoke up. "It seems our water reserves have run out already. I have already told Ashe but I was hoping you both would go and get some water from the spring."

Florian gave Alaric a questioning look.

Alaric saw his confusion and continued to explain. "I spoke to some of the villagers this morning, they have informed me of some sort of leak occurring at the water tower. So I told them that I would send You and Ashe to gather some water for them."

Florian hated the way Alaric would speak of the townsfolk. It felt as if Alaric did not belong with the rest of them.

"Very well, I will quickly gather my things and head out," Florian said.

Alaric nodded at him. "Do make haste however, the townsfolk are getting rather impatient."

Florian rolled his eyes. The townsfolk are usually very care-free. Alaric is probably exaggerating once again.

He turned his back towards Alaric and walked towards his large chest. He heard the door close behind him. He then got dressed. He now wore a brown leather tunic, brown trousers and ended with a pair of brown boots. He reached for the sheathed dagger that lay on the small desk. He quickly slipped the dagger under his belt and exited his room. His room had been on the end of a long hallway. Three other equally spaced wooden doors made up the left side of the hallway.

On the right side towards the middle of the hallway were downward facing wooden stairs. He made his way down the stairs. The bottom floor was large. The floor and walls were made of cobblestone. There were rows and rows of wooden chairs leading up to an altar situated on the north side of the room. The townsfolk led by Priest Able held a ceremony in this room on the dawn of every third day.

Florian attended these ceremonies but never understood their importance. At the southern end of the room in front of two large wooden doors stood Alaric and Ashe. With the exception of Priest Able, they were the only family he knew. The strict, older Alaric and the carefree, younger Ashe. He often wondered what it would be like to have an actual family but always concluded that he prefers his patchwork family.

Alaric eyed him as he descended the staircase. Ashe was the shortest of the group. She had shoulder-length blond hair and brown eyes. She was dressed similarly to Florian however she had a large wooden barrel strapped to her back.

"Greetings sleepyhead," Ashe said with a smile

"Greetings" He returned the smile.

Alaric brought another wooden barrel over to the group and began strapping it to Florian's back.

"What are you going to be doing?" Florian asked, glancing at Alaric.

"I promised Lady Alfreda that I would help teach her kids how to read and write." Alaric finished tying the barrel and stepped to the side

The weight of the barrel was not anything new for Ashe and Florian as they were accustomed to transporting items for the townsfolk, be it water or food.

Ashe pulled on the wooden doors and cool fresh air entered the room.

"Best get going," Ashe said.

Florian followed her as they exited the building.

"Be sure to dawdle!" Alaric yelled behind them.

Never heard that from him before.

The cool air bit at Florian's face as he walked through the town. He greeted the townsfolk as he followed behind Ashe. The small town of Diable, situated on Diable Island, was home to only about seventy-five people. Priest Able had once told him that every person that lived here was outcasted from the mainland. He never understood why, every person on the island was abundantly polite. Besides what would that say about him and Ashe were they supposedly outcasts at birth.

He had asked Priest Able that exact question, the reply he got was that Priest Able found him as a baby on the mainland. Life on the island had been lonely at first, for the first two years of his life it had just been him and Priest Able. He was then joined by Ashe who was still a baby at the time, Priest Able said he found her in the same way as he had with Florian. When Florian had been four years old, their family grew again as Alaric was brought into their house. Alaric had been a year older than him.

Alaric had been very dismissive at the beginning but as time continued he opened up. The only subject Alaric never spoke about was his parents. He had once snapped at Florian and Ashe when they asked him about it.

Ashe and Florian reached the entrance to the forest. The spring was situated amid a forest to the south of the town. Florian could see that Ashe was immensely happy by the expression on her face.

"If only I could find the bliss in doing Alaric's chores as you can," Florian said.

Ashe chuckled. "It is not so much the chores as it is the freedom these chores give me."

He expected this answer. She had always loved going outside and exploring the forest. She had begged Priest Able to allow her to travel with him to the mainland many times, he always told her that one day she would get the opportunity. She had always been saddened when heard that. He thought about the time she ran into the house crying stating that she had seen a gigantic black gooey spider in the forest. The entire town went into the forest that night searching for the spider only to find nothing. Florian chuckled at the memory.

"You're thinking about the spider again, aren't you," Ashe said.

"How'd you know?" Florian asked stifling laughter.

"Whenever we are traversing the forest, you always seem to bring it up."

"Come on, it was funny, you even had Old Dunstan up on his feet ready to hunt spiders."

Ashe flushed.

He knew that she felt guilty about that night.

"Now I wish Alaric joined me instead," Ashe said.

"We both know that is untrue unless you wanted to get lectured the entire way."

"You're definitely right about that one."

They were making steady progress into the forest, the spring was quite a decent distance away from the town.

"Has he been acting strangely?" Ashe asked.

"Who?"

"Alaric."

"You have noticed as well."

Ashe nodded slowly.

"He hates when we meddle with his business. He is most probably stuck on some arithmetic question Priest gave him." They both laughed as they continued to walk.

An hour later they had reached the spring. The spring was a beautiful sight. It was large, the water had been translucent with a tinge of blue and green. Florian, Ashe and Alaric played here many times when they were younger. It had been a place of fond memories for Florian. It represented his happiness, a place where his family were joyous.

Florian helped remove the barrel off of Ashe's back. Ashe was about to do the same with Florian's barrel when a loud screech attacked their ears. Both had placed their hands over their ears. After a couple of seconds, the screech ended. Both Florian and Ashe gave each other worried looks. That has never happened before. Ashe then immediately began to sprint in the direction from whence they had come. Florian withdrew his dagger, cut the rope that strapped the barrel onto his body and took off after Ashe.

CHAPTER 3

Alaric slowly opened his eyes. The cloudy sky and his cobblestone house came into view. He could hear someone sniffling to his right side. Realisation swiftly hit him, he got up and rushed down the stone steps past the figure that sat there and viciously began to throw up onto the gravel.

" A-Alaric...You...alive."

Alaric recognized the voice but remained hunched over heaving. Alaric looked like a mess. His white linen shirt had been stained red. His hands and a portion of his face was bloodied. Alaric took a few moments to recompose himself and then turned to face the figure behind him. Florian's face had been damp, most probably from the tears, thought Alaric. Florian ran up towards him and embraced him tightly.

"Thank heavens, I...thought you were gone." Florian cried into his shoulder.

He gently rubbed the back of Florian's head.

He waited for Florian to compose himself before letting go of his embrace.

"Where is Ashe?" Alaric asked.

"I left her at the southern entrance of town," Florian whispered.

Alaric nodded and headed off. He avoided the corpses as he walked. He dared not to look at any of the familiar faces on the ground. He had a glance at a deceased caster, his body began trembling and he struggled to breathe. Alaric steeled himself and continued forward.

He saw the figure of Ashe right where Florian said he left her. She sat on the ground with her knees tucked firmly behind her arms, she buried her face into her knees. Alaric walked up to her and crouched before her.

"This must be equally as terrifying as that spider, to have you this stunned," Alaric said. He had tried to make a joke but he couldn't hide the tremble in his voice. Ashe looked up towards him. Her once vibrant face was completely replaced by a distraught one.

"A-A-A" She had struggled to speak.

"It is okay, don't speak."

Alaric turned so his back faced Ashe. She knew what this meant, when they were kids she always enjoyed the piggyback rides he would give her. She wrapped herself onto Alaric's back and he swiftly stood up.

"Keep your eyes closed, okay?"

Ashe nodded as she closed her eyes tightly.

They met up with Florian then entered their house.

Ashe dashed straight to her room.

Florian and Alaric stood awkwardly in the middle of the room.

"What happens now," Florian whispered.

"Wait here while I go find freshwater to wash up."

Florian nodded slowly.

A few moments later, Alaric returned with two wooden buckets filled with water. Florian noticed that Alaric had removed his bloodied shirt and walked bare-chested. He examined Alaric's body for wounds but found none.

"What are we going to do about them?" Florian asked.

"I will handle it, just try to get some rest," Alaric answered.

Three days passed at a snail's pace for Florian. He had been immensely exhausted due to the lack of sleep he got. No one spoke a word to each other, they barely ate. The only person to have left the house had been Alaric. A knock came from his door, followed by Alaric's muffled voice.

"Downstairs, now."

By the time Florian reached the bottom floor, Alaric and Ashe had already been seated on their respectful wooden chairs. They had both looked exhausted. Ashe sat with her bare feet on the chair making herself as small as possible. Florian sat on the chair next to hers opposite Alaric.

"What is this all about?" Florian asked.

"We cannot continue as we have, we must speak about what occurred," Alaric answered.

Florian agreed with this.

"What did you do with the bodies?" Ashe's voice came in a whisper.

"I have burnt them."

Ashe nodded at Alaric's response.

"What happened to our town?" Florian asked.

Alaric broke eye contact with him, out of the corner of his eye Florian could notice Alaric clenching his fists. This must be hard for him.

"We got attacked..." They waited for him to continue.

"Casters from the mainland. They ambushed us and used some sort of magic to propel rocks through the chest of the villagers."

"How'd the casters die?" Florian asked.

Alaric was uncomfortable; he shifted many times in his chair.

"The...villagers fought back. It was almost as if they were prepared for this very moment to occur. Alas, they died trying to protect me. Losing the majority of their men, the remaining casters fled leaving me alive." This was not the whole truth. Then Ashe brought up something that plagued Florian's mind as well.

"You knew about the attack, did you not?"

Alaric paused then nodded.

Florian rushed to his feet and grabbed Alaric by the collar of his shirt.

"Why...why did you not warn everyone, why only protect the two of us? This town has been our home for many years!" Tears streamed as he yelled.

"Your home but never my home," Alaric whispered.

As soon as the words left Alaric's mouth he felt a force hit the left side of his face. Florian had punched him square in the jaw. He was about to go for another before Ashe got in between them.

After a moment Alaric spoke up.

"Old Dunstan visited early that morning. He had told me that some of the fishermen had spotted a foreign ship that was approaching the island. He said that I should hide within the forest along with the two of you."

"You should have just told us," Ashe whispered.

"Why did you stay in the town when you got the warning," Florian asked.

Alaric was about to answer when the doors to the home swung open.

Priest Able walked into his home flanked by two identical muscular men. His black robe swayed steadily with the wind, his usual slick thin grey hair was ruffled by the forces of nature. He watched his beloved children as he walked leisurely towards them. Ashe rushed up and embraced him. He wrapped his arms around her.

"It seems as if the situation has turned rather dire," Able said as he glanced at his other two children. They had both been staring daggers at the men flanking him.

"Fret not my dear children. These two men are my dear associates. To my left stands Eros and to my right, Anteros. It will bode well for you to treat them with a little bit of respect."

The two men said nothing, they had been eyeing Alaric with a smile on their face.

Ashe had moved to the side of Able. "Where have you been?" She asked.

"My dear Ashe, during my time within the mainland I had heard word spread that the king intends to raid Diable Island. I rapidly called for my two associates and headed here alas it would seem I was too late," Able explained. "Was Dunstan able to send you a warning?"

Alaric nodded at him, clearly still wary of the twins.

"It is quite a shame the old fool had to die then." "It appears that now might be the correct time for the three of you to commence your mission."

"Mission?" Alaric gave him a questioning look.

"Yes, there had been a reason I brought you three to Diable Island. I will explain shortly, firstly I would like to gather my things." Able motion to the twins and they followed him upstairs.

Moments later they had returned, Eros and Anteros carried a wide wooden box between them. It seemed immensely heavy as the two muscular men struggled to carry it. They placed it in front of the three confused members of the house. Able followed shortly after them, a rolled-up parchment under his right arm and three velvet boxes that he struggled to balance within his hands. The twins removed the boxes from his hands. "Thank you" Able then took the parchment and unrolled it onto the large box. It had been familiar to all of them. It showed the continent that they lived upon.

"Before I explain your mission, I would like to reiterate the history of the land we call Hominus." "Hominus hadn't always been separated in two. It had been one large mass filled with many different races and countries. Alongside Drakenskav to the west and Ysgafyn to the northeast, the realm as we know it had been at peace. Five thousand years ago, however, calamity struck within Hominus. The land itself broke into pieces, and vile dark creatures emerged from the cracks between the land.

Creatures we call 'The Nixum'. The shapeshifting creatures nearly destroyed half of the life on Hominus. As the Nixum emerged, Drakenskav with their incredible technology erected a forcefield around their land. Ysgafyn had closed off their borders, leaving poor Hominus to waste away."

Ashe, Florian and Alaric listened intently as they watched the man who raised them explain history.

"The fire of this land was about to be extinguished when suddenly a young human man emerged showing incredible and mystical powers. This young man was known to everyone as Heinzidal the Saviour. He had fought the Nixum using his abilities. One day he had fought the largest and fiercest Nixum ever witnessed. The battle raged on for days, It had decimated the lands between West and East Hominus leaving only a single island. Both Heinzidal and the Nixum had been killed at the end of it. Saddened by the loss of their saviour and the threat of the Nixum still about, the people of Hominus thought it had been the end. Alas, Heinzidal had offspring that showcased the exact powers he had once wielded. As the generations continued it had seemed that anyone born from the line of Heinzidal had the ability to wield the power. This was how Hominus got introduced to Casters."

"What does this have to do with us?" Florian asked.

"It has everything to do with you, my dear son. For you, three will have to save the world once again."

The statement had stunned them. Able chuckled before continuing.

"With the Nixum threat contained, Hominus was at peace for four thousand years. However, under the rule of the then King

Balthander, the peace fell. He had ordered that all non-powered individuals, whom he called Mysurs, be subjugated to only slave work. Thus the great Zidal Empire became the home of oppression. The other races that resided on West Hominus fled to Ysgafyn. The Sku'al on East Hominus was not that lucky, however. Before King Balthander passed on he had cursed the land with a powerful cast. The cast blocked any child that was born from a caster-mysur relationship from wielding the power. These half-breeds or cursed children are usually killed or exiled. But you would know all about that wouldn't you Alaric?"

Alaric could sense the stares he received but he just nodded along.

"The casters of the empire monopolised Hominus, Diable Island was our last free land until they took that away from us. Those blue-robed casters were soldiers from the imperial force sent to eliminate us."

"That is nice and all but how do we fit into the picture?" Alaric asked.

"You three will be responsible for freeing the mysurs from the clutches of King Godric and imperial forces."

"Impossible, we are just three mysurs." Alaric scoffed.

Able began laughing loudly, the twins followed after him laughing as well.

The rest looked between each other with confusion.

"We have a plan of course. It would be foolish to make an enemy out of the entire continent without a well thought out plan." As Able spoke the twins laid out the three velvet boxes over the map.

"And what if we do not want to take part in your plan?" Alaric asked.

"Then you are welcome to remain living with the ghosts of Diable Island."

Ashe's eyes lit up by this.

"Does this mean we get to go to the mainland?" She asked.

"Yes, my dear. You may not all want to participate in this plan but I know all of you have a reason to journey to the mainland." Able then began to point at Ashe.

"Freedom." He then pointed at Florian.

"Revenge for destroying your beloved community." He then pointed at Alaric and smiled.

"Answers."

One of the twins opened the velvet boxes. It revealed three golden amulets each had ten small black jewels positioned in concentric circles.

"What are these supposed to be," Florian asked.

"Power. It is called a Rixa amulet. A rare artefact that gives the wearer power that rivals that of the casters. Try it on."

After a brief moment of scepticism, Alaric made the first movement. He had grabbed the amulet closest to him. The amulet had been connected to a thin gold chain. Alaric slowly placed the amulet around his neck.

The world went dark for Alaric, his home replaced by a dark abyss. He attempted to move his body but he felt sluggish. It was a familiar feeling, it felt as if he had been underwater. Alaric tried to move his body upwards but paused as he heard a sound. He had not been alone. He slowly turned to face the opposite direction. This had been when he had noticed it. Three larger than life eyes stared back at him. Alaric had been a speck of dust compared to one of the eyeballs. The iris of the eyes had been a dark shade of red. Its pupils had been sharp. Alaric had tried to move away from the mysterious creature but was pulled towards it via some sort of black tendrils until darkness had completely enveloped him.

He woke up to the concerned faces of Florian and Ashe. He had been drenched in sweat lying on the stone floor.

"What happened?" Florian asked.

"Do not be alarmed, it is simply the Rixa amulet binding with one's soul," Able explained.

Alaric did not feel anything different, he took a glance at the amulet around his neck. Half of the black jewels now shone a bright yellow.

Alaric then got back onto his feet and sat back down on his chair.

"Do you feel anything...special?" Ashe asked.

Alaric shook his head.

Florian put on one of the amulets. Alaric watched as his body went into shock. His eyes rolled back until only white remained. He then fell to the floor shaking vigorously. Alaric watched him with concern. After a minute he had completely stopped and returned to consciousness. Alaric helped him to his feet. His amulet shone with a green light.

Ashe seemed cautious about taking the final amulet.

"What is amiss, my dear?" Able asked.

Ashe shook her head.

"I am just a little afraid."

Florian then placed his hand on her shoulder and nodded. This had seemed to give her more courage and eventually she took the amulet. She had experienced the same event as the rest of them. Her amulet shone green as well.

"Before we commence, I will have to warn you that once the Rixa separates from your body it will take your soul with it. You should never remove it."

Rage washed over Alaric's face as he dashed to his feet staring into Able's eyes.

"Before you, outrage, answer me this. Would you have put it on the amulet if you had known the consequences?" Able asked.

Florian pulled Alaric back into his seat.

"If you ever pull something like that again, I will never forgive you," Alaric said.

Able scoffed.

"Be careful with how you speak to me, boy. Do not forget that I was the one to raise you."

"What do we need to do now?" Ashe asked.

"Simple, we train you how to use the amulet effectively." Able motioned to the twins.

The twins then removed everything that lay on top of the box and then opened the box. Revealing many different weapons from shortswords, spears and sickles to polearms and even a pitchfork.

Godric sat comfortably on his throne admiring the structure of the room. He had designed the entirety of the room himself and he could never be prouder. For in this room he was invincible, there was nothing this world could offer that would faze him as long as he was in this room. Godric had spiky, grey hair. His eyes had shone a cold blue. His face had been wrinkled however the most standout feature had been the large scar across his nose. He was dressed in full body armour, it had been mostly silver with a few blue accents. His admiration stopped when the large metal doors swung open. An old man, dressed in a velvet tunic. The old man bowed before Godric.

"My lord, I have a few soldiers that returned from our attack on the Scaev on Diable island." The old man spoke with confidence.

"Good, I have been waiting to hear of our triumphant victory. Send them in, Dalton," Godric instructed. His voice had been very deep and commanding.

"Very well, my lord." Dalton left the room and returned shortly after with two soldiers. They looked incredibly terrified. Strange, I sent twenty soldiers to the island. Godric thought.

The two men still dressed in their blue robes bowed before Godric. One of the soldiers then spoke.

"My King, the Scaev on the island, had been successfully eliminated."

"What happened to the rest of your party?" Godric asked.

Both soldiers swallowed heavily.

"They were brutally massacred, my lord. We only escaped because he let us."

"Who massacred my men?" Godric asked angrily.

"He called himself, Jerial. He was an incredibly powerful caster."

Godric had been stunned. He began rubbing at the scar across his face.

"Dalton."

"Yes, my lord?" Dalton had been equally stunned.

"Call for a meeting, I do not care what they are doing. Gather the Great Lords. " Godric ordered. He looked completely enraged.

Chapter 4

Alaric stood within the forest along with one of the twins, the one called Anteros. They had been separated to train. Florian went with Eros while Ashe went with Priest Able. They had been told that it would be six months until they got to leave the island.

"What are we doing here?" Alaric asked. He hated how Anteros looked at him.

"This shall be your home until you are ready," Anteros said motioning toward the forest surrounding them.

"And the rest?"

"Just as you, they will spend their time gathering strength." "You were foolish to not accept a weapon."

Alaric shrugged. "I do not need to wield a weapon. I will not kill anyone."

"Your enemy shall not think twice to slice off that wise head of yours," Anteros warned.

"I don't need to be lectured on the cruelty of the world."

Anteros laughed loudly.

"You look just like him, act like it too sometimes."

The anger pent up within Alaric.

"Don't you dare say that ever again!"

Anteros just laughed once again. Alaric just gave him a dead-pan look.

After a moment Anteros walked over to Alaric and handed him a few parchments.

Alaric had tried to read the letters on the parchment but he couldn't make anything out. There had been many strange symbols, words not written in any language he had ever seen and a few symbols that looked like a pair of hands gesturing in a variety of ways.

Anteros suddenly spoke up.

"The Rixa emulates the energy that exists naturally within a caster. Essentially transforming a mysur into a caster."

Alaric glanced at his amulet. Where did they get this?

"It is an immensely rare item. Banned from the land of Hominus, it can only be bought from specific...characters." Anteros explained noticing Alaric's glance.

Alaric's discomfort showed on his face allowing Anteros to laugh.

"Why does my amulet shine a different colour to the rest?" Alaric asked.

"That displays your type of casting. Before we get ahead of ourselves, shall I explain the fundamentals of casting?"

Alaric nodded.

"There are four requirements to begin casting." Anteros raised one finger.

"Firstly, to cast one needs stria. Stria is the energy that flows within all casters, the amount differs from caster to caster. It flows like the air we breathe, all around us. It is the only difference between us, mysurs, and them. The Rixa provides us with the energy we lack."

"Is there no method mysurs can use the stria that occurs naturally?" Alaric asked.

Anteros shook his head. "Not at least on Hominus, there are reports that Drakenskav has found a way to utilise it. That is not important though. The next requirement is stamina. Casting is energy-draining, therefore the best casters are always physically fit. Something you have to work on."

Alaric hated the way Anteros analysed his body.

"Is the stamina usage fixed or does it drain depending on the specific cast?" Alaric had been fascinated with the mechanics of casting for a long time. He had often made up many different theories while he sat in his room.

"The more complex the cast the more energy is required. Not that you would be able to cast anything other than beginner casts."

Alaric had been fed up with the insults that were being hurled at him and just started walking away.

Anteros ran after him and placed a hand on his shoulder.

"Where are you going? The boss doesn't like rebellious retainers. You should know all about that." Anteros cupped Alaric's face with one hand then proceeded to knee him in the gut. Alaric fell over and began heaving heavily.

Anteros smiled strangely at Alaric.

"Back to the lesson. The third requirement is material. This could be anything from the ground we stand on, the water that exists in lakes or even the natural existing stria. I am sure you saw the casters using the gravel to slaughter the villagers. They used gravel as the material. The material differs depending on your surroundings, I suggest sticking to using the earth and natural stria."

Alaric was in immense pain but got back on his feet trying to hide his discomfort.

"And the fourth," Alaric asked.

Anteros pointed at the parchment Alaric dropped to the floor.

"The fourth requirement is an incantation of some sort. The language you find on that parchment is known as Heinzidal Text. A language that is known only to casters. The incantations can be done in many different forms. It can be spoken, it can be drawn as a rune, it can be carved onto special items or it is performed via a series of hand gestures. As you are a Phen type, you would only need to learn runes and hand gestures."

"Phen type?"

Anteros pointed at Alaric's amulet.

"There are three types of casters. Sio, Phen and Ilium. Each offers a different aspect. Sio is the type that consists of offensive casts. Phen consists of defensive casts while Ilium casters use supportive casts."

"How'd you know which type I was," Alaric asked.

"The colour of the Rixa. Yellow is usually linked with Phen type caster. Your friends however are both Ilium casters. Phen casters are quite rare, so you should be happy."

"Is it possible to be able to cast two types?"

Anteros shook a finger at Alaric.

"That is impossible. Many have tried, alas one type of caster cannot even comprehend another type.."

Alaric picked up the parchments that lay on the ground.

"We will be cycling between combat training and studying the text until the day of your departure," Anteros instructed.

Klink-Klink. Godric walked down the hallways of his palace. It had been a week since he had received the unsettling news. He had called for the Great Lords to meet and today had been the day. The Great Lords were currently gathered in the palace. It was a rare occurrence for the Lords to be gathered under one roof. At least it hadn't happened since the last King's Rite. The thought made Godric rub at his scar. He arrived at his destination. He motioned for a servant to open the doors for him.

The room was eerily quiet. Five figures sat around a table. Dalton stood next to a chair that was placed at the head of the table. The room had been rather large. Large bookshelves lined the walls. The room had been well lit by many candelabras as well as a flame that engulfed the arm of one of the figures. With Godric entering, the number of people in the room was now eight. Godric sat down. He scanned the others at the table. Three sat to his left and two sat on his right. The Figure on the far left spoke up first.

"The situation must be dire for the King to summon us."

"Quite dire, Umbra," Godric said.

Damiana the Umbra had been the youngest at the table. She was a beautiful woman, she had long auburn hair with green eyes. She was dressed in noble clothing opting to not wear armour.

"Oooo-To have the great King Godric quivering in his boots. This will be quite enjoyable." Damiana said with a large smile.

The rest sat in silence.

Godric glared at her.

"There is no time for your games, Umbra." "Hominus has thrived under my rule. The Nixum has been constrained within the Nix and the Sku'al has been made subservient and possesses no threat. We seemed poised to invade Ysgafyn at the turn of the new year."

"And the Scaev?" A figure to his left piped up.

"Under control, Ivo," Godric answered.

Ivo the Eyes had been dressed in similar armour as Godric but instead of blue accents, his had been green. He had unruly black hair. His eyes had been the most standout feature. It looked like his eyelids had been burnt closed. Large burn scars covered both his eyes and a bit of his forehead. The scars seemed to glow with a tinge of red. Behind him stood a woman in the same armour as him. A mace had been attached to the back of her armour.

"Have you just called this meeting to gloat?" Damiana asked, rolling her eyes.

"Great Lord Damiana, it would be preferable if you would let King Godric finish." Dalton interrupted.

Godric lifted a hand. Dalton noticed it and offered a quiet apology.

"A new threat emerged on Diable Island. A powerful caster took out all of my men. You should all be familiar with him."

The Lords watched Godric with intrigue.

"Jerial the Merciless has risen from the grave," Godric announced ominously. The discomfort clearly showed in his voice.

All the Lords were stunned. Ivo specifically was hysterical.

"Lies...you speak lies. My master died sixteen years ago. We all saw the body. You have to be mistaken." Ivo had been banging his fists onto the table. The armoured woman attempted to calm him down.

"Ivo, my men said he told them his name and let them go. Jerial is out there and sent a message to all of us. We might not know what he is planning but whatever it is, it threatens the current state of Hominus." Godric explained.

Ivo seemed to calm down.

"Adhu Aqua...it is his home he will most probably show up there first," Ivo said.

Godric nodded.

"Ivo, I know he was the man who gave you everything. However, do not let nostalgia take over your common sense. Kill the bastard before you are killed by the bastard. Adhu Aqua is your city, he no longer has any hold on it." Godric added.

Ivo slowly nodded. The armoured woman behind him placed a hand on his shoulder.

A couple of hours after the meeting concluded, Ivo sat in his darkened bedroom.

"Cressela?" Ivo called.

An armoured woman entered the room.

"Yes, my Lord?"

"Once we arrive home, have the soldiers search West Hominus for a man named Alaric. He should have black hair and blue eyes. He should be twenty-one years old."

Cresselia looked unsure.

"My Lord, we have tried to search for him already for years. What makes you so sure he will pop up now?" She asked.

"I am not certain however if my master is still alive, there is hope. Alaric was a smart kid, I will not believe he had simply died that day." Ivo answered. Despite being blind Cressela could feel Ivo had been staring at her.

"Yes, my Lord. I will have my men search all of Hominus if they have to."

Alaric's clothes had been in tatters. His shirt ripped to shreds hung loosely over his body. Over the last six months, he had become very muscular. Gone were the days when he would rely on Florian to do some heavy lifting for he was too skinny to lift anything remotely heavy. These past six months have gone extremely quickly. I cannot believe we get to leave at dawn. His hair grew and he had a messy beard.

Anteros told him that they would meet at the house at night, so he had the rest of the day free. There had always been one thing bothering him while he lived on Diable Island. So he had set out to try and resolve it. This was how he found himself on the southwest edge of the island. The townsfolk rarely went to this part of the island but one event occurred here that stood out to Alaric.

This was the section of the island where Ashe claimed to have seen a gigantic spider. Alaric himself had never been to this part of the island so he did not know exactly what he was looking for. After a few hours of searching, he noticed a small entrance to the cavern. Strange, no one ever spoke of this.

As he approached the cavern, the ground beneath him shook vigorously. Alaric hopped a few paces backwards.

Two black gooey appendages erupted from the ground. The two appendages stood taller than Alaric but they hadn't been wide. The entire monstrosity lifted itself out of the ground. The gooey monster stood many heads above Alaric. It had eight legs and eight red eyes. It had not only looked like a spider, in all aspects this should be a spider if not for the black goo that dripped off of it. Alaric had heard only fairy tales of such monsters. A Nixum.

One so close, how had nobody seen this? The spider charged towards him, lifting its two front appendages to strike Alaric. Alaric panicked trying to remember his training. He then lifted both his hands and then performed a few gestures. The ground before him arched upwards and into a curve protecting Alaric. The spider's appendages struck the lifted ground and stopped moving. A wave of exhaustion ran through Alaric. It is a lot stronger than me. I cannot keep blocking. Alaric stopped his hand gesture and the ground returned to normality. The spider got ready to strike again however Alaric had expected this and rolled out of the way.

He began to run underneath the spider. The spider did not move to face Alaric. It had pointed its romp towards the ground, black goo started to drip onto the floor. Alaric was not bothered by the black goo as he tried to sprint towards the cavern. The black goo began to morph into many smaller spiders, with each spider looking like an identical copy to the large one. Alaric froze dead in his tracks as the smaller spiders walked towards him. The larger spider had begun to turn around. The spiders had almost been upon Alaric when he decided to move. He had sprinted towards one of the large appendages of the spider.

He grabbed the appendage and began to scale it. The gooey consistency made it difficult but he made steady progress.

Halfway up the appendage, he felt a tingling feeling on his skin. He noticed the black goo on his hands and body formed many tiny spiders. The spiders below him had also begun scaling the large spider. Alaric ignored the spiders on his body and began to scale faster. The spiders began to bite at his skin. Once Alaric reached the top of the spider, it began to move vigorously attempting to throw him off.

The black goo hadn't had the best grip but it held as Alaric was swung wildly from one side to the other. He could feel a thousand pricks on his body while he tried to find balance on the swaying spider. Let's hope this works. He steadily made his way towards the spider's face. The red eyes watched him carefully. Alaric looked behind him and saw that the smaller spiders were almost upon him. He then commenced stomping on one of the spider's large red eyes. The spider screeched. So you can get hurt.

Alaric kept his foot on the spider's eye and began to perform different hand gestures. A yellow translucent barrier formed around Alaric, the barrier cleaved a large portion of the spider's face along with all eight of its red eyes. The spiders lost their form and turned into a puddle of goo. Alaric stood on top of the spider, took a huge fall and landed back first onto the ground.

Alaric lay on the ground heaving. His exhaustion outweighed his pain. He watched as the black goo puddle transformed into grey flakes and floated away with the wind. After he had regained some energy Alaric got up, he wiped off the grey flakes that plagued his body. He then began to move towards the cavern. As he got closer he could see that the cavern had been lit. People have been here. The cavern hadn't been very deep, it had also been lit by a series of lamps. When Alaric had reached the end of the cavern he froze.

The room was small, a simple pedestal stood in the middle of the room. Around the pedestal, was the reason Alaric froze. Decomposed corpses lay stationary on the ground, all dressed in blue robes. Casters? And so many of them. Alaric scanned the room, and he found a large carving on the wall behind the pedestal. A symbol had been carved into the wall, a symbol he had recognized.

It was a symbol that was found in his home as well as every house on the island. Able never told them what it meant.

What happens on this island?

The evening had come and Alaric found himself standing in front of his cobblestone home. He could hear some commotion inside so he decided to open the doors. Once he entered everyone stared at him. Ashe and Florian both smiled at him as he entered. They looked much neater than he did. Ashe's hair had been longer than usual while Florian's hair was still a curly mess. Florian had a similar messy beard as Alaric. He made his way to them and embraced them.

"I am glad to see both of you well," He said.

"Compared to you, we both look in perfect condition," Ashe said.

"I had one hell of a day but I will tell both of you about it once we leave this island," Alaric whispered.

They nodded at him.

"Never thought I would ever get to see a muscular Alaric," Florian teased.

Ashe chuckled.

"Do not let me order you guys to do chores again."

They both visibly paled. The group laughed.

Anteros, Eros and Able stood towards the back of the room seemingly discussing something. Alaric noticed the symbol on the altar that stood at the end of the room. The same symbol as in the cavern.

As the night went along, Able and the twins went upstairs, they had stated that they needed to discuss a few matters. Alaric stood behind Ashe trimming her hair.

"I apologise for hiding things from you both," Alaric blurted out.

"You are probably hiding a million more issues from us. But it doesn't matter anymore." Florian said. He had been cleanly shaven.

"Florian is right, you may be smart but most of the time you are dumb. But that is who you are." Ashe added.

"Hey, you better watch yourselves." Alaric chuckled.

"Cursed child or not, you are still Alaric who grew up alongside us here in this village," Florian said.

Alaric's smiling face slowly turned sombre.

"I had wanted to die that day." He stated.

Ashe turned around and watched him.

"Why?" She asked.

Alaric shook his head.

"Just promise me that when I need saving you will be there to help me."

Florian and Ashe nodded at him.

"That needn't even be addressed. We shall always be there for you." Florian stated.

Alaric had finished trimming Ashe's hair and went on to cut his hair before they retreated to their quarters.

Before heading to bed they had each noticed a new set of clothes set out in their room.

The night passed by quietly.

CHAPTER 5

Able stood alongside the northeastern coast of the island. The sound of the waves crashing onto the coast had been soothing. Early signs of light began penetrating the sky.

"I hope they have not changed their minds," Eros said.

"They'll be here. Regardless, he will be here. It is just a matter of time." Able responded.

Able could hear a small bit of chatter in the distance.

"Here they are!" He called.

Three figures clad in black emerged in the distance.

Ashe wore a black tunic, with black trousers and black boots. She also wore a black robe that had a hood. She carried a spear in one hand, using it as a cane as she walked.

Florian had been dressed similarly, however, he hadn't worn a robe and instead of a spear, a short sword hung from his belt.

Alaric had worn similar items however he had cut the sleeves off of his robe revealing his muscular arms. He carried no weapons. Each of them had large packs on their backs.

The group arrived before Able.

It had been a cold morning, if Alaric had been getting cold he hadn't been showing it.

"Greetings, my dear children."

They had responded to his greeting.

"Will we not stand out wearing this...glamorous clothing?" Ashe asked.

"Not at all, my dear. For one to look upon you they will just assume you are a travelling caster."

"Aren't we fighting for the mysurs, why should we look like casters?" Florian asked.

Before Able answered Alaric interrupted.

"We will get nowhere if we are viewed as mysurs. The only way to infiltrate the Zidal Empire is to act as we are casters."

"Zidal Empire?" Ashe looked confused.

"Yes...you know the empire that controls all of Hominus. Led by King Godric. You should know this." Alaric explained.

Ashe flushed.

"Alaric is correct, you do not want to stand out as a mysur who can suddenly use casts. Therefore you should probably hide those." Able said pointing at their amulets.

"Rixa is...taboo within the empire. Anyone seen with it is immediately executed."

They then hid their amulets underneath their clothes.

"What is this mission you want us to do?" Alaric asked.

Able handed a parchment to Alaric, a small pouch to Ashe and an envelope to Florian.

Alaric unrolled the parchment to reveal the map of Hominus.

"Your mission will be simple: find a way to infiltrate the city of Meinspir and then cast the spell within that envelope." Able explained.

"Sounds simple enough," Florian added.

"It is not simple at all," Alaric whispered.

"He is correct. The journey will not be as simple as I made it out to be. It shall be long and arduous. It shall be painful even. You might die. However, you shall learn, get stronger only then shall you accomplish your mission." Able warned.

"Aren't we strong already? What was the training for?" Florian asked.

The twins laughed from behind Able.

"That training only made you as strong as a regular soldier. There are many casters with immense power that exist on the mainland."

Florian visibly paled.

"What is the cast in the envelope supposed to do?" Alaric asked.

"Good question. According to my master, it shall change the realm forever."

Master? Alaric thought.

Ashe opened the small pouch revealing several small jade beads.

"Those are sentz, it is used to purchase goods within the homeland. Use it sparingly." Able pointed out noticing Ashe's curiosity.

"There is still one issue bothering me?" Florian piped up. "How will we get to the mainland, we have no boat to cross the ocean?"

Able moved before them revealing the twins, who were digging into the sand on the beach. They revealed stone steps that lead downwards.

"These steps lead to a portal that transports you to the closest coast on the mainland." Able explained.

"Who built this?" Florian asked.

"Our Master." Able nodded at the twins who returned the nod.

Able led them down the steps revealing a cobblestone wall with a few symbols on it.

"Runes..." Alaric said as he got pushed into the wall.

The wall hadn't stopped him, instead, he felt his body phase through it. He tumbled forward. He turned around to look who had pushed him; however, he was met with a familiar cobblestone wall. Suddenly, through the wall, Florian and Ashe tumbled through it. After they had tumbled through the wall, the runes upon the wall started disappearing one by one. Alaric attempted to put his arm back through the wall but the wall was solid.

"Where are we?" Ashe asked.

Alaric turned to examine their surroundings.

They had been in a narrow cave, it had been dark and there had been no visible exit straight ahead.

"We are in a cave on the coast of the mainland, I have been here before. We have been blocked off from going back. We have to go forward." Alaric said.

The cave was only wide enough for two people to walk alongside each other. Florian and Alaric led the way as Ashe followed behind them.

Occasionally they would walk past skeletal remains that lay on the ground.

"Who built this place?" Ashe asked.

"Most probably the people of Diable," Alaric stated.

"What makes you think that?" Florian asked.

"There are many things they hadn't told us." "Yesterday, I searched the southwestern coast of the island."

Ashe flushed.

"What did you find?"

"A nixum, a large nixum that was shaped like a spider."

"I told you it was real." Ashe poked Florian in the back.

"A...nixum, you got to be joking. Why hadn't it ever attacked the village?" Florian had been in disbelief.

"I had been confused as well. Throughout history, nixum has been shown to be highly volatile and dangerous. There is more to it than that. The nixum seemed to be protecting a cavern."

"I have seen a cavern there once before. I was too scared of the spider back then to pay it any mind." Ashe said.

"What did you do then?" Florian asked.

"I killed the nixum and entered the cavern."

"You have to be lying. It is said that it takes ten men to destroy a single nixum." Florian stated.

"Just how strong have you become, Alaric?" Ashe asked.

Alaric snorted.

"No, it wasn't because I am so strong. Even as I fought it, I felt as if it could've done more. Like it had held back."

"Impossible. Nixum were supposed to be mindless creatures. It wouldn't know how to hold back or to even guard a cavern." Florian retorted.

"I know it should be impossible, that makes it even more perplexing." "The cavern also held some shocking revelations. I found a room filled with the remains of caster soldiers as well as the symbol carved into the cavern's walls."

"Symbol?" Ashe asked.

"Yes, the symbol that is present within all the houses on the island."

"You thinking that things were happening right under our noses?" Florian asked.

Alaric nodded. "Not just thinking, I am pretty confident."

The group walked through the cave in silence for a few moments before Florian brought up a question.

"Do we follow along with this mission?"

Ashe gave him a look of uncertainty.

"Yes, we do. Regardless of Priest Able's other motives, he had been correct on one thing. We all had some sort of reason to travel to the homeland. And if you are uncertain about your goals, we can figure it out on the way." Alaric answered.

They walked for a long time until light broke into the cave in the distance. Ashe squeezed her way past Florian and Alaric, as she sprinted towards the light. Florian and Alaric smiled at each other as they took off behind her. The end of the cave had stone steps that led upward. Crashing waves could be heard in the distance. As they got closer to the exit, the coolness of the cave had been replaced with an extreme warmness. Ashe had reached the top first and stopped. Florian and Alaric tiredly caught up to her.

"It seems we are still no match for her," Florian said between breaths.

"I will never be a match for her." Alaric jokes. "Ain't this a nostalgic sight."

Before they stood vast amounts of sand, it formed large mounds and continued until past their eyes could see. Behind them, the ocean stretched for thousands of metres.

"Nostalgic? Does that mean you have been here?" Ashe asked.

Alaric nodded. "Once, when Priest Able took me to the island."

"You would never see this scenery anywhere on the island," Ashe said. Her sense of amazement had been palpable.

"Which direction do we head first?" Florian asked.

Alaric grabbed his map and unrolled it.

"The most efficient method is to head east and follow the coastline until we reach a river then follow the river until we arrive at Adhu Aqua."

Florian looked confused. "Which way is...east?"

Alaric pointed to the sky. "The direction that Ysgafyn's twin arrives every morning is east."

Florian watched the white ball of light in the sky. "It is a good thing you came along with us. We would've probably been lost without you."

Alaric shook his head. "This is common knowledge. If you listened to Priest Able's lessons you would have known this."

"This is not the time, Alaric. We have the world to ourselves. Let's go and explore." Ashe said as she walked along the coast to the right of them.

Alaric and Florian followed behind her as Alaric continued to berate his lack of knowledge.

After walking for long hours, the evening had come and on Alaric's instructions, they had stopped to take a break for the day. They had all unfurled the bedrolls that they received from Able. The night had been quite chilly compared to the blistering heat they had experienced during the day. At Alaric's request, they have agreed for one person to keep watch at intervals. Ashe had volunteered to go first, then followed by Alaric and Florian would take the last watch.

During the night some mumblings woke Florian up. He glanced at where the other two bedrolls had been. He saw that Ashe had been fast asleep but Alaric had been missing from his bedroll. He looked around and noticed Alaric had been standing on the beach. Florian could hear talking but could not make anything out. He then decided to get out of his bedroll and make his way towards Alaric. As he got closer the mumbling got quieter. Alaric had been standing with his back towards Florian. "Alaric?" Florian called out. Alaric swiftly put his hand to Florian's throat and began choking him.

A flash of purple shone from Alaric's face. As quickly as it shone, it had dissipated.

Alaric released him from the chokehold.

"I am sorry..." Alaric said. His guilt showed on his face.

"Do not worry about it. I was the one who snuck up behind you." Florian explained trying to lift the mood.

Alaric returned to his bedroll.

Florian was left to ponder the event for the rest of the night.

Morning arrived and they took off again. They had brought along dried fruit and nuts from the island, each of them had a flask filled with water as well. Florian watched Alaric as they walked. Unusually quiet. Occasionally Florian would notice him take a few swigs from his flask.

"Be careful, you do not want to run out of water out here," Florian said.

Alaric looked towards him, gave him a half-smile and continued to walk onwards.

Florian patted him on the shoulder. "You don't have to be troubled by what happened last night. Let's just move on as nothing happened."

"I did not mean to hurt you, " Alaric whispered.

Florian smiled. "There is no way you ever would mean to hurt me. I startled you and you retaliated. Can we just go back to how things were?"

Alaric nodded.

Chapter 6

After a few days of walking, the sandy dunes along the coast slowly transformed into marshy green lands.

Ashe pointed at something off in the distance.

"Civilisation. Finally, I was beginning to lose hope." Ashe said.

"We prioritise food and water. We do not want to waste time on unnecessary activities." Alaric said.

"It is not unnecessary, it is called exploring." Ashe retorted.

Florian snorted. "I have to agree with Ashe."

Alaric rolled his eyes.

It took the group about half a day to reach their destination.

The village they had arrived in hadn't been large. It consisted of many wooden houses built extremely close to one another. One wide road separated the village into two. As they entered the village, they saw many people bundled up amid the road. There had been a handful of blue-robed men sitting atop horses looking down upon the villagers that surrounded them. Alaric pulled up the hood of his robe, Ashe had done the same. Alaric turned to Florian and Ashe and placed a finger onto his lips.

They had followed Alaric as he casually walked up to the group forming in the middle of the village and stood on the outskirts.

"...Lord Chapman does not receive his payment, this village shall be torn apart!" One of the blue-robed men yelled.

Florian scanned the faces of the people in the crowd. He noticed that most of them had been women and children. There had been a handful of men but they had been elderly. He also noticed that everyone looked towards the ground, no one was looking at the blue-robed men. Everyone in the crowd had been incredibly thin and wore ragged clothing. Some of the people had been coughing horribly.

After a few more threats towards the crowd the robed men left. The crowd quickly dissipated, leaving only a few people in the street.

"What was that all about?" Ashe asked.

"It seems like this is a mysur-village. And it seems that they are not in the greatest of situations." Alaric whispered.

"These people...are incredibly sad," Florian said.

Alaric nodded. "I sense it too."

"Can we help them?" Ashe asked, looking at Alaric.

Alaric looked unsure. "We...cannot help everyone that is in trouble, if we do that we will never reach Meinspir. We should focus on procuring food and water."

Florian and Ashe both gave him disapproving stares.

"Listen, we prioritise our wellbeing. However, if there is enough information and the risk is minimum then we step in to help. Is that okay with the both of you?" Alaric suggested.

They nodded at him gleefully.

Alaric walked towards an elderly man who stood on the road.

Once the elderly man noticed Alaric, he immediately looked towards the ground.

They think we are casters.

"Pardon me, where can we purchase some cuisine?" Alaric asked.

"Yes, milord. You can find some at that house over there, milord." The elderly man said while pointing at a larger wooden building. "If the food is not to your liking, milord. I can show you to the fields for some fresh harvest."

"That will not be necessary, I am certain the food here shall be great," Alaric said.

The elderly man bowed slightly. "You are too kind, milord."

Alaric rejoined the group.

"This is not right. We are the same as them. They don't have to be acting like this." Florian stated

"It is something we have to get acquainted with. We cannot change a thousand years of oppression overnight." "We lived happily on the island for years while these people suffered. Don't forget that. Suffering comes naturally to mysurs on the homeland. Strange kindness from unknown casters will only confuse them. It is harsh but it is the truth." Alaric explained.

Florian looked downcast.

"Maybe for now, but I want to do as many good things for these people, so they can feel the same joy I felt when I first stepped foot on the mainland," Ashe said.

Alaric nodded. "Once the mission is complete, we can come back and help these people. But for now, let's get some food."

They followed as Alaric led them into the large wooden house. They entered a large room that was filled with wooden tables and chairs. Opposite the entrance stood a wide wooden counter behind which stood an elderly woman wiping the counter with a cloth. She noticed them and immediately bowed.

Alaric led them straight to the counter where they sat.

"It is not every day, we are visited by adventurers. What shall I get you, milords?" The elderly woman asked.

"Adventurers?" Florian asked.

Alaric pointed at his black robe. "Black-robed casters are known as adventurers. Sorry for my comrade, he is a little bit uneducated."

Florian glared at Alaric.

The woman looked at Florian. "I didn't mean to offend you, milord"

Florian shook his head. "You have done none of the sorts."

"What type of food gets served here?" Ashe asked.

The woman kept looking at the floor as she spoke. "Harvest has not been great recently, milady. I can only offer stew. If it is not up to your tastes you are free to beat me."

Ashe shook her head vigorously. "We shall never do such a thing. Stew is perfectly fine."

The woman hadn't been expecting that answer and froze for a minute before walking into a nearby room.

The woman returned with three wooden bowls and set them before the three of them.

Florian analysed the stew. Steam steadily wafted upwards. The stew had been a milky white with a few chunks of orange pieces. It had not been appetising to look at.

Ashe took out her pouch and handed the woman three sentz.

"This far too much sentz, milady. Only one shall suffice."

Ashe looked at the woman with confusion and then at Alaric. Alaric held up two fingers and Ashe gave the woman two sentz.

The woman bowed continuously.

The stew hadn't been the most appetising, however, it had been an upgrade from living on dried fruit and nuts for days.

"What was that gathering about earlier?" Florian asked.

The lady seemed to hesitate. "Ummm...it was Lord Chapman's men. They have come to collect, milord."

"Lord Chapman? Is he one of the five Great Lords?" Alaric asked.

The woman shook her head. "No, milord. Lord Chapman is a rich nobleman that owns these lands. He insists we call him Lord."

"And what do they collect?" Florian asked.

The woman pointed at Ashe's pouch."We grow our crops and sell them to adventurers or merchants that arrive. Lord Chapman takes a portion of the profit as we are renting his land."

"And what happens when you cannot pay?" Alaric asked.

The woman did not answer, instead, she looked towards the ground.

Ashe finished her stew and set the bowl back on the counter. "The stew was really good, miss."

The woman bowed. "I do not need the praise, milady."

"Stop calling me milady, my name is Ashe and what might yours be?"

The woman flushed. "Y-y-you may refer to me as Thea, mil-Ashe."

Ashe smiled at Thea.

"Who are you? Most casters aren't nice to us mysurs." Thea stated.

Before Florian could speak Alaric interrupted him.

"Our town is quite far from the big cities, where we are from, everyone just cares for one another." Alaric lied.

"Then you three come from the barren lands beyond Versus?" Thea asked.

Alaric nodded. Florian looked at him confused but played along.

"Can I have some water, Miss Thea?" Ashe asked.

The woman paused and then shook her head.

"The water here is not healthy, milady. Our folk have gotten sick recently."

Alaric raised an eyebrow. "Where do you regularly receive your water?" He asked.

"The Gwyn River, milord. It is situated a few paces out of the village. Most villages around here use the river for water."

"Have you brought up the issue to Lord Chapman?" Florian asked.

"Lord Chapman just waves us off, milord."

Florian clenched his fists.

"You stated that there are other villages around the river. How do they fare?" Alaric asked.

"There are many villages that are situated along the river that are in the same situation as our village. As you follow the river to the north, the more affluent the villages become. The large town of Isern sits at the north end of the river. It is where Lord Chapman resides."

"That should be close to Adhu Aqua," Alaric stated.

Thea nodded. "Yes, milord. The town sits a few days away from the great city."

The chatter continued as evening drew closer. Thea seemed to dodge most questions about the repercussions of not paying Chapman's taxes.

"Miss Thea, do you know of a place where we may slumber?" Alaric asked.

"One of you can reside in my room and I shall ask some other villagers if they are willing to give up their rooms."

Alaric stopped her. "We do not want to kick you out of your room, Miss Thea. If it is appropriate may we slumber here?"

Thea slowly nodded.

Alaric and Florian began moving the tables out of the way and began unfurling their bedrolls.

Ashe felt a tug on her shoulder as she slept. She groggily opened her eyes. Alaric crouched before her telling her to be silent.

"Florian is missing. Do not panic." Alaric said in a hushed tone. He had pointed at the robe he wore.

Ashe quietly got up and put her robe on as Alaric suggested. She grabbed her spear and followed him out of Thea's tavern. Alaric motioned for her to follow him.

"Where did he go?" Ashe whispered.

"He probably went to the river. I am sure he suspects some foul-play from Chapman's soldiers." Alaric explained.

"Why'd he go alone?"

"Because I would've stopped him. We shouldn't get involved with the issues in this village. We don't want to be making enemies with the wrong people."

They walked in silence for a few moments.

"We can't just ignore them as well. I understand you, Alaric, but Florian and I think differently."

"You both are naive. I have seen what they can do. We are not invincible. We have to take on our battles strategically. We only get involved when our victory is guaranteed."

Ashe decided not to prod any further.

At the edge of the village large trees began to dominate the land. A makeshift path seemed to be carved through the forest of trees.

Alaric motioned for them to go off the path. They walked among the trees just to the side of the path.

Ten minutes later they noticed an orange light in the distance. Alaric slowed his pace and crouch-walked. Ashe had followed him.

Four blue-robed men stood alongside the bank of the river with their arms stretched out towards the river. The area around them had been lit up by a few lanterns. Four horses stood nearby them as well. They had been chanting in a different language.

"They are speaking in Heinzidal Text. What are they doing?" Ashe whispered.

Alaric thought for a bit before answering. "Stria poisoning. I will explain once we get back, for now, we have to get Florian before they get him."

It was difficult to see within the forest at night. Ashe could barely see Alaric who had been directly in front of her. She searched for a few moments when she noticed something out of the corner of her eye. Far towards her right side, she could barely make out a figure behind a tree. The glint of his shortsword caught Ashe's eye. She tugged at Alaric's robe. Alaric looked towards her and she pointed at Florian. He needed to squint to locate Florian.

"This is bad." "Do you have any casts that can distract or stun him?" Alaric whispered.

Ashe nodded. She focused her mind and started chanting in a quiet tone.

It sounded like complete gibberish to Alaric as he watched her cast.

Ashe finished her cast and watched as Florian seemed to move wildly in the distance.

Alaric then moved swiftly and quietly towards him. Alaric put a hand around Florian's mouth. Florian's lower half had been covered by long strands of grass that seemed to grow from the earth. The grass seemed to twist around his legs, rooting him in place.

"Do not do anything foolish," Alaric whispered into Florian's ear.

Florian's tense body seemed to relax as he recognised the voice.

Alaric then slowly removed his hand from Florian's mouth.

"They are doing something to the water here. We need to stop them." Florian whispered.

"I know. We cannot however act rashly and go in with no plan. We regroup at the tavern then we can discuss further. This is too dangerous." Alaric explained.

Florian reluctantly agreed and followed them back to the tavern.

They walked back to the village in silence. They arrived at the tavern, where Alaric set out three chairs.

They all sat facing each other in the dimly lit room.

"Because both of you insist on helping these people. Let's first discuss what we know about this place." Alaric said.

"Chapman and his soldiers are poisoning the people of this town," Florian stated.

Ashe frowned. "Why would he poison the people if he needs them to collect sentz?"

Florian scowled then looked at Alaric who scoffed at him.

Ashe waited for Alaric's explanation.

Alaric sighed before explaining. "I do not think Chapman intends to poison the people."

"Then what does he intend to do?" Ashe asked.

"He intends to poison the crops." "For crops to grow it requires water for nutrition," Alaric said.

"But if he poisons the crops then the harvest will not be plentiful. That means less sentz for Chapman." Florian stated.

Alaric shook his head. "Chapman never intends to collect sentz from this village."

"This is incredibly confusing," Ashe said. Florian nodded in agreement.

"It is quite simple. Chapman sabotages the harvest, then he requests his collection. Once they are unable to pay the sentz, he takes something from this village. What he takes, I am still uncertain." Alaric explained.

They pondered this for a while.

"Men," Florian whispered.

"What?" Ashe asked.

"Think about it. He steals the men from the village. Most of the folk are either women or children with a handful of elderly men."

Alaric chuckled. "Why didn't I think of that?"

"You are not the only one who can think." Florian jokes.

"Why does he need men?"And why doesn't he just take them? This is a rather roundabout way of doing things," Ashe said.

"They are probably used as Chapman's slaves. There is probably a larger reason as to why he cannot just take the men, however that is not of importance at this current stage. We need to determine what we are going to do," Alaric answered.

"I say we take on Chapman's soldiers and force them to take us to him. There we force him to help these people." Florian suggested.

"Incredibly stupid idea. We don't know how many men Chapman has or even how strong they are. And anything we do he will probably make sure these villagers get hurt for it." Alaric said.

It was quiet for a few moments before Ashe turned to Alaric.

"You said those casters were performing something called Stria poisoning. What did you mean by that?" She asked.

"It is a tactic that was popularised during the reign of King Balthander. It involves casters pouring their stria into consumables. While casters will not be affected by ingesting something that is stria enhanced, it is quite poisonous for mysurs. It is probably the reason for the illness amongst the folk." Alaric explained.

Ashe thought for a moment. "I think I have a solution for this place."

Alaric and Florian gave her a curious look.

She then proceeded to explain to them her idea.

Once she was done, Alaric gave her a huge smile. She loved seeing him smile since they were children he had hardly smiled. She used to team up with Florian attempting to make him smile only succeeding a few times.

"That is a great idea. Are you certain you both are up to it?" Alaric asked.

Florian and Ashe nodded at him.

"Great. We move at first light." He stated.

Chapter 7

The villagers gathered in the middle of the road similarly to the previous day, only now they have been gathered around Florian. He had been slightly nervous, but he put on a smile as he faced the folk.

"Hear me, people of Nezzagwyn. You are being fooled by Lord Chapman. He sabotages your harvest, making sure you cannot pay once it is collection hour!" Florian exclaimed.

He heard a few gasps within the audience. The elderly man from the previous day spoke up. "I apologise for what I am about to say, milord. But how can we trust what you are saying?"

Florian grabbed the pouch attached to his belt and emptied its contents onto the road.

The crowd gawked at the floor. Thirty green beads lay sprawled out on the ground.

"I swear that if you cannot pay Lord Chapman's tax at the next collection, you shall have my sentz as well as my head," Florian stated.

Florian could feel the tension lifting within the crowd.

"If what you are saying is true, how do you fix our harvest, milord," Thea stated.

Florian smiled at her. "My associates are handling that as we speak. Alas, our plan will only work in secrecy. Lord Chapman cannot find out about our plan or all our heads shall be on his plate."

The crowd shivered at the thought.

"I suggest we believe in him," Thea stated.

The crowd gave her questioning looks.

"Mysurs has been ruled over by casters for many ages. What difference does it make trusting one caster over another? I believe we choose the lesser of two evils." She continued.

Thereafter the crowd had many questions and he answered them as Alaric instructed.

Alaric and Ashe stood at the bank of the river.

"Why didn't you address the people yourself?" Ashe asked.

Alaric shrugged. "As much as I hate to admit it. Florian is more charismatic. If anything this was your plan you should've addressed the people."

Ashe flushed. "No-no-no, all I did was come up with an idea. You set this whole plan up."

Alaric chuckled as he kneeled.

"How certain are you that this will work?"

"Not certain at all, this is still just a theory," Alaric stated.

Alaric revealed his Rixa amulet and dipped a part of the amulet into the river.

Immense pain.

Red eyes.

Pain.

Breathe, you imbecile. His voice called.

Alaric regained consciousness to a teary-eyed Ashe standing over him.

"Are...you alright?" She asked.

"What happened?" He asked as Ashe helped him to his feet.

"I am not certain...you started screaming and started shaking."

Alaric shook his head. "Let's find out if it worked." Alaric grabbed the bucket they had borrowed from Thea and filled it up with water.

"There was..one more thing...your eyes turned purple for a few seconds," Ashe said.

Alaric paused for a moment. "Must've been from the Rixa, I guess."

They made their way back to the village.

When they arrived the streets were filled with only a handful of people glancing at them.

They entered Thea's tavern where Florian sat at the counter.

"Did it work?" He asked.

"We will not be able to know if it did for a few days," Alaric replied. "Miss Thea, would you be so kind and drink some of this water?"

Thea bowed before him. "Yes, milord." She then proceeded to dip a small bowl into the bucket and drink some of the water.

"What is this theory of yours again, Alaric?" Florian asked.

"We were told the amulet was a substitute for stria. Therefore there might be a possibility that it might be able to absorb stria out of the river." Alaric explained.

"If this does work, won't Chapman's soldiers just poison the river again?"

Alaric nodded. "I am certain that they will, but as long as we are here we will be able to counteract them. This gives us time to stockpile as much clean water as we can."

Florian noticed that Ashe had a very concerned look on her face. "What is the matter, Ashe?"

She shook her head. "It's just that-"

"She is concerned about what happened to me. Let's just say I went through quite a painful experience." Alaric interrupted.

"If that is the case, let's collect more of the water right now," Florian said.

Alaric shook his head. "No, we are not certain if it worked ." Alaric then turned to Thea.

"How often does Lord Chapman collect?"

"I believe he does it once every 30 lights, milord," Thea answered.

"And how often do merchants pass through Nezzagwyn?"

"Merchants arrive from Adhu Aqua once every 7 lights, milord."

Alaric thought for a while. "If Chapman planned to collect yesterday, we have twenty-nine days to obtain the required sentz. Regarding the merchants, only four will arrive before the next collection."

"Milord, I apologise for asking but how will you get to the merchants to purchase our decrepit crops."

Alaric smiled and pointed towards Ashe. "That is where her idea comes in."

Miss Thea and a few other women led the group towards the area they use as a farm. It had been a decent distance from the village. Stood before they were acres of brown crops. Rows and rows of dead plants plagued the fields.

"This is bad," Alaric said. "Tell me, Ashe, that cast you were planning on using won't add any colour to the crops?"

Ashe shook her head.

"Are we stumped?" Florian asked.

"Not quite, We can try the same thing I did with the river," Alaric answered.

"No, you are going to get hurt," Ashe said.

"I will be fine, the stria within the crops will only be a fraction of the stria found in the river. And this will be the perfect test to see if it works." Alaric said in a reassuring tone.

Alaric crouched beside one of the dead plants. He turned his back to the group behind him, hiding the amulet that hung around his neck. He held the amulet against the plant. The pain hadn't been the same as earlier, this time it had only felt like a thousand pricks on his body. Colour returned to the plant. Brown was replaced by a beautiful green. Alaric moved away revealing the results to the group.

Ashe and Florian had been ecstatic while the women had been shocked. Alaric could hear some murmuring amongst themselves.

"Are you hurt?" Ashe asked.

Alaric shook his head. "I told you it would be okay. But we have some work to do, hundreds of crops need to be purified."

Alaric ordered Miss Thea to gather the rest of the villagers and collect as much river water as they can.

The day came to a close as Alaric, Florian and Ashe spent the entire day restoring the crops.

The next morning, the entire village alongside Alaric and Florian stood at the now green farm. They had been watching Ashe who stood in the middle of the farm. She had placed her hands before her. She began chanting, it had been the same cast she used on Florian, the night at the river. In response to her cast, a few crops in front of her grew at a rapid rate. Orange ovals began to appear on the plants. Must be what Miss Thea used to put in the stew.

The villagers did not know how to react to what happened before them. A few bowed, a few cried and a few even dared to smile.

Florian leaned over to Alaric. "Won't casting have the same effect as using stria poisoning on the plants?"

"No, casting influences the stria that exists naturally allowing the plants to grow. Stria poisoning is the direct injection of stria into the plants."

Florian acted as if he understood Alaric's explanation and continued to watch Ashe. Even from this distance, it was noticeable that Ashe had been tiring. She had been casting for an hour. A few crops had been fully grown and ready for harvest.

"Learn that cast," Alaric told Florian. "We need much more crops if the plan is going to succeed. Ashe might be extremely fit however she cannot do more than an hour at a time."

Florian nodded as he headed towards Ashe. At this point, she could barely walk. He helped her walk as they headed back towards Thea's tavern. Alaric stayed behind discussing matters with the villagers.

Once they arrived at the tavern, Florian set Ashe onto a wooden chair. He then grabbed two wooden mugs, poured water into it and gave one to Ashe, who downed it in one swift movement.

"Hey Florian?" Ashe said.

Florian turned towards her. "What is wrong?"

"Did you ever notice Alaric's eye colour changing?" She asked.

Florian froze. "Yes, once before, on the road here. His eyes shone purple for a moment."

"That is strange, back at the river two lights ago, his eyes turned purple for a few moments. He claims it is from the Rixa, but I am not certain of that."

"Strange, knowing Alaric he probably has it under control. I have never seen much that fazed him before."

Ashe nodded. "True though I still worry about him."

The door to Thea's tavern opened a few minutes later. Alaric entered carrying a bucket of the orange ovals.

"What are those?" Ashe asked.

"They are called Khalt, it is a vegetable found only in southern West Hominus," Alaric said. "It is what we had in the stew the other day as well."

"Is that the only thing they grow here?" Florian asked.

Alaric nodded. "It appears that the people of Adhu Aqua rely on villages along the Gwyn River to grow Khalt. It is probably then sold to other cities."

"You know a lot about the mainland," Ashe stated.

"Yes...I have studied the mainland religiously while on the island. But I too know this because...the Great City of Adhu Aqua is my home." Alaric said.

Florian almost got out of his seat. "Impossible, you are saying you lived in one of the six great cities before arriving at the island."

"Yes, but it wasn't as glorious as you made it out to be."

"What is Adhu Aqua like?" Ashe asked.

"Big. Larger than anything you can imagine. It is sad as well, there is a deep sadness as well."

"I wanna go!" Ashe exclaimed.

"Milady Ashe, I am afraid going there shall bring Master Alaric only pain," Thea stated as she entered the tavern. Instead of looking to the ground as she normally did, she stared directly into Alaric's eyes.

"I was afraid that you would be old enough to remember, Miss Thea," Alaric said.

Thea chuckled. "A few of us elders spoke about it. You do resemble him, Master Alaric."

Alaric frowned.

"Maybe you should visit Adhu Aqua. The city has changed since the last reign. And you need to face your past, Master Alaric."

"You have gotten quite cheeky these past few days, Miss Thea."

Thea laughed. "I believe it is the hope you three have given us."

"Who do you resemble? What is going on?" Florian asked.

As Alaric was about to speak, the doors to the tavern creaked open. Four blue-robed men entered. Alaric immediately lifted his hood and went to sit next to Ashe and Florian.

"Old lady, go make some of that terrible stew." One of the men said.

Alaric recognized the men from the first visit to town.

Thea looked to the ground. "Yes, milords." She made her way behind the counter and into the room she claimed was the kitchen.

The four men sat at the counter. They spoke in a hushed tone.

Florian noticed that the men occasionally looked toward where they were sitting.

"Don't do anything foolish, if they speak to us just make your answer short and concise," Alaric whispered.

They nodded at him.

Thea brought four bowls of stew. The men began eating.

"Absolutely disgusting as usual." One man stated.

"Jugz, what would expect from mysurs? Disgusting food from disgusting people." Another stated.

"I apologise if the food is not to your tastes, my milords" Thea bowed.

"Get us some water to wash down this awful taste." The one they called Jugz said.

Thea bowed again. "I am afraid I cannot do that, milord. The water of this town has been making the folk ill."

Jugz snorted. "Useless village, useless people." Jugz was about to hit Thea when something caught his arm.

Florian stood behind Jugz and held his arm in place.

"I am afraid it is terribly ill-mannered to cause a scene while we are enjoying our morning," Florian said.

Jugz and the other three men stood up and faced Florian.

"I beg your pardon, do you know who you are talking to?" Jugz asked.

Alaric walked up and stood in between Florian and Jugz. Jugz had stood at the same height at Alaric. That meant he had been quite tall compared to the rest. Jugz had also been more muscular than Alaric.

"I apologise on my associate's behalf. I believe you are Lord Chapman's soldiers?" Alaric said.

Jugz scoffed. "You need to control your man, adventurer. You do not want to be messing with Lord Chapman."

"I apologise once again. I am afraid we are new to town." Alaric grabbed Florian and headed back towards Ashe.

Jugz followed them and placed an arm around Alaric's shoulder.

"You know what, I apologise for ruining your morning," Jugz revealed a dagger he had been carrying with him. "We had come here to kill the old lady, but I would like to give you the honour," Jugz whispered into Alaric's ear as he shoved the blade into Alaric's hands. Jugz headed back to the counter.

"They call you, Jugz. Am I right?" Alaric said.

"Master Jugz, for someone of low rank like you." One of the other men said.

"How much do you know about Rites?" Alaric asked.

Jugz and his men paused a bit before laughing.

"Rites, a duelling practice popularised in the Great Fire City of Impestra. It is quite an ancient practice back when Impestra was still untamable. Where two casters disagreed and fought righteously to prove their point. Once the duel is concluded both parties are rebuked from mentioning it ever again." Alaric stated.

"I know what a Rite is, young man. Are you suggesting we hold a Rite right now?" Jugz asked.

Alaric shrugged. "Why not, you wanted me to do something and I refuse. I see no other way to settle it. Or are you afraid of embarrassing yourself to Lord Chapman?"

Jugz laughed. "I will do it but I will not face you, I will face him." Jugz pointed at Florian.

"That is perfectly fine by me," Alaric replied.

Alaric turned to Florian who scowled.

"What is this Rite thing about?" Florian whispered.

"You will have to duel him, don't worry about it. Just focus on your training." Alaric said.

Alaric left the tavern following behind him was Florian and Ashe. A few moments later Jugz exited the tavern alongside his men.

"Is one of your men a Phen type?" Alaric asked.

Jugz nodded. He called for one of his men and the soldier stepped forward.

Along with the soldier, Alaric began to carve runes onto the road. He remembered asking Anteros to teach him the runic text specifically for Rites. The runes had formed a wide circle around which stood Florian and Jugz.

"You were the one insisting we don't cause trouble, why'd you antagonise him?" Ashe asked. She still seemed fatigued.

"Curiosity," Alaric answered.

"Is that it?"

"I wanted to find a way to determine just how strong we'd become compared to regular casters."

"And you are willing to put Florian's life on the line because of your curiosity?"

"You are worrying too much. Rites are usually not a fight to the death. If the situation becomes too dire, I will pull Florian out."

Ashe looked unconvinced.

A crowd quickly gathered around the commotion.

"Do not waste my time!" Jugz called out.

Alaric turned towards them. He stood behind Forian and at the opposite end, the other Phen caster stood behind Jugz. They began moving in tandem. They have done various hand gestures before placing one hand on the ground. The runes on the ground shone a light yellow as a yellow translucent barrier separated Florian and Jugz from the rest of the crowd. Alaric knelt, maintaining his hand on the ground.

Florian watched Jugz as he removed his shortsword from his belt. Jugz held his sword in his hand.

He probably has more strength than me.

Once the barrier around them was erected, Jugz immediately began to chant. A portion of the road broke off and floated in the air before Jugz. The solidified gravel then shot towards Florian, who ducked. A second projectile shot at him. He had no time to dodge. He parried the gravel away with his sword. Florian hadn't been prepared for a third projectile. He moved slightly out of the way but the gravel scraped his left shoulder.

He doesn't intend to give me any time. His shoulder had drawn blood, which now had slowly begun to travel down his arm. Florian gripped his blade tight as he charged at Jugz. He had been murmuring words as he charged. Jugz shot more gravel projectiles at him. Florian had sidestepped them as he got closer to his foe. Once Florian had been within distance, Jugz got prepared to strike him down with his blade.

As Jugz was about to strike, his body suddenly lost balance. He took his eyes off of Florian for a second to look at what had happened. The ground under his left foot liquidated. Jugz reacted just in time as he leaned his torso backwards. Florian had slashed at his chest. Not deep enough. Florian had cut through Jugz's blue robe and left a long shallow cut across his chest.

Florian hadn't expected Jugz to recover as quickly as he did. Jugz caught him with his right boot. Florian was flung backwards by the force of the kick. Florian landed on his back. He made sure not to let go of his sword. His abdominal area had hurt.

"Ilium users, tricky little bastards. Alas, you would need to do more to beat me." Jugz exclaimed.

Florian got to his feet as Jugz attempted to strike him. Florian brought up his sword to parry the strike. His whole body swayed to the side as he parried the strike. He is too strong. He had been tired already, sweat dripped down his forehead. The difference in swordsmanship skill was evident. Jugz gave no time for Florian to cast, he was overwhelming him with his strength. Think Florian, what would Alaric do?

"You are a persistent little rat," Jugz called out.

Florian was too tired to reply. Wait, how'd they find me that night in the forest. Florian eyed his sword as he blocked Jugz's next flurry.

Of course.

Instead of parrying Jugz's next attack, he had jumped backwards. His back had almost been against the barrier. He lifted his sword awkwardly. His stance changed. He held the sword close to his face and angled towards the ground. Jugz closed in on him. Florian closed his eyes. He chanted as fast as he could. Jugz was upon him in a flash however he stopped just inches in front of Florian. An incredible white light shone from Florian's blade. It had blinded Jugz as well as everyone in the crowd. The light only lasted a few seconds. Florian opened his eyes. Jugz held one hand to his eyes. Florian took the opportunity to slash at him. Florian slashed right across his torso. Jugz yelled in pain as he fell to his knees.

"Tricky...bastard." Jugz groaned.

Florian had barely been conscious, he limply held his blade towards Jugz. He watched as the yellow barrier dissipated around them. Jugz men unsheathed their blades and charged towards Florian. This is the end. As they were about to strike him, a yellow barrier appeared around him. Alaric appeared next to him. His arms had been crossed and he made some sort of sign with his hands. The blades struck the barrier and ricocheted off of it.

"You men intend to disregard a Rite. You would dare to demean your lord's name!" Alaric exclaimed.

The soldiers looked confused at one another.

"He...is...correct. Stand...down." Jugz coughed. He had been losing blood at a rapid rate. Following Jugz 'command, they had sheathed their weapons.

"Fetch the horses!" One caster called out. Once the horses arrived, the casters sped away along with the injured Jugz.

Ashe walked towards Florian when he had suddenly collapsed. Luckily Alaric caught him before he fell to the ground.

"Well done, you made everyone on Diable proud today," Alaric whispered.

The crowd cheered as Alaric carried him back towards the tavern.

CHAPTER 8

It had been evening when Florian regained consciousness. He had been laying on a straw bed, not unlike the one found in his room. He had been in a small room. He felt a sharp pain in his left shoulder as he moved. He noticed that his left shoulder had been wrapped in some sort of cloth.

He exited the cramped room and headed down the stairs that followed. Familiar surroundings met him as the bottom floor had been Miss Thea's tavern. Ashe was asleep on her bedroll softly snoring. Alaric and Miss Thea had sat at the counter discussing amongst each other. He slowly made his way to the counter and sat next to Alaric. Miss Thea bowed to him as he sat down.

"Has that battle taught you anything?" Alaric asked.

"Yeah, do not go along with your crazy plans," Florian stated.

Alaric chuckled. "Yes, and I wanted to show you that casters from the mainland are strong. I am certain Jugz is not a high-ranked caster."

Florian nodded. "I thought I was going to die...and I..."

"Almost killed him?" Alaric asked.

Florian nodded.

"I know, it is something that you will have to get acquainted with. You chose to wield the blade, you have to take responsibility," Alaric said sternly.

"Master Alaric, perhaps you shouldn't be too harsh on Master Florian."

Florian smiled at Miss Thea. "Do not worry about it, Miss Thea. He has always been like this, even when he was a child. It would be out of character if he had said anything else."

The trio sat in silence for a moment.

"What cast did you use to blind Jugz?" Alaric asked.

"It was a simple enhancement cast. It is not dissimilar to Ashe's plant enhance cast." Florian explained.

"Can you enhance anything?"

Florian shook his head. "Enhance is one of the most basic Ilium casts. Enhancing the light as I had done earlier is usually used to light up dark areas. Using enhance for more complicated tasks requires a large stria consumption, which is not normally present in regular casters."

Alaric had been incredibly invested in Florian's explanations. At some point, Miss Thea left. They had discussed their casting ability until they had grown tired.

The following morning, Alaric stood in the middle of the road. Alongside him had been many of the women of the village. Each had been carrying a bucket filled with Khalt.

"Are you certain he will be here?" Alaric asked,

"Yes, Master Alaric." One of the women said.

A few moments later, a large carriage rode into the village pulled by two horses. A stout man sat at the head of the carriage.

The carriage stopped right before Alaric. The stout man got off the carriage. The man had been incredibly short, he wore a suit but it appeared too tight on him.

"Greetings, mysurs of Nezzagwyn." The merchant said. The women bowed. The man eyed Alaric cautiously.

"I assume the harvest is still bad?" He asked.

"That is not quite the case...Noble..." Alaric said.

"Gerboud, the name is Gerboud." The merchant said.

Alaric allowed the women to showcase the Khalt in the baskets.

Gerboud had been stunned. "Impossible..."

"What perhaps do you mean by 'Impossible', mister Gerboud?" Alaric asked.

"What have you done?" Gerboud seems terrified.

"Let's discuss matters in private, Mister Gerboud."

Gerboud nodded.

Alaric ordered the women to transfer the buckets onto Gerboud's carriage. He then led Gerboud into Miss Thea's tavern.

Alaric pulled out a wooden chair gesturing for Gerboud to sit. Gerboud hobbled towards the chair.

"Mister Gerboud, we will have to negotiate the price you are going to pay for the Khalt," Alaric said. He put one hand onto Gerboud's shoulder, he then moved to sit opposite him.

"You must be mistaken, sir. This village has no Khalt, the harvest should be bad."

"My, my. How could you have been so certain of that? Have you gone to the fields to check for yourself?" Alaric asked.

"But Lord Chap-" Gerboud paused.

Alaric acted shocked. "Are you telling me that Lord Chapman has told you lies about the harvest? Are you calling Lord Chapman a liar? I am pretty sure Lord Chapman wouldn't like that."

Gerboud began sweating. "You, this is your doing. Who are you?"

Exactly, what I wanted. Alaric smiled. "Some call me merciless, some call me insane, some even dare to call me a genius. Alas, most know me by the name Jerial."

Gerboud froze.

Alaric got up and moved behind Gerboud. "You are going to buy all the Khalt this village has to offer for well over market price." Alaric ran a finger across Gerboud's neck. Gerboud shivered under the touch. "If you don't buy whatever they offer, dead. If you squeal to Chapman, you and whatever you love, dead." Alaric whispered.

Gerboud didn't say anything.

Alaric grabbed his shoulder and put some pressure on it. "Well...Gerboud."

"Yes...My Lord. I-I will do as you say!" Gerboud exclaimed.

"Very good, now we demand fifty sentz."

"But my L-"

Alaric tightened his grip on his shoulder.

"Very well, My Lord."

Gerboud brought out a large sack, he then proceeded to count out fifty jade pieces. Once he was done, Gerboud immediately returned to his carriage and took off with the Khalt.

Alaric left the tavern where more villagers gathered. They looked at him with wandering eyes.

"We have successfully procured fifty sentz for our harvest!" Alaric announced.

The folk cheered.

"Alas, our battle is not over yet. We may have already acquired enough to avoid the first collection, however, Nezzagwyn still has some journey to get through. We shall not leave until your land is stable."

The cheering continued. Some even chanted his name.

Alaric headed back into the tavern.

I am just like him.

Alaric felt the bile rise to her throat as he emptied the contents of his stomach onto the wooden floor.

"Oh, dear. Master Alaric, are you ok?" Miss Thea said as she entered the room.

"I...am...perfectly...fine," Alaric said between pants.

Thea swiftly fetched a bucket of water and a cloth. "Was it the stew? Or the water?" She asked.

Alaric shook his head. "It is truly nothing, Miss Thea. Thank you for your concern." Alaric composed himself and began to help Miss Thea clean up his mess.

"That will not be necessary, Master Alaric," She said.

"I insist, it was my mess."

Florian and Ashe stood in the middle of the field of crops. Florian stood in front of an overgrown brown plant with his arms straightened out in front of him.

"You are using too much stria," Ashe instructed.

"You can control the amount of stria you use when casting?" Florian asked innocently.

Ashe gave him a deadpan look. "What did you learn back on the island?"

Florian scratched his head. "Uhm...to understand the Heinzidal Text and cast. The rest of the time was spent training my athletic ability."

"Oh, Heinzidal's grace...maybe I shall ask Alaric to lecture you about the intricacies of casting," Ashe said.

"That's unfair...you already had amazing athletic ability, all you had to learn was the casting. What did I have before the training?"

"Nothing." Ashe laughed.

"Not funny at all." He chuckled.

They quickly fell into silence as Florian attempted and failed the cast once again.

"How strong do you think Alaric is?" He asked as he wiped the sweat off of his forehead. It had been warmer here than on the island. It had been a change they had still been adapting to.

Ashe shrugged. "He said he fought a Nixum so I would guess he is pretty strong." "He always had an untouchable aura around him."

Florian nodded. "He can't be fazed, in his mind at least." "You noticed how the people look at him?"

Ashe nodded.

"They think of him as a messiah, Ashe." "It is not right. They are no different to us. We help them through a guise of lies."

"Maybe...it's time we left this place. Alaric warned us against helping these people. We were the ones who convinced him." Ashe said.

Florian sighed. "Maybe we deserve to feel this guilt."

"Just maybe we do," Ashe replied.

The duo worked in the field until dusk whence they returned to the tavern.

When they arrived, Alaric had been sitting at the counter as per usual. They joined him as Miss Thea brought them stew to eat. They ate their stew in silence. Miss Thea left as they ate.

"Alaric?" Ashe piped up.

Alaric did not respond, he stared into nothing as he seemed unfocused.

Ashe shook his shoulder.

"What is the matter?" Alaric asked.

Ashe paused before speaking. "Florian and I...were wondering if we can leave Nezzagwyn soon."

Alaric burst out with laughter. "What had I said that first night? Naive. That is what both of you are. You cannot back out now, we've only begun. What will the people of Nezzagwyn think, us casters leaving them to rot after giving them a glimpse of hope." Alaric mocked.

Ashe knew what he had said had been correct but the way he had said it made her angry.

The doors to the tavern suddenly opened, Miss Thea entered alongside a dozen or so women.

They bowed before the trio.

"We have come with a request. Master Alaric." Miss Thea said.

Alaric raised an eyebrow.

"We may sound selfish and what we request may be disobedient." She continued.

"What is this about?" Alaric asked.

"Us, folk have been discussing." "We wish for you three to leave Nezzagwyn and find a way to return our husbands, fathers and sons to us."

Alaric shook his head. "Impossible. That would require facing Chapman, we do not have the strength to perform such a task. And that would mean you would go back to how things were before."

"We understand the task may be extremely difficult. But what Master Alaric showed us these past few days, us mysurs had never had a reason to hope."

"No, I am just one man...there's just no way."

The women began looking downcast.

"I believe you underestimate yourself too much, Master. You are an astute young man, you remind me of-"

"No!" Alaric interrupted abruptly.

His tone shook everyone.

"I have a suggestion," Ashe stated as she stared at Alaric. "A Rite, me and you. I win and we do as these people say. If I lose, we will continue your plan and stay here."

Alaric snorted. "You cannot be serious."

Ashe looked at him sternly. "Deadly serious."

"I don't want to hurt you, Ashe."

"Then surrender," Ashe suggested.

Alaric thought for a moment. "Fine, I agree to the rite."

Ashe nodded.

"We do not wish to cause harm between you masters." Miss Thea said.

"Do not fret, this is a happenstance that needed to occur," Alaric said as he headed out.

Ashe went to grab her spear.

"Are you sure about this?" Florian asked.

"He is too stubborn and too smart to change his mind. This is the only way to get him to change his mind." Ashe responded while doing a few stretches.

"Don't do anything reckless, you have been casting all day."

"I will be fine. You know, I am confident I can overwhelm him with my athletic ability." Ashe smiled. She carried her spear with the bladed edge pointed to the ground.

"Be safe, okay."

Ashe waved him off as she exited the tavern.

The evening was young. The sky was illuminated with a dark shade of blue. The night sky was clear. The light of Ysgafyn's twin had been enough to illuminate the realm even after it had dispersed for the night. The town of Nezzagwyn had been lit up with a handful of lanterns.

Many of the townsfolk stood outside their respective houses.

Alaric stood in the middle of the road, his black robe and dark hair made him look like a shadow in the night. He eyed Ashe as she exited the tavern and walked towards him. She stood opposite him about fifteen feet away.

"I cannot cast a barrier and fight you! Be careful with your casts!" Alaric yelled.

Ashe nodded.

"Well then, let's begin!"

Ashe immediately charged toward him. She kept her body low and once he was in range she struck with the blunt side of her spear. Alaric dodged to the side and attempted to grab her spear but she had been too fast and whisked it away.

Don't give him time to think. She quickly tried to strike him down. He rolled out of the way of her strike. He created some distance between them. He waved his hands around. Ashe paused.

What is he going to cast?

Alaric smiled as he stopped the gestures and charged her. Ashe hesitated as Alaric's right boot viciously kicked at her left knee. She planted the bladed side of her spear into the ground to prevent her fall. Her left knee throbbed. He is not holding back.

Ashe didn't have time to think as Alaric went for another strike. She quickly spun around her rooted spear and aimed a kick at Alaric's head. A few centimetres from his head she felt her foot strike something. There had been a pale yellow barrier blocking her from striking him. But he is not doing any gestures. She followed his eyes as he revealed something to her. At his feet, there had been a symbol carved into the gravel. Runes. He baited me.

Alaric swiftly struck her torso with a firm punch. The air disappeared from her lungs. She let go of her spear as she was tossed back from the blow. Alaric hadn't moved, instead, he opted to remove her spear from the ground and tossed it towards her. It landed a few metres away from her.

Ashe regained composure. Her torso and knee had brought her great discomfort. She grabbed a few stones from the gravel road. She got to her feet and began to chant. She grabbed her spear and tossed the stones at Alaric. In midair, the stones enlarged. The stones hit Alaric's barrier and fell to the ground. Alaric however was too focused on the stones that he didn't notice Ashe's charge.

Instead of attempting to strike him, she opted to disrupt the symbol on the ground. With his rune destroyed, Alaric swung a kick at Ashe. It had hit the left side of her torso. Ashe was once again tossed back by the force of the blow. She heard the clink of her spear hitting the ground.

She had been panting. I can't beat him. She attempted to move. Everything hurts. She hobbled to her spear and picked it up. She held the blunt tip of her spear towards Alaric's chest. This is my only chance. She began chanting. Suddenly her spear began to stretch forward. Alaric's eyes widened in shock. The spear was going to strike him in the chest. Instead of striking him, it appeared to have passed through him.

Alaric's appearance went ghostly. His body appeared to be incorporeal. Ashe glanced at his hands. His fingers had been twisted in weird ways. The spear passed back through Alaric as it shrinked and returned to its regular form. Alaric let go of his gesture and his body went back to normal again. She noticed him walking towards her; however, another figure blocked her vision.

He is untouchable. She thought as she lost consciousness.

She woke up to Alaric wrapping some cloth around her torso. Her body ached as he wrapped the cloth. The sadness in his eyes seemed magnified.

"I am so sorry." He whispered.

Ashe tried her best to muster a smile through her discomfort. "I would have hated you if you hadn't taken the rite seriously." "Now don't feel bad, I will not be able to hide my frustration."

Alaric smiled at her. "We are leaving the day after tomorrow."

"What? But our agreement was..."

"If I had won, we would stay in the town. You never stated how long we have to stay." "We will be staying for one more day."

Ashe was lost for words.

"We have a lot of work to do tomorrow, get some rest."

Once Alaric had been done treating her, he began to leave the room.

"Alaric," Ashe called out.

Alaric hummed in response.

"You are not untouchable, one day when you are vulnerable allow us in, okay?"

"I know," Alaric said as he left the room.

Ashe allowed her fatigue to wash over her as darkness crept into her eyes.

CHAPTER 9

Ashe and Florian stood in the fields just as they had the previous day. Ashe's body had still been in pain. She cast and the plants grew. Florian had helped some of the villagers cultivate the Khalt. Once Florian had been close enough Ashe spoke up.

"You didn't say anything dumb to Alaric, right?"

Florian shook his head. "At first, I was angry when he struck you down the first time. But once I saw you try so hard to beat him. I felt that if he had shown you mercy, that would have been disrespectful." "I wouldn't have known what to do if I was in his shoes."

Ashe chuckled. "You would've done the same." "Alaric is strong, he might not have the brute strength of that Jugz guy but he sees the battle differently to you and me."

"What do you mean by that?" Florian asked.

"It is hard to explain. It is like he rigs the battle from the start." "He left the tavern earlier last night to draw the rune onto the road. He knew I had to grab my spear."

"He cheated?"

Ashe shook her head. "No, he just planned better. I think we can get stronger if we begin to think like he does when we battle."

"I don't think that is what you want to do." Another voice popped up.

Alaric walked between the fields holding buckets filled with water. A few women stood behind him with their buckets.

"Do not try to fight like me," Alaric said once again as he sprinkled some water over the plants.

"Why not?" Ashe asked.

"My way of fighting has its weaknesses as well." "Take Florian's fight for example. I wouldn't have fared any better than Florian had against Jugz."

"You could use your barriers to block his attacks though." Florian brought it up.

Alaric shook a finger at Florian. "I can't block everything. If the attack is powerful, it takes a large toll on my body. I get extremely fatigued if I constantly erect barriers as well. And I cannot move when I cast a barrier." "There are many weaknesses that I have, the best way to improve is to adapt to your weaknesses."

"Great, this is turning into another lecture," Florian said.

Alaric chuckled. "My point being, that you should use your strengths to the best of your abilities. That means Ashe, continue using your ever-impressive athleticness. And Florian, use your quick wits. Only when you do this well, will you overwhelm your opponents."

"Where did you learn all this?" Ashe asked.

"I read it in a book I found in Priest Able's room."

"Maybe we should've read more." Ashe laughed.

Florian shuddered at the thought.

The trio laughed as they continued to work.

The twins' light was dissipating as the trio got back to the village. Florian had helped Ashe walk. The village was different this evening. Wooden tables stood spread out on the road. The people of Nezzagwyn looked incredibly busy but they had smiles on their faces.

"What is happening?" Ashe asked.

Alaric spotted Miss Thea and went up to her.

"Oh, Master Alaric. You are early, we are still preparing." Miss Thea bowed.

"Preparing what exactly?" He asked.

"A feast."

"A feast for what?"

"For our three masters."

"Why?" Ashe asked.

"There is a tradition amongst the Gwyn people, whenever a prosperous time ends we celebrate with a feast." Miss Thea explained.

"That cannot be good for the state of the village, Miss Thea. We do not need a feast." Alaric argued.

"This cannot be argued against, Master Alaric. Everyone in the village agreed to the feast. We are thankful for the hope you continue to give us each passing day."

Alaric looked to argue further but Ashe stopped him.

"Some things do not have to be explained by logic but rather from the heart. And these people wish to share their heart with us." Ashe said.

Alaric reluctantly nodded.

Miss Thea led the trio to a table and brought three wooden mugs. Ashe drank it but almost spit it out. It had been bitter.

"What Is this?" She asked. She stared at the dark yellow liquid.

"This is Adhu Aqua Ale. I have kept it for special occasions. Is it not to your liking, dear Ashe." Miss Thea asked.

Ashe shook her head.

Alaric and Florian seemed to enjoy the drink.

"This is a fascinating drink, Miss Thea," Alaric said as Florian agreed with him.

"I can't drink this, it tastes terrible," Ashe said.

Miss Thea bowed. "I apologise, I shall bring another beverage shortly."

Once everything had been set up, the townsfolk joined the trio. The feast had not been very large but the atmosphere oozed joy. People had been dancing and people had been laughing.

Ashe smiled as she watched her brothers. Florian had way too much ale and had been swaying as he tried to dance with the folk. She watched as Alaric downed another ale but looked as stern as ever. The celebration was halted as a voice exclaimed.

"What is the meaning of this?" A woman stood on the road looking at the feast. Her hair had been cut short, and she had a rugged look to her. Her clothes had been torn in places. She held a blade in her left hand. She walked up to Florian with her blade pointed at him. Alaric stepped between them.

"What did you, casters, do to my village?" She asked.

"We have done nothing. You are the one pointing the blade." Alaric replied, his voice did not have the sharp edge as it normally did.

The woman swung her sword at Alaric. Her sword bounced off Alaric's yellow barrier as he swiftly cast.

"Thorin! Stop that right now!" A voice called.

The woman, named Thorin, paused.

Miss Thea slowly walked up to her.

"You cannot harm these people." Miss Thea said.

"But grandma, they are casters. How can you feast while they are here." "Did you forget what they did to us? Us mysurs."

Miss Thea shook her head.

"Master Alaric and his friends are not like the rest of them." "They helped us greatly."

Thorin was shocked. "This can't be! They are manipulating you. They have to be!"

Alaric put a firm hand on Miss Thea's shoulder. "It seems our time here has run out. We shall retire for the night. We wouldn't want to cause trouble."

Thorin held her blade towards Alaric the entire time. Alaric helped Florian walk as he gestured for Ashe to follow. They went into the tavern.

"What was that all about?" Ashe asked.

"She is a brave mysur. It takes a lot of courage to stand up against a caster." Alaric answered.

"Why didn't you stand up for yourself?"

Alaric rubbed at the stubble on his chin. "Nothing I explain would put her at ease. More trouble would've brewed had I opened my mouth."

Florian had passed out immediately as Alaric carried him to his bedroll. Miss Thea entered the tavern later, standing with her had been Thorin.

Miss Thea bowed. "I apologise for the happenings this evening, Master Alaric."

Thorin scowled at Alaric.

"It had been no bother to us. We quite enjoyed the feast but it had grown late and we were going to retire regardless." Alaric stated as he smiled.

"Don't let my grandma fool you, I do not trust people like you," Thorin said.

Alaric chuckled. "That is something we have in common." "Now if you will excuse us, we will like to rest for the night."

"Very well, Master Alaric."

Thorin glared at Alaric as she left with her grandmother.

"Won't she try and...kill us while we sleep," Ashe asked.

Alaric shook his head. "She might be brave but let's hope she is not stupid."

Thorin stood staring at fields outside Nezzargwyn. Orange vegetables stood proudly in the early light.

"How?" Thorin asked.

"This is only a portion of what they had done for us." Miss Thea said. Thea revealed a pouch filled with sentz.

"Why would they do this?"

Thea smiled. "I think they are just good people sent to us by Heinzidal's grace."

"Casters are not good people. They took papa." Thorin said.

Thea placed a reassuring hand on Thorin's shoulder. "Master Alaric is journeying to Isern to attempt to free our people." "Why don't you travel alongside them? It is much safer than having you here, antagonising Lord Chapman's forces."

Thorin scowled. "Why do you trust this Master Alaric so much?"

"He has a good head on his shoulders." "You could learn a thing or two from him."

Thorin sighed. "You are too trusting."

Thea chuckled. "It is a far easier way to live." "Come on, let's go home."

Thea walked back to town followed by Thorin.

Alaric, Florian and Ashe stood in front of the tavern.

"Miss Thea, you have returned. We did not want to leave without bidding you farewell." Florian said.

Thorin glared at Florian.

"Thank you for allowing us into your home," Alaric said as he bowed.

Thea shook her head. "It has been my pleasure, masters." "Travel safely and return to visit us in the future."

"We will definitely return and have a feast once again," Ashe said excitedly.

The trio waved their goodbyes and took off onto the gravel road. A voice called out behind them.

"Are you headed to Isern?" Thorin asked.

Alaric turned around to face her. "That is part of the plan."

"I am familiar with these parts, I can guide you there."

Alaric shrugged. "Are you sure you want to travel with casters?"

Thorin scoffed. "I have to determine if you all are serious about facing Chapman."

Ashe smiled at her. "Just join us!"

Thorin said farewell to her grandma and joined the trio along the road.

The quartet left the village.

"Did you not bring anything along?" Florian asked.

Thorin did not answer. Her face had been in a permanent scowl.

The group walked along the banks of the Gwyn river.

"Do you know anything particular about Chapman?" Ashe asked Thorin.

Once again she didn't answer.

Alaric chuckled. "A helpful guide indeed."

Thorin sighed. "I have never met Chapman myself, all I know about him is that he is a good friend of King Godric." She spoke dismissively.

"That makes our mission even more difficult," Alaric said.

"It is the reason he gets away with what he does. Not even Great Lord Ivo bothers to intervene."

"Great Lord Ivo?" Florian asked.

Thorin stared at him with confusion.

"What? Is he someone I should know?" Florian asked.

Alaric flinched at the mention of the name.

"Sorry about him. We are from a land far from here." Alaric interrupted.

"Great Lord Ivo the Eyes, ruler of the Great City of Adhu Aqua. These are his lands." Thorin explained. "Anyone who resides on Hominus should know this."

Florian scratched the back of his head. "Let's say I haven't paid enough attention."

"How many Great Lords are there?" Ashe asked.

"There are five Great Lords, each ruling over a Great City," Alaric explained further.

"Who rules over Meinspir?" Florian answered.

Thorin gave him a weird look causing Alaric to chuckle.

"Meinspir is the capital city of the Zidal Empire. It is where the King resides." Alaric explained.

"What kind of casters does not know this?" Thorin asked.

The trio did not know how to answer the question.

Thorin shook her head.

As dusk arrived the quartet still walked along the banks of the river.

"There should be villages around here, right? Shouldn't we find a place to stay?" Florian asked.

"No, we have to spare our sentz. We might have to use it later. We will sleep outside tonight." Alaric answered.

Florian grumbled.

"Look there is someone there!" Ashe exclaimed while pointing at a figure sitting on the ground in the distance.

Thorin immediately dashed to the figure. Alaric gestured for the rest to follow her. The figure had been a young boy. The boy had been conscious. He had worn similar ragged clothes like Thorin.

"What happened to you?" Thorin asked. Her tone had been much more relaxed when she spoke to the boy.

As the boy tried to speak, black symbols appeared around his mouth. The boy looked as if had been struggling to speak.

Thorin patted the boy on the cheek. "Shhh, don't speak. It will be fine. I know you are scared but you have to go back to your village."

The boy froze before he nodded. The boy got up and stared at the rest of the group before taking off in the opposite direction.

"Did Heinzidal Text form around that child's mouth?" Alaric asked.

Thorin nodded. "He is afflicted with the Versus Curse." She spoke again with a hostile tone.

"Like the Mountains of Versus?" Ashe asked.

Thorin did not respond.

"Those who set foot within the cursed mountain range shall never return the same man. Or so the old tale goes." Alaric stated solemnly. "The old history stated that Versus was a haven for those who lived prior to Heinzidal's death. Some old scripts believe that the curse was brought to the land as a cost for Heinzidal's ultimate sacrifice." Alaric looked at the sky. "Why don't we rest here for the night."

After collecting some kindle for a fire. Ashe and Florian unfurled their bedrolls and sat on them. Alaric offered his bedroll to Thorin, who swiftly shut him down.

"Us mysurs are used to sleeping on the ground," Thorin said offhandedly.

Alaric rolled his eyes. "That may be true but I don't think I would be able to sleep knowing a woman is sleeping on the ground while I sleep comfortably."

Thorin still refused to take the bedroll.

"Think of it as payment. Tell us everything you know about the Versus Curse." Alaric said.

Thorin sighed and grabbed the bedroll.

The quartet sat around the fire as Thorin began to explain.

"Recently there has been more and more people appearing who have this curse. Most of their families claim that they have never set foot in those mountains."

"How does the curse affect you?" Ashe asked.

"As we witnessed earlier, it takes away your ability to speak," Thorin said.

"Is there a reason for the sudden increase of the curse?" Florian asked.

"I...am not sure. Some state that there is a hooded man who comes out at night and passes on the curse."

"That would make the Versus curse more of a cast than a curse," Alaric stated.

"Yes, but that is just hearsay." "Those who have been cursed are treated as outcasts, for people who reside along The Gwyn believe that entry into the mountains is forbidden."

The fire crackled as she spoke.

"Why don't we just head into the mountains?" Florian asked.

Thorin almost burst out with laughter.

"The risk is too high. If the two of you are cursed, you won't be able to cast ever again." Alaric said. "For once I am curious as well, but we cannot go."

"What about if we caught the culprit?" Ashe asked.

"That is a possibility however we have a mission right now." "We can't afford to stop anytime people require help," Alaric stated.

They are strange casters.

The night passed silently.

A few days passed without any issues. One night, Florian woke them up when he heard sounds. Alaric stomped out the fire.

They could hear a person yelling in a language none of them could understand. Alaric suggested they follow the origin of the sound. The quartet walked quietly through the trees that surrounded them. The sound led them to two figures. One was a young woman who had her back faced to a rock and the other had been a hooded figure. The figure's robe had an interesting design, it looked like a patchwork of many different materials. The figure began chanting.

"He is a caster." Thorin heard someone say. Suddenly black symbols appeared on the woman's face. Thorin grabbed her blade and was about to charge at the hooded figure when Alaric grabbed her.

"Let go of me," Thorin whispered.

"I will if you listen closely," Alaric whispered.

Thorin attempted to break free of his hold but once she couldn't she gave in.

"You distract the hooded guy, while we ambush him from the other side. Got it?" Alaric stated.

Thorin scowled but nodded. Why would I listen to you?

"Don't aim to kill, we want whoever is under there alive," Alaric whispered as he sneaked away.

Thorin waited for the rest to get a decent distance away before she revealed herself to the figure.

"What did you do to her?" Thorin yelled.

The figure mumbled something.

"What are you mumbling for?" "Don't be a coward and show yourself!"

The figure was about to run when Alaric appeared behind and grabbed the figure in a chokehold. The person struggled for a while before eventually falling unconscious.

Alaric took off the figure's hood. It revealed a middle-aged man. The man had been bald, replacing his hair with many black symbols.

"We need a way to constrain him," Alaric said.

Ashe held the man's hands close together and cast. Pale yellow light appeared along the man's wrists binding them together. She has done the same to the man's ankles.

"This should hold for now," Ashe said.

Thorin immediately ran to the woman who was now sitting against the rock looking terrified. The woman tried to speak but the black symbols prevented her.

"Gesture if you know this man," Thorin said while pointing at the bald man.

The woman shook her head.

After handing the man over to Florian, Alaric joined Thorin. He pulled out his Rixa amulet and placed it against the woman's face.

Nothing occurred. Alaric cursed.

"What is that?" Thorin asked.

"It is an amulet that can absorb stria. But it seems it cannot undo this curse." Alaric answered as he hid the amulet.

Alaric whispered to the woman. "Show us to your home, we will make sure you get there safely."

The woman, who had been crying, nodded.

Thorin watched as Alaric carried the woman on his back as she pointed when he should go.

There is something different about them.

They had returned the woman to her family and returned to the campsite. Her family seemed to be acquainted with Thorin.

"Have you ever seen anyone that looks like this, Thorin?" Alaric asked, pointing at the captive.

Thorin shook her head. "This is the first time I have seen such a man. That robe too is not like any of the other caster robes."

"I guess we will only get answers once he regains consciousness," Alaric said.

The quartet fell silent as they watched the fire.

"What is the deal with you three? You are not regular casters." Thorin asked.

The trio did not say anything.

Alaric sighed, he then revealed his Rixa amulet.

"Is it okay to tell her?" Florian asked.

"She will be travelling with us, it is better to get this out now before she finds out later," Alaric said. "We are not casters. All three of us are mysurs just like you."

Thorin paused.

"The ability to cast comes from this amulet," Alaric explained.

Thorin grabbed her blade before scurrying backwards.

"I have been travelling with Scaev, this whole time. You disgusting pigs." Thorin exclaimed.

"What is Scaev?" Ashe asked

"Those are Rixa amulets. You aren't going to convince me to join your ranks." Thorin said. She sounded scared.

"Calm down! We have no idea what you are talking about. What is a Scaev?" Alaric asked.

Thorin had been conflicted at the questions. How do they not know?

Thorin then slowly made a way back to the campsite. "Are you telling me the truth? You do not know about the Scaev?"

The trio shook their heads.

Thorin sighed. "The Scaev is a group of heretics both caster and mysur alike. They worship the Nixum and believe the realm should have ended when the Nixum invaded.

I am no expert on the subject, but I have been told to never associate myself with a Scaev. Scaev's are known to wear an amulet that gives them power. An amulet that is created using the blood of hundreds of Heinzidal's offspring." "I ask where did you get those amulets?"

"Our guardian gave us the amulets..." Alaric said.

"Then the-" Florian had been interrupted by Ashe.

"There is no way. Not Priest Able."

Alaric was about to speak when they heard some rustling. The bald man had woken up and attempted to break free of his restraints.

"We speak about this later, first we deal with him," Alaric said.

Alaric kneeled before the man who glared at him.

"What is your name?" Alaric asked.

The man yelled in a foreign language before spitting in Alaric's face. Alaric wiped the spit off his face and turned to Thorin. "You recognise the language?"

"No, I haven't heard anything like it before." She answered.

Alaric turned back to the man. "Where did you come from?"

The man continued yelling in another language.

"We are not going to get anywhere if we can't understand him," Florian said.

Alaric watched Ashe as she seemed down.

The man yelled continuously for hours while trying desperately to break free. The group was silent until they heard a word they understood in their language.

Versus.

"He said 'Versus'. Right?" Florian asked. Thorin nodded.

"This might be a wild idea but I think we should go to the cursed mountains," Alaric suggested.

"No-no-no. There is no way I will ever set foot there." Thorin said.

"I agree with her, Alaric. Like you said a few days ago, the risk is just too high." Florian said.

"We cannot keep this guy with us the entire way and we do not know if there are more people like him out there. The only thing we know is that he is related somehow to the mountains of Versus." Alaric explained.

"Why don't we just kill him?" Thorin asked.

"No!" Alaric exclaimed. "We are not savages." Alaric shakily rubbed his right hand.

The group looked at Alaric with confusion.

"I mean...maybe there are still some things we can fish out of him," Alaric said. "For now let's just get some rest."

Chapter 10

When Florian woke up, he saw that Thorin had been up already. Thorin stared at him.

"What is wrong?" Florian asked.

"He is gone." She had said.

"What?" He looked around and noticed what she meant. The bald man as well as Alaric had been missing. Left in his place was a pouch of sentz.

"Why didn't you wake us?"

Thorin shrugged. "If he is headed to Versus, I want no part in it. I need at least one of you to rescue my people."

Florian woke up Ashe.

"What are you doing?" Thorin asked.

"We are going to rescue him."

Thorin raised her blade towards Florian. "I don't think you are. We are heading towards Isern."

"What is going on?" Ashe asked.

"Alaric is heading towards Versus. Come on, we need to go get him." Florian explained.

Thorin brought her blade to Florian's neck. "As I said, we are not going to Versus."

Florian sighed. "We are not abandoning him. You need him as well, we will never rescue the people from Chapman's grasp without him."

Ashe got between Thorin and Florian. "He is our brother as well. And just like you, we are not going to abandon our loved ones."

Thorin sighed. "If it gets too dangerous, I will be dragging both of you to Isern."

Ashe and Florian nodded.

"Let's head to the village. We need to get some horses." Thorin instructed.

The trio headed to the village where they'd returned the woman from the previous night.

The village had been similar to Nezzagwyn but far smaller. The young woman from the previous night spotted them and shook another older woman, presumably her mother. The older woman called them over.

"Thank you again for saving my daughter, milords" The woman bowed.

"There is no need to thank us, we couldn't stop her from getting cursed," Florian said.

"I'd rather have a cursed child than a dead one, milord." "It is rare to see you with casters, Thorin. Are you in trouble again?"

Thorin's expression softened. "No, it is nothing like that, Miss Olyve. We are just temporarily working together." "We came to ask if you have seen another caster. He is tall, has a black robe and is possibly travelling with a bald man with weird symbols on his head."

The younger woman shook her mother gently as she tried to speak. "I know dear." Miss Olyve whispered. "You are talking about the kind young man who visited us late last night. My daughter is quite infatuated with him." The younger woman blushed as her mother laughed.

"Do you know where he was headed?" Ashe asked.

"He mentioned that he needed a horse, so I showed him to the stables. Did I do something wrong, milady? Is he in trouble?" Miss Olyve asked.

Ashe shook her head. "No, he is fine. We were wondering if you could show us to the stables as well."

"It would be my honour, milady."

MIss Olyve instructed them to follow her. As Florian followed, a hand reached out and grabbed his. It had been the younger woman. She had been sulking. Florian reached out and patted her on the head. "Do not worry, he will be fine. I will make sure of it."

The woman gave a small smile and headed back to her house.

Florian caught up with the rest.

"Was Otsana giving you trouble, milord?" Miss Olyve asked.

"Not at all, she was just a bit worried is all."

Miss Olyve brought them to the stablehand, whom they paid.

"This may be a bad time to bring this up, but how does one ride a horse?" Ashe asked.

"You have got to be joking. Where'd you people even come from?" Thorin asked.

"Diable Island," Florian answered.

"Diable Island? Never heard of the place."

Ashe and Florian looked at one another.

"Anyway, you are going to have to learn how to ride a horse as we head to Versus. You will have to beware of the desolate lands around Versus." Thorin warned.

"What do we have to be wary about?" Florian asked.

"Not many dare to step foot close to Versus, those that do have become bandits ready to strike at unsuspecting travellers. Being close to the Nix, there might be an occasional Nixum spotting."

"The Nix?" Ashe asked.

"I swear you do not know anything. The Nix is a walled-off region to the north, where the Nixum are allowed to roam freely. Nobody lives there."

Thorin then hopped onto her horse and instructed the rest. They said their farewells to Miss Olyve as they strode out of town.

As they rode between the trees, Thorin brought up a question. "What is the deal with Alaric?" She stared at Florian who chuckled at the question.

"What do you mean by that?"

"He is just...weird. He acts like he knows everything and is most of the time stone-faced. Why would he act rashly all of a sudden?"

"He had been acting differently ever since we left the island. But this is rather out of character for him, he would not do something this risky." Florian answered.

"I don't think that is the truth," Ashe said.

"What do you mean by that?" Florian asked.

"I think he has acted differently since the day of the massacre." She answered.

"Massacre?" Thorin asked.

Florian hadn't answered, he kept his eyes forward.

"Touchy subject, I guess?" Thorin asked.

Ashe nodded.

After a few days of travelling, they reached the lands around Versus. Florian now understood why Thorin called it barren. There had been nothing but dirt. There had been no hills or grass. The land had been flat, so they could see further than usual. In the distance there had been a large concentration of mist gathering. There had been no sign of Alaric. It had been raining constantly.

"Does the rain ever stop?" Ashe asked.

"No! No one understands but the rain here does not ever stop!" Thorin yelled. Her voice was barely louder than the pouring rain.

"Shouldn't we be seeing Versus by now?" Florian asked.

Thorin used her blade to point forward. "Those mists are Versus!"

"I thought it was a mountain!" Ashe yelled.

"This is the closest I have been to it, I am as clueless as you are!" Thorin yelled.

Florian's horse came to an abrupt stop, cries of equine pain emanated from Florian's horse.

Florian scanned his horse for the cause of the issue. A black goo-like creature hung from the bottom of the horse. The creature resembled a miniature shark. Florian looked behind him and noticed the predicament they had been in. Behind them, hopping out of the dirt like a fish out of water, had been dozens of goo-sharks.

"Nixum behind us!" Florian yelled.

Thorin and Ashe had both turned to witness the attack. "Faster!" Thorin yelled as her horse sped up.

Florian manoeuvred his body so that he leaned on the side of the horse. He swiped his shortsword at the creature nibbling on his horse. After a few swipes, the creature let go of the horse. The horse calmed down from his panic. At Florian's instruction, his horse sped forward again. He had been far away from the other two. His horse had been in pain from its cries as it ran.

Florian did not bother looking backwards. This came at his demise as he felt a sharp pain on his left bicep. He yelled a curse. He glanced at the origin of the pain. The Nixum hung from his bicep, its sharp teeth gnawing at his skin. Black goo oozed down his left arm, it stung as it moved. Florian held his balance on the horse with his legs as he cleaved the nixum. Once the blade passed through, the nixum just turned completely into goo. Florian slowly and carefully changed the way he sat on the horse.

With the horse heading forwards, Florian sat facing the rear of the horse. The nixum hadn't been far behind. Some tried to jump at Florian who used his sword to keep them at bay. Things went from bad to worse when Florian heard more horse gallops to the east of him. There had been men dressed in rags, their faces were covered by cloth and they all wielded crossbows.

While Florian took his eyes off of the nixum, one had dived at him and caught his right shoulder. He cried in pain as he dropped his sword to the ground. He grabbed the nixum and attempted to yank it out of his shoulder to no avail. Both of his arms had been a bloody, gooey mess.

An arrow whistled through the air. Florian heard a cry as his horse collapsed under him. Florian fell face-first onto the dirt. This is the end. The nixum hadn't attacked immediately. They used the dirt as an ocean and circled Florian, only their black fins protruding the dirt.

Florian laid there with a muddied face waiting for his demise. The crossbowmen had waited far to the east. Probably to pick up the scraps. The nixum stopped circling and began combining into each other. Florian watched as the fin grew larger and larger. Once there was only one fin, it jumped out of the dirt towards Florian. It had been shaped like one large shark made of goo.

Florian closed his eyes, falling to notice the elongating spear pushing the air. The spear pierced the nixum causing it to return to the goo-like substance. He opened his eyes just in time to see Thorin yanking him up and onto her horse.

"You guys better reimburse me for this!" Thorin yelled.

Ashe hadn't been far away from them trying to keep hold of her now shrinking spear. "We have to move before it reforms!" She yelled.

They set off.

"We have another problem! How do we deal with those guys?" Thorin asked.

The crossbowmen had their sights aimed at the two horses.

"I will deal with them." Florian groans. He chanted quickly.

The ground around the crossbow men's horses liquidated causing them to tumble. The group watched as the nixum turned their sights to the easier targets. The large shark massacred the men.

"I...killed...those people," Florian whispered as he rode behind Thorin.

"They tried to kill you. Do not worry about it." "You look really bad."

Florian could not move his arms much and the little he could come at immense pain.

"I feel bad too."

The rest of the way had not been as stressful. It seemed like the closer they got to Versus less and fewer bandits started appearing.

Eventually, their trip came to an abrupt end when a huge gaping abyss stopped them from a few paces from the gigantic concentration of mists that reached the sky.

"How are we going to cross that?" Thorin asked.

Ashe shrugged.

Florian hadn't said anything, he had been trying to preserve his strength.

"If he isn't here, I swear I am going to rip his head off when I find him," Thorin said.

"He'll be here," Florian whispered.

"How about we follow this edge and observe for an entrance?" Ashe suggested.

Thorin nodded along as they headed east alongside the abyss.

Half a day passed when they saw a horse standing close to the abyss. There had been no rider.

"That has to be Alaric's horse," Ashe said.

"That would mean there has to be an entrance somewhere close," Thorin said.

They dismounted their horses and scanned the edge on foot. It did not take them long to find the entrance. It had been an old run-down rope bridge. Half of it hovered over the bridge while the rest of the bridge crossed in the mists.

"We are not crossing that. One misstep and splat." Thorin said.

Ashe chuckled.

"I agree with Thorin." Florian groaned.

"Come on, we have no time to be cowards," Ashe said.

Ashe stepped on the first plank of the bridge and it creaked under her foot.

Thorin helped Florian walk. "You know, I think I will just stay here," Thorin said.

"Are you perhaps afraid of heights?" Ashe asked.

Thorin flushed causing Ashe to laugh. "Not afraid to stand up to casters but deathly afraid of heights."

"I am not afraid of anything," Thorin said as she followed behind Ashe.

Progress across the bridge had been slow. Most of the planks had been wet from the constant rain, some even broke. Once they entered the mist-covered segment of the bridge it had become even harder for they could only see what was directly in front of them. Sounds could be heard within the mist. It was loud grumblings, it sounded as if something had been dragged across a stone floor.

"What in Heinzidal's name is that?" Thorin asked.

"Whatever it is, it is at least a sign of life," Ashe said unconvincingly.

"Or a sign that we are about to die," Thorin said.

Ashe gulped as she took the next step.

A painfully loud zing went through her head. She held her head while trying to maintain her balance.

"You feel that too?" Thorin yelled.

"Yes!"

"I don't like this."

"We're going to have to power through!"

"Remind me to never travel with loonies from whatever island!"

Ashe didn't have the mental capacity to laugh. She just continued forward. The sound in her head got worse as she went. Eventually, the end of the bridge was in sight.

"Land!" Ashe yelled.

Ashe stepped onto the stone ground. Suddenly the mists around her cleared. The sight had been other-worldly. A larger than life green serpent towered before her. The snake hissed loudly at her. As it hissed the sound in her head grew larger. It had shown its large fangs. The serpent had large runes carved into its green scales, where the mists seemed to swirl around. The serpent had been large but what stood behind it was even larger.

Three mountains stood proudly behind the serpent. Unlike regular mountains, the three mountains had flat peaks and instead of widening, they became extremely narrow as they went to the base. How these mountains even stood without collapse had been a mystery. Also unlike regular mountains, these mountains had been slowly made up of stone. The largest of the three stood in the middle, Ashe noticed that she could make out tiny squares carved into the mountain. This is Versus.

Thorin and Florian joined her and paused as they witnessed what she had. Ashe felt a prick at her skin and the world suddenly became dark.

Ashe woke up in a panic. Her panic made her surroundings sway.

"Calm down. Don't move too much." A voice to her left.

She analysed her surroundings. She had been in a wooden cage. Thorin had been alongside her in the cage. There had been no sight of Florian. The cage had been floating high above a chasm. The mist made it difficult to see how high they had been. The cage had been attached via metal chains to a metal spike that had been stuck in a stone high above. In front of her had been a large square room that had been carved into the stone. She couldn't make out anything in the room due to the darkness.

Where are we?

"Versus." A voice to the left as if it read her mind. "Near the peak."

Ashe looked towards her left. A similar cage hung there. A figure sat with crossed legs.

"Alaric?" Ashe asked.

"You shouldn't have come," Alaric said.

"Where is Florian?" She asked.

Alaric raised an eyebrow. "He came with you did he not? You should know where he is."

Ashe cursed.

They hung in the cages perilously with only uncertainty below them.

Chapter 11

Alaric rode his horse through the barren lands towards the large mists, he thought had been Versus. The bald man he had knocked out had laid limply in front of him.

You'd better be right about this.

When have I ever been wrong?

Shut up.

Now that is not the attitude to have with the person that saved your life.

Shut up. You only saved me because you need me.

Foolish boy, you assume I need you.

If I find nothing of interest, I am tossing myself off of Versus.

You are a coward, there is no way you'd do such a thing.

Shut up.

Regardless, you are sure to find some interesting things. You wouldn't be here if you weren't the least bit as curious as I was when I first came here.

I am nothing like you.

Why are you here then?

Shut up.

Masked men on horseback shadowed Alaric. They drew their crossbows and fired at Alaric. Alaric stared at them. His eyes shone a bright purple. The crossbow bolts suddenly decreased speed and moved through the air as if in slow motion. Alaric caught the bolts as they got close to him and tossed them off to the side. The masked men looked between each other.

Alaric looked forward. Black fins protruded out of the dirt. Dozens of them.

Nixum.

That makes it easier then.

The nixum hopped out of the dirt. They seemed to respond to Alaric's purple gaze and moved past him. The masked men seemed to turn around and sped the opposite way.

How'd you do that?

Some of us have to keep our secrets. You are an expert in that field as well.

Shut up.

Alaric reached his destination. He lifted the bald man over his shoulder. He slowly stepped onto the bridge.

Don't slip and fall now.

Alaric carefully walked across the bridge. Halfway across the bridge, a loud sharp sound rang in his head.

Slavio is still at it. It seems.

Slavio?

You will find out soon.

Alaric withstood the sound as he crossed the bridge. Alaric froze at what waited for him. The sound in his head calmed down. It was replaced with faint whispers in his head.

What is happening?

The large serpent hadn't hissed, instead, it brought its gigantic head towards Alaric.

This is strange.

Alaric put a hand on the serpent's head and rubbed it.

Alaric felt a prick on his skin and fell unconscious.

Alaric woke up to a startle. The world began spinning. It took a few moments to get his bearings and analyse the situation. First, he saw a few dozen people staring at him from a platform carved into some sort of rock face. The people had all been bald with black symbols scattered across their heads.

They all wore patchwork robes. There had been a mix of men and women and a few children. They all looked at him with cold expressions. He heard a creaking to his left and glanced at it. A similar cage had hung to the left of him, the bald man they had captured sat within it. A scowl could be found on his face.

The group of people made way for an old shorter man to take the foreground. The man's skin had been extremely wrinkled. He had looked closer to death than actually being alive. The man opened his mouth and began to speak. His voice sounded in a sharp shrill.

"What has brought you to the Mountains of Versus?" He asked.

Alaric was shocked. "You speak the language, good."

"Answer the question, trespasser."

"You locked me up, I am the one who needs to ask the questions."

"You are in no position to talk back, child." The old man pointed to the metal spike that currently held Alaric's life. "We can end you whenever we'd like."

N'gata, still the old bastard.

"As you can see, I have come to return something that belongs here." Alaric motioned to the man in the adjacent cage.

The old man yelled at the other man in a different language. He had been furious. He turned to Alaric.

"Yes, I have to thank you for bringing my foolish great-grandson back."

"Can you let me go now?" Alaric asked.

The old man laughed. The others looked at him with confusion.

"You are a fool, you knowingly came to Versus despite its reputation. You cannot leave without getting cursed."

Alaric sighed. "Before you curse me, can you at least explain what happens here?"

"Of course." The old man began explaining the history of Versus. "Our people are known as the Nitio, record keepers of the history of Hominus. Versus was a haven for our people during the Nixum invasion thousands of years ago. Like all other races, we were seeking a safe place as we waited for the Great Heinzidal to eradicate the threat of the nixum."

"One day right before the great battle that shaped our land, Great Heinzidal visited Versus. He gave the Nitio an expectation of sorts. He predicted the happenings of the battle that was to follow." "Like everything, the Nitio recorded his prediction. And as it happened the battle ensued exactly as Heinzidal predicted. However, that was not the only reason Heinzidal came to Versus. Heinzidal instructed us that we should protect the ancient history and that no one should ever uncover what truly occurred in ages past. He left us with his companion, Slavio. Who protects us from invaders"

"Let me get this straight, the Nitio lives within these mountains in secrecy, protecting the ancient history of the world. Who are you and what happens when someone invades Versus?" Alaric asked.

"I am N'gata, the chieftain of the Nitio." "Those that enter Versus are cursed. The ability to speak is a dangerous one."

"Certainly." Alaric gulped.

"We are bound by our duty."

"What about those who mistakenly enter Versus?"

"We do not make any exceptions."

N'gata began to chant before he halted and grabbed his head as if he was in agony. The other Nitio looked at him with concern. Alaric heard the faint whispers in his head once again. N'gata yelled in a different language. The only word that sounded familiar to Alaric had been 'Slavio'.

N'gata calmed down and glared at Alaric. "It seems the great serpent says cursing you is against Heinzidal's will."

"Heinzidal's will?" Alaric asked.

N'gata shrugged. "I am as confused as you are. The great serpent has never intervened ever." "But that does not matter, we shall soon witness your death."

"You're going to kill me?"

"Execute you, yes. The Nitio cannot have another one of you running around."

"Another?"

N'gata calm demeanour turned sour. "A few years back, the Nitio failed at protecting history. A man infiltrated Versus and had a glimpse at the ancient text. We, Nitio, despise that man. He represents our greatest failure."

"You specifically mentioned 'another one of me', what did you mean by that?"

"That man had been your father, Jerial the Merciless."

Just great.

"We shall see to your execution, at the brightest light."

The Nitio slowly departed the platform.

Chapter 12

Florian felt a slight warmth as he woke up. He had been laying on a stone table of sorts. He had been shirtless, the Rixa amulet hung cooly against his chest. Green leaf-like objects had been wrapped around certain parts of his arms. He noticed that this was where the warmth emanated from. He had been in a small stone room that had been dimly lit by a torch.

He had not been alone, there had been an older woman alongside him. She had been bald with black symbols on her head. When she realised that he woke up, she began yelling in a different language. A few moments later a larger man entered the room. He had been bald as well. He lifted Florian easily and carried him over his shoulder. Florian tried to fight back but quickly learned that he had not been strong enough.

The larger man carried him through stone corridors. Eventually, they reached a stop in front of a large wooden door. The man opened the doors slowly. Beyond the doors was a wide stone platform that stood before a large opening. The opening had revealed three cages dangling over nothingness. The large man placed him down on the ground. Florian heard the man chant.

Mist gathered at the man's fingertips and swirled around his forearms. The man held his mist-covered arm forwards. The mist stretched and collided with one of the cages. The man retracted his arm as if he had been pulling on an object. The cage got yanked towards them. The man opened the cage carefully observing the figures within them. Now that the cage had been moved closer, Florian saw Ashe and Thorin sat in it.

They had not attempted to escape. The man grabbed Florian and tossed him violently into the cage. "You could be a little bit more careful, he is injured. Asshole." Thorin yelled. The man closed the cage. The mists pushed them back, once again dangling over nothing.

"I am glad you are okay," Ashe said.

"There was a lady that healed me," Florian explained. His arms were numb. "Why didn't you attempt to escape?"

Thorin pointed at the cage adjacent to them. Florian finally noticed Alaric.

"They took our weapons and we don't know how many of them there are. Fighting now will be foolish." Alaric explained.

Florian smiled. "It is nice to have you back."

"Can you explain why we are here?" Thorin asked.

Alaric shook his head. "You shouldn't have come here."

Thorin scoffed at Alaric. "Are you going to keep saying that?"

Alaric nodded. "Tomorrow, they are going to execute me. I will do my best to make sure that you three get to leave safely."

"What nonsense are you spewing? We all are going to leave together." Ashe said.

Alaric remained quiet.

Florian piped up. "What about that promise you asked of us? We will help you when you need saving."

"It seems that will not be necessary anymore." Alaric smiled.

"I did not come here just to see you die and leave. I was told that I could learn from you but it just seems that you are a selfish prick."

Alaric laughed. "I guess that is true."

The quartet could not sleep that night. They watched the platform as light began to flood slowly into their senses.

Ashe sat with her face tugged into her knees. She had still been puzzled about the revelations of the Scaev. Now she had more things to worry about. How would she save her brother from certain death? Ashe thought and thought, to no avail. Every method she could come up with ended in a full-on battle in which they would probably lose. Then she thought about Alaric.

In many ways, they had been opposites. He had always been quiet and broody while she had been loud and carefree. He rarely laughed and she spent hours trying to make him. He had always stood up for her when she did something wrong but then turned around and lectured her behind Priest Able's back. But above all, he had been her older brother, one that despite everything. she will standby until the end. She then remembered one key aspect of Alaric.

He is smart, he has a plan. He won't leave us. Her thoughts of encouragement made her worry less. She glanced at him. He sat quietly with his eyes closed. Definitely has a plan.

After what felt like hours, there had finally been movement on the platform. An incredibly old man entered first and stood at the edge of the platform. He was followed by dozens of people that filled out the platform. The old man analysed her as well as the other two in the cage.

"Son of Jerial, I have seen that your friends have come to witness your death." The old man said. Jerial, who is that?

"N'gata, would you humour me with a request?" Alaric said. Ashe watched his expression. He hadn't shown anything, for a man about to be executed he had been very calm.

The old man who she assumed had been named N'gata laughed.

"A request? There is nothing we have to give to you." N'gata said.

"Then how about you do your job and protect history," Alaric answered.

N'gata scowled. "What do you mean by that?"

"I have brought your great-grandson back to you, alas he has been doing incredibly bad deeds. He cursed innocent people, women and children who had no intention of invading your land."

N'gata spat at his great-grandson. "What are you suggesting, Son of Jerial?"

"The Nitio has to protect history and it has almost been exposed by one of your kind. Luckily, I put a stop to it. And all I wish is that you let my friends go safely and curseless."

N'gata thought about it for a while. "What relations do they have with Jerial?"

"None, they do not even know who he is. I pose the biggest threat, kill me but let them go."

N'gata looked towards another Nitio woman. She nodded before speaking. N'gata nodded and looked at Alaric.

"It seems you are telling the truth. You are correct the Nitio cannot escape judgement for our wrongdoings. The Great Heinzidal wouldn't allow us to." "Fine, I agree to your terms." N'gata motioned to a few Nitio men. They then used the same mist technique and dragged Ashe's cage towards the platform. They opened the cage and mists swirled around Ashe's body. Her arms had been tight against her body as the mists restrained her.

The men led her as well as Florian and Thorin, who both had been restrained, onto the platform. A man stood behind them. Most probably the one who casted. They were turned to watch the other cages. The bald man had laid within his cage, he looked on as if he had been carefree. From this side of the platform, Ashe could see that the platform had a second level high above. A man stood on the second level with a large hammer. The second level stood before three large metal spikes.

"Any last words, Son of Jerial?" N'gata asked.

Alaric looked at Thorin, then at Florian and finally at Ashe. He softly smiled. "Don't be mad at me."

A loud clang could be heard as Alaric's cage jerked violently. Ashe looked up and saw the man hammering away at a large spike. Florian and Thorin had been yelling. Ashe could only watch, tears had already begun to invade her eyes. She had never seen Alaric with such a soft expression. He does not have a plan.

She cried as the last clang rang out. She watched as his wooden cage plummeted and disappeared into the mists.

She sniffled as she walked through the stone corridors. A large man had been guiding them through the stone maze that was Versus. Finally, they reached a large stone staircase. The trio had been silent. Ashe noticed Florian had dry tears on his face matching hers. He had still been shirtless. His Rixa amulet swung side to side as he walked. Thorin had been uncharacteristically quiet.

"He let them down," Thorin whispered.

Ashe didn't ask who she was talking about.

"Nezzagwyn...my grandmother. They all put our hopes in him." She continued.

"They're not the only ones. The people of...Diable...protected him against the casters. All...for nothing." Florian added.

Don't speak ill of him. He did this for us.

"Believe in him," Ashe said. "He sacrificed himself so that we can live. He lives through us now."

Florian shook his head. "He abandoned us. Then dies protecting us. I always thought he was smart but it turns out he is a fool."

Ashe scoffed at Florian. "He is your brother, how can you say things like that."

"If he really was our brother he wouldn't have kept secrets from us. Who in Heinzidal's name is Jerial?"

"Jerial..." Thorin whispered.

"Do you recognize the name?" Ashe asked.

"Only slightly. My grandmother and father mentioned it before. Jerial the Merciless was the Great Lord of Adhu Aqua before Great Lord Ivo." Thorin explained.

"Alaric...mentioned that Adhu Aqua was his home," Florian said.

"That means he is the son of the previous Great Lord," Ashe said.

"No-no-no impossible, there is no way. I refuse to believe that he was someone as important as that." Thorin said.

"What happened to Great Lord Jerial?" Ashe asked.

Thorin thought for a bit. "My grandma said that he got poisoned and died, however, she also stated that she did not truly believe that."

"Maybe that is why Miss Thea said that visiting Adhu Aqua will only bring Alaric sadness," Florian said.

They had finally reached the bottom of the staircase. The man led them out into the mists. Mist surrounded them. The man ahead yelled something, she couldn't understand. They followed him regardless. She wondered how this man knew how to traverse through the mists. After a few minutes, the man ahead of them suddenly held his hands to his head and began screaming. The mists that restrained them swiftly dissipated.

"What is happening?" Ashe asked.

"No clue but we have to get out of here before we suffer a similar fate," Thorin said.

"And how do we know which direction we should go?" Florian asked.

"We just run straight, I am certain we will find something," Thorin answered.

"Let's not run, remember the abyss as we got here?" Ashe said.

"Good point."

"We could use one of Alaric's plans right now," Florian said.

They briskly walked forward.

Chapter 13

Alaric cast a barrier made of mist as he fell. He was aware that the barrier was not going to withstand the force of the fall but he felt that it was necessary for some reason. The faint whispers had returned in the morning and hadn't stopped since. He has been quiet.

Mist engulfed his vision as he fell, the platform could no longer be seen. Suddenly the wooden cage crashed into something. Alaric felt a heavy force at the back of his barrier. A wave of exhaustion arose. His body stopped falling. Alaric let go of his barrier. The cage had been broken into pieces around him. He got up to his feet and analysed the floor. Instead of the stone of Versus, he had been standing on something green and scaly. A large head popped up to Alaric's side. It was the large serpent he had seen when he first arrived. "Did you save me?" Alaric asked.

The whispers in his head had become louder. You are trying to communicate with me.

The serpent brought its head close to Alaric. They said your name was 'Slavio'. You forever have my gratitude. Alaric began scaling the giant serpent's head and sat on top of it. The serpent began moving. Instead of going up towards the platform, it went towards the ground and along the side of the stone mountain. Where are you taking me Slavio? Alaric struggled to keep his balance atop the serpent's head.

Whenever he was about to fall, the serpent adjusted its head to make sure he did not fall to his death. Slavio stopped at a square opening. The opening led into a room. I guess you want me to enter this room. Alaric made the short jump from the serpent's head into the room. The room had been lit by lanterns. A large mural was drawn onto one of the room's walls. It depicted three Nitio men bowing before a man who had been dressed in a rainbow robe.

Behind the robed man was a serpent who had runes carved into its scales. Is that you, Slavio. Whispers once again rang in his head. I need to figure out what you are actually saying. Alaric looked around the room. It had been filled with large tomes. There had been one tome that stood out. It had been separated from the other books. It sat squarely in the middle of a desk.

It had gold inscriptions on the cover. Above the tome was a sword that had been sheathed. Alaric picked up the tome and paged through it. The text within the tome had been foreign to him. He almost put the book down until he noticed a few illustrations. The illustrations showcased the same man dressed in a rainbow robe having a fierce fight with a large three-eyed black creature. The final illustration showed the rainbow-robed man being defeated by the creature. Alaric analysed the creature.

Why does it look familiar? The creature had red eyes and black tendrils that flowed up towards the rainbow man. Below the illustration, there was one word written in the regular tongue.

It read 'Angh'. Alaric flipped through more pages searching for more illustrations. A bit of parchment fell out of the book and onto the desk. Alaric unfurled the paper and read its contents. Take the sword, Alaric.

Is this the reason you wanted me to come here?

No response.

Alaric sighed. He picked up the sheathed blade. There had been a strap attached to the sheath. He strapped the blade to his back when the door suddenly opened. N'gata stepped into the room. N'gata froze. Alaric froze.

"You devil child. I am going to kill you!" N'gata yelled. N'gata was about to cast when he began to hold his head. Alaric grabbed the tome and proceeded to boot N'gata to the face. The old man grunted as he was struck to the floor. His nose had been gushing blood. Thanks, Slavio. He looked at the creature. Are you smiling at me?

"You are going to tell me where I can find my friends and their weapons." Alaric threatened.

N'gata had just been crying in pain. Alaric quickly realised that he was not going to be helpful. Slavio, try to find my friends and protect them. Alaric hadn't known if Slavio would follow his orders but he had to try. Alaric watched as the great serpent moved away from the window. Alaric stepped into the corridor. Far to the left, he saw men rushing down the corridor towards him.

He held the tome firmly in his left hand and sprinted down the right side of the corridor. I can't cast with the tome in one hand. I have to get out of here soon. Luckily, most of the rooms he passed had no doors attached, therefore he could glance at them as he ran past. Some of the rooms had people within them who yelled as he ran past. Stairs, need to find stairs. As he turned one corner, he ran directly into a large burly man. They both froze. Alaric reacted first. He kicked at the man's knee.

The large man grunted a little but wasn't very fazed. The man prepared to strike. Alaric tried to brace for the impact, however, it never came. The man had been holding his head. Slavio, you are a lifesaver. Alaric used the right side of the wall as a platform as he punched the man in the face. The large man dropped to his knees. Alaric grabbed the man's head with his right hand and pushed it against the walls of the stone corridor. The man grunted as he fell unconscious.

Alaric glanced behind him to notice that the other Nitio were very close behind him. No time to catch my breath. Alaric sprinted. The stone corridors were very narrow and winding. Alaric finally reached a staircase. Nitio men were rushing up the staircase. What should I do? Alaric grabbed the blade on his back and unsheathed it. The blade's hilt had been golden with intricate details carved into it. The blade itself was crimson. Bright gold runes were drawn on the flat side of the blade.

He could feel the blade sapping his energy as he held it. And his energy was draining fast. The Nitio men suddenly paused. They then screamed and ran away from Alaric. He glanced behind him and the same was happening to the chasing pack. He ran down the staircase. I can't hold this for much longer. He sheathed the blade again. He reached the end of the staircase. He was met with many corridors leading in all directions.

He just continued straight. As he ran he noticed something in the corner of his eye. He turned around and headed towards it. A woman stood cleaning a large stone table. She turned around when she heard him enter the room. She froze at the sight of him. She quickly hid behind the stone tablet. Alaric ignored the woman and instead walked over to Ashe's spear. He noticed Thorin's blade and Florian tunic were also situated in the room. He also grabbed the sentz pouch. He looked for Florian's shortsword but could not find it.

He nodded to the woman as he left the room. He searched for an exit as he ran. The Nitio he had encountered along the way seemed terrified of him. Was it the sword? Eventually, he arrived at a large stone staircase. Alaric sped through the staircase, skipping steps where he could. He reached an opening but he was surrounded by mist. Which direction should I go? Alaric headed straight. After a while, Slavio's whispers could be heard. This time however it seemed Alaric could hear its origin.

He followed the whispers. He could see a hint of green through the mists. You best have found them. As he got closer he could hear Thorin yelling. The large body of the serpent moved as Alaric arrived, revealing Ashe, Thorin and Florian. They were stunned at the sight of him. Ashe ran up to him and gave him a tight hug. She had begun to cry again.

"How?" She asked.

"I will explain everything later, for now, we have to get out of here," Alaric said.

Alaric gave Ashe her spear, he then tossed Florian's tunic and handed Thorin her blade.

"Sorry, I couldn't find your sword. Have this one instead." Alaric said as he took off the blade strapped to his back and handed it to Florian. Florian nodded at him. They were still speechless.

Slavio's head protruded through the mists and came close to the group. Thorin aimed her blade at the serpent's head. Alaric walked up to the snake and rubbed his hand on the serpent's head. Thank you, Slavio. I have one final request. Make sure the Nitio never leaves this place. The rest of the group watched Alaric with confusion.

"Okay, let's head out," Alaric said.

"How will we traverse the mist?" Thorin asked.

"Don't worry, he will show me the way." Alaric pointed at Slavio.

"The giant snake?" Florian asked.

"Yes, it is a bit complicated but he is on our side."

Thorin shook her head. "Death made you crazy."

Alaric chuckled as he walked through the mists.

CHAPTER 14

The group rode on horseback through the barren lands. Florian sat behind Ashe as they rode. Alaric had explained the circumstances of how he escaped certain death.

"Why did the snake help you?" Thorin asked.

"I don't know," Alaric answered.

"So the snake just helped you for no reason?" Thorin continued.

Alaric shrugged. "I felt Slavio trying to communicate with me but I couldn't understand anything." Alaric glanced at Florian who till this point had not spoken to him yet. Florian just kept his glance over Ashe's shoulder. He also noticed Ashe glancing at him strangely.

"You want to ask me anything, Ashe?" Alaric asked.

Ashe hesitated before she spoke. "Yes, it is about Jerial."

"Can't say I did not see this coming," Alaric said. "Yes, Jerial is my father or at least was my father."

The group fell silent.

"My father, Jerial the Merciless, Great Lord of Adhu Aqua. One of the strongest casters to ever exist. Some would even argue for the strongest. He was loved by many and feared by all. What made him stand apart from all other Great Lords at the time was his great intellect. Under his control, Adhu Aqua was prosperous. Alas, his untimely death threw the city in turmoil."

The rest listened to his story intensely.

"Do not be fooled, however, my father was a horrible man. He treated me and my... never mind that wasn't important. After his death, I had nowhere to go. Priest Able found me and the rest is history."

"Why'd you never tell us about him?" Florian asked. He still looked forward.

"Simple, it was never important. We all have dead parents."

Before anyone could speak, Alaric sped up with his horse and now rode ahead of the group. "Nixum, ahead! Stay behind me!" He yelled.

Thorin and Ashe rode their horses closer to Alaric.

"What are you going to do?" Ashe asked.

"A trick I learned from my father," Alaric whispered.

Come on, you have been too quiet.

Out of sight to the others, Alaric's eyes shone a bright purple. The shark-like nixum seemed to respond to him. They separated, seemingly making a path for them to cross through.

Happy?

Extremely.

Once they were past the nixum, Thorin piped up. "How did you do that? Caster's tried to tame the nixum for years."

"It is a curse," Alaric answered.

Florian scoffed.

After they passed the nixum threat, Thorin took the lead once again. She led them toward a different direction, claiming that the new way will lead them directly to Isern.

"I don't think I can trust you anymore," Florian said. He said it while staring ahead. Nobody questioned who he was talking about.

"Florian, that is-"

"It is okay, Ashe. I understand completely. None of you has any reason to trust me." Alaric stated.

The mood turned sombre.

A few hours later, a tall building broke into the distance.

"What is that?" Ashe asked.

"Isern. That tall building is where we will find Chapman." Thorin explained.

"How far?" Alaric asked.

"I would say still a few hours but we are close."

"What is Isern like?" Ashe asked.

Thorin scowled. "A place where scum lives."

"Sounds like a great place," Alaric said. "Is that a person?"

Thorin squinted trying to see what Alaric had been talking about.

A figure stood clad in black in the pouring rain. The figure's face had been covered but just stood still as the horses approached.

"A bandit?" Ashe asked.

Thorin shrugged.

"If he tries anything, I will just block it," Alaric said.

As they approached the figure, they saw that it held a gloved hand towards its chest.

"Just move past," Alaric said.

Thorin sped up. The figure ignored her.

As Alaric was approaching, it jumped towards him. The jump had been unnaturally high. The figure raised an arm to strike him.

Alaric cast a barrier around him.

The figure's arm seemed to phase through the barrier and strike Alaric in the chest. Alaric was thrown backwards, he fell from his horse and onto the dirt. The figure landed in front of him immaculately. Alaric groaned in pain. How'd he do that? "What do you want?" Alaric asked. The figure pointed at its chest.

Alaric noticed Ashe's elongating spear approaching. She had caught it off-guard. Before the tip of her spear struck, it suddenly retracted. Alaric got back to his feet. His clothes had been all muddied. He hoped the tome that he attached to his belt had been safe. The figure readied another attack. Instead of casting a barrier, Alaric parried the blow. It had been aimed at his chest once again.

The blow had been powerful but Alaric kept his composure. Alaric retaliated with a few punches and kicks. The figure blocked, dodged a few but not all. As the figure got hit, it had not made any significant noise. It had just stumbled backwards. Alaric and the black-clad figure attacked one another relentlessly. It looked like a beautiful dance in the rain. Ashe interrupted the two, she swung her spear at the figure, who expertly dodged.

It grabbed her spear and wrestled it out of her hands. It then tried to strike her with the blunt end of the spear. Ashe responded quickly as she got low to the ground and tried to swipe at its legs. Before Ashe could connect, it jumped off the ground and with incredible athleticism, flipped through the air and landed perfectly a couple of paces from them. It spun Ashe's spear a few times in a taunt. Alaric saw Florian charge at the figure with the crimson blade.

Before Florian could strike however he stumbled and fell. He cannot handle it. The figure let go of Ashe's spear and rushed towards Florian, who had been defenceless. A blade flew through the sky. Alaric recognized it quickly as Thorin's blade. The figure flipped into the air once again but this time he had caught blade midair.

Thorin charged at the figure swinging her fists wildly, like an animal. The figure did not seem to fight back, instead, it just dodged her attacks. Alaric walked over to Ashe who was ready to charge as well. He put a hand on her shoulder. "We can't win this."

She nodded. "What do we do then?"

"You regroup with Thorin and Florian and head to Isern."

"And what about you?" Ashe scowled.

"I will be right behind you. I just need to buy some time so you can escape."

"I don't agree with you. We will fight together."

"There is no time to argue, we don't have much time."

"Promise, you will return to us safely."

"I promise." Alaric tied the pouch of sentz to Ashe's belt and gave her the tome. "Keep this safe for me."

Alaric and Ashe charged at the figure. Thorin had been tiring and attacking slowly. Alaric entered with a high kick that threw the figure off-guard. It couldn't dodge in time and was thrown backwards. Thorin's blade was tossed out of its hand. Ashe grabbed Florian who was getting back to his feet and then grabbed her spear off the ground. Alaric kicked Thorin's blade towards her. "Keep them out of trouble until I get there." He yelled at Thorin.

Alaric then charged at the recovering figure. Alaric crossed his arms then placed his hands on the ground. His fingers were placed so that it looked like a triangle. The ground around Alaric and the figure began to morph. A dome of dirt surrounded them, removing them from the surroundings.

Within the dome had been dark, Alaric could barely make out where the figure had been. Just have to keep this up until they are a good distance away. Alaric realised that the figure could probably break out of the dirt when it wanted to if it could break through his barrier. He was not going to give it a chance though. Alaric could feel the dome sapping his stamina already. Alaric's eyes shone a bright purple. Alaric was the first one to move. They had continued their dance of limbs within the darkness.

Chapter 15

Isern had been situated at the base of a mountain range. The mountain range had not been as impressive as Versus, however. The Gwyn River ran through the centre of the town, presumably originating from the mountains. Isern was large, larger than anything Ashe had ever seen in her life.

Even now during the night, there had been many people outside seemingly just because they wanted to. The trio stood at one entrance of Isern. Isern was made up of many stone buildings mixed with a few wooden houses. Ashe stared at the stone buildings, she had never seen this many before. Isern was also made of many streets and alleyways. A large stone building could be seen towering over the rest of the town.

She followed Thorin's lead as they walked through the city. People eyed them as they walked. The people of Isern felt different to Ashe. They seemed...happy. "I get a different feel to this town. It feels different compared to Nezzagwyn." Ashe said.

"The majority of people are casters. That is why it is different." Thorin answered.

As they passed an alleyway, a person bumped into Ashe. She quickly apologised but the person just continued forward. "What was that about?" Florian asked.

"Probably a slave that is trying to escape," Thorin said.

"A slave?"

Thorin nodded. "It is more common in the more affluent areas. Casters buy mysur-slaves from different slave traders."

"What do these slaves do?" Ashe asked.

"Anything their owner bids them to do."

"And if they refuse?"

Thorin hesitated before she answered. "A painful death."

"Why don't they just fight back?" Florian asked.

Thorin glared at him. "Such a misguided question." She didn't speak further, she just walked forward. Ashe watched as Thorin walked a bit faster than before. She whispered to Florian. "I think you are being a little insensitive. Casters are much more powerful than mysurs. And I don't think it is so simple as to fight when mysurs have been oppressed for a thousand years." Florian did not say anything, he just frowned.

Thorin paused ahead of them, she then dragged them into an alleyway.

"What is wrong?" Ashe asked.

Thorin pointed to the street. "Watch."

They watched the street. At first, a blue-robed soldier entered their view. He held a whip in one hand. Hitting it occasionally against the ground. The soldier walked confidently. Following the soldier were men. They had metal cuffs around their hands. Their feet had also been cuffed with a loose chain. Ashe thought that it might be to refrain them from running. The men also had a large metal cuff around their neck which was attached to one another.

The men had been shirtless, their bodies had been bruised. Ashe could make out slash marks. The men looked to the ground as they walked. They had sad expressions on their faces. A soldier walked behind them as well, equipped with a whip. As the men passed, Ashe noticed the street being filled once again with people. "What was that about?" She asked. She watched as Thorin rubbed her eyes.

"Metalworkers." "They are the ones we are going to save," Thorin said.

Ashe noticed that her voice had been softer than usual.

Thorin walked out into the road. "Come on, let's find an inn."

Thorin led them to a stone building that had a small drawing of a house on it. As they entered the inn, they were met with a young man that stood behind a counter.

"Welcome to the Lockler Inn!" The young man said with a smile. The young man eyed the trio. "We offer rooms at 2 sentz per person. You shall not have to pay for your slave." He said while gesturing at Thorin. Florian was about to interject but he was stopped by Thorin. Ashe reached for the pouch that hung from her belt. She soon realised that something had been wrong. The pouch that had to be there was missing. When did it go missing? Ashe turned to the group and whispered what had happened.

Thorin sighed. She then took off one of her shoes revealing a few hidden pieces of sentz. She then handed it to the young man. He reluctantly accepted the jade pieces. They then followed him upstairs where he showed them to their rooms. Ashe could hear that there had been other people staying here. Some had been talking loudly within their rooms while others made weird...so unds.

They had two rooms, which were right next to each other. The rooms were different from what she was accustomed to. It was made of a bed that was lifted by some sort of wooden foundation. There had been a writing desk with parchment and ink prepared. There had also been buckets filled with water as well as a variety of mugs. They decided that before sleeping they would discuss the plans for the next day.

"This is going to be bad," Thorin said. "I used the last of my sentz for these rooms."

Ashe apologised for losing the pouch.

"That is just the way this town works. Just be more careful next time." Thorin said.

Ashe nodded.

"How are we going to free those metalworkers?" Florian asked.

"I don't think we can plan anything until Alaric arrives," Ashe said, causing Florian to roll his eyes. Thorin watched the exchange.

"I have to agree with Ashe. There is nothing we can do right now. We need to get our hands on some sentz as well. We only have this room for the night." Thorin said.

Florian sighed. "What if he doesn't make it?"

"What happened to you?" Ashe asked angrily.

Florian shrugged.

"He will be here. He survived a fall from Versus, unscathed. One man is not going to stop him." Thorin said.

Ashe noted how Thorin changed in her opinions of Alaric.

"We separate at first light. We try to find out any information on Chapman or how to infiltrate his factory. We also need to find ways to make money." Thorin explained.

"Factory?" Ashe asked.

Thorin nodded. "The tall building, it is Chapman's metal factory." Thorin eyed the tome that was attached to Ashe. "What is that?"

Ashe grabbed the tome. It had been damp. "Alaric gave this to me. I think he got it at Versus." They paged through the large book. They could not read the strange text. Ashe paused on one page that had text that looked familiar to her. She tapped Florian. "Does this portion look familiar?" She asked. Florian looked at the text then saw what she meant. "It resembles the 'enhance' cast. But there are parts I cannot read." He said.

Ashe nodded. "That means this entire book is written in Heinzidal text."

"Then why can you not read it?" Thorin asked.

Florian shrugged.

Ashe thought before answering. "Perhaps it is written in all forms of the text." Alaric would be proud of me.

Thorin and Florian still looked confused.

"I assume, both Florian and I can only read 'Ilium' Heinzidal text. Therefore we can make out a few symbols. Alaric would only be able to read 'Phen' text. Since we can't comprehend most of the text, it is probably written in all three text forms."

"Did you get any of that?" Florian asked as he turned to Thorin, who shook her head. Alaric would understand.

Ashe spent a few minutes trying to decipher the text.

"There is another problem," Florian said.

Ashe looked at him, eyebrows raised.

Florian then placed his sheathed sword in his hands. "I can't use this sword."

Ashe and Thorin waited for him to explain further.

"I tried to use it on the masked person earlier, but when I grabbed the blade...it sucked all my energy."

Ashe held her hands out. "Let me try."

Florian placed the blade in her hands. She pulled at the golden hilt revealing the crimson blade with golden runes. Once the blade had been fully removed from the sheath, she felt what Florian had spoken about. She felt her energy draining rapidly. She nearly lost consciousness when she finally dropped the blade. The draining stopped immediately.

"What in the world is that?" Ashe asked.

Thorin picked up the blade. She held it firmly. "I do not feel anything," She said.

"Strange." "You can keep it then," Florian said.

"No, this blade is way too...blatant. I prefer my own."

Florian sighed but took the blade. He sheathed it and placed it against his back.

"We should head to bed," Ashe announced. The rest nodded. Florian left for his room. Thorin and Ashe shared a bed. The room was dark. She did not face Thorin.

"Your opinion on Alaric has changed," Ashe whispered. She heard no response for a while. She thought Thorin had been asleep before a voice whispered back.

"He is different to what I thought him to be." "At first, I thought he was a stuck up caster who believed that he was better than everyone else. But...now I guess...he is a little more relatable. Yes, he still has rude tendencies but I don't think we understand all the pain under his mask."

Ashe chuckled lightly. "I feel a similar way to you."

Thorin went quiet again. "There's another we have to worry about."

"I know."

Ashe allowed the dark of the night to wash over her and finally fell asleep.

CHAPTER 16

Alaric arrived at the edge of Isern. Light peaked through the mountains. Alaric had his hood up to block the light. There had only been a few people within the streets. As early as it had been, it was a surprise to see life within the town. If there had been one word to describe the way he looked, it would be dirty. His clothes as well as his arms and face had been covered in mud.

He felt bad as well. His body ached, specifically his chest. He had been famished and dehydrated. The people that loitered on the street eyed him carefully. He hadn't walked very fast, he kept his eyes on the road and focused on putting one step ahead of the other. A man came up to him.

"Are you okay?" He asked. Alaric walked past him without a glance.

The man called out from behind him.

A shorter figure bumped into him from a nearby alleyway. He had almost lost his balance. He locked eyes with the figure as they crossed him. He saw something that caught his attention. The figure had been around Ashe's height. They wore a tattered grey-brown cloak and hid their hands within the cloak. The cloak's hood had been pulled tight to obscure the face. Alaric began to follow.

The cloaked figure walked fast and kept from the centre of the streets, Instead chose to walk through back roads and alleyways. He struggled to keep up and almost lost them on many occasions. Occasionally the figure would look behind themselves to check if anybody was following.

Alaric hadn't exactly been stealthy but kept a decent distance. Alaric watched as they turned into another alley. Alaric waited a moment then entered the alley. As he turned he was swiftly shoved into a wall. A dagger was swiftly placed at his neck. In a hushed tone, they spoke. "Who are you and why are you following me?"

Alaric stared at the figure threatening him. Her black eyes stared angrily back at him. Her face told Alaric that she was a beautiful woman around his age.

"Answer me or I will slit your throat." She barked.

"You have something that belongs to me." Alaric's voice came out dry and hoarse.

"That is a lie. I took nothing from you," She said. "Why are you here?" "Did she send you?"

"Where did you get that pouch?" Alaric asked as he glanced down.

She followed his glance when he suddenly shoved her away from him. The shove lacked power. He attempted to move away but could not get very far. She began chanting. A caster...I am done for. The woman pulled out another dagger and stabbed both daggers into the ground. Alaric watched as spikes began forming from the floor getting closer and closer toward him. He tried his best to get away but the spikes were soon upon him. He cast a barrier around him. He felt the spikes hit his barrier and ran out of stamina. The barrier dissipated and Alaric lost consciousness.

He woke up to an unfamiliar ceiling. He woke up feeling much better however his throat had still been dry and he had still been hungry. He had been half-naked, only dressed in his black trousers. The mud had also been cleaned off of him. The Rixa was cool to his skin. Movement to his left caught his attention. She held a wooden mug in one hand and a dagger in the other. She put the mug down next to Alaric, without breaking eye contact, and retreated to a corner of the room.

She had been staring at him. Alaric got a good look at her, now that the cloak's hood was down. She had long, straight brown hair that framed her face. She had been skinny and her clothes were loose on her body. The woman had been beautiful and that is a fact that he couldn't ignore. The room they had been in had been cramped. It had only one door and one window. The rest of the room was bare, it hadn't even had a bed. He grabbed the mug and drank whatever it held with haste. Luckily for him, it had been water. She watched him carefully and waited for him to finish the water before speaking.

"Scaev, what do you want from me?" She asked.

"I am not a Scaev," Alaric replied. His voice had gone back to normal.

She pointed with her dagger at Alaric's amulet.

Alaric rolled his eyes. "This amulet was forced onto me. I can't take it off or I'll die."

"Why should I believe you?" She quickly retorted.

"You have no reason to. Just like you had no reason to not kill me."

She flushed. "What did you want from me?"

"The pouch that you stole from me."

"I stole nothing from you, Scaev."

"I am not a Scaev!" Alaric sighed. "You stole a pouch from a short blonde woman dressed in all black, right?"

The woman just raised an eyebrow.

"That was my younger sister. Now I need that pouch back."

"Not gonna happen," She said.

Alaric stood up and moved.

"You are not going anywhere!" She yelled. Alaric complied and sat back down.

"Do you know how much sentz I will get if I report a Scaev to the empire?" She asked.

"All you casters are the same. You prefer power or sentz over people's lives. It is disgusting."

"You scaev's do not have the right to claim we are disgusting."

Alaric rolled his eyes. He stood up again, ignoring her protests. He scanned the cramped room for his clothes. He spotted his clothes and went to grab them when he felt a dagger at his throat. She's fast. I did not even hear her.

"You are not going anywhere." She ordered.

Alaric sighed and raised his hands in defeat. Once she removed the dagger, he used the chance to kick her against the torso. She fell onto her back but got back to her feet by doing an impressive kickflip. She held her daggers ready to strike.

"We do not have to do this," Alaric said. She threw a dagger directly at him. He cast a barrier and the dagger ricocheted off of the barrier. She quickly rushed to grab her dagger and attacked once again. She kept her body low to the ground. Alaric changed his cast and his body suddenly became translucent. Her attack phased right through him.

He took the opportunity to dash the door. He reached for the door but something knocked his feet right out from under him. He fell headfirst into the door. He was dazed for a few seconds. She dragged him by the feet back to the centre of the room. She used her knees to pin down his arms to the floor. She also brought a dagger close to his face.

"I called over some blues, they will be here shortly to take you away," She said.

Many possibilities ran through Alaric's mind.

"Fine." He said. "I will not try to run away."

She kept her position firm on him. Not believing him.

He relaxed his body. She didn't move from her position.

"What is a young woman like you, living alone in the city like this? What are you twenty or twenty-one?" He asked.

She did not respond.

Great.

"You do not seem to be having the best living arrangements, not what I would expect from a caster."

No response.

"There has to be something more important to you than sentz. What about your dreams, your family, your well-being?"

Something he had said weakened her grip on him slightly. He took the opportunity to lift himself off the ground. She yelped as she was thrown backwards. Her dagger fell to the ground. Alaric grabbed both her wrists in his hand and pinned her against the wall. The other dagger fell out of her hand and He swiped a foot at it. It slid across the floor. She was angry and she was struggling. Alaric held his grip firm.

"I can't afford to get captured." He said. She threw weak kicks at him. They were weak as she couldn't generate enough power.

"As much as I hate casters, how about we make a deal?" He said.

She spat at him. She braced herself for an incoming strike. Alaric did nothing.

"Look, I am not going to hurt you." He said.

She looked at him unconvinced.

"Why did you come to this town?" She asked.

"We came to free the mysurs under Chapman's rule."

"Impossible."

"Maybe, but I will die trying."

"Why?"

"Simple, the people of Nezzagwyn are counting on me." "So, how about that deal?"

She did not resist anymore.

"You don't hand me over to the soldiers and I will do anything you request, as long as it is within my power."

She did not seem convinced.

Alaric sighed. "You are in some sort of bad circumstances, right? I will fix it, whatever it is."

"Promise..." She whispered.

Alaric could barely hear it. "Promise, if I don't you can kill me and give my head to the soldiers."

She didn't say anything. Alaric released his grip on her. He half expected her to try and kill him, but she did not. She just stood there. Alaric slowly made his way to his clothes and got dressed. He heard her shuffle around behind him. He turned back toward her. She had again sat in the corner of the room with her daggers ready to strike.

"Alaric, that is my name."

He had expected her to introduce herself.

"I know," She said.

Alaric was stunned.

"There is a bounty for a man that fits your description, his name is Alaric and should be brought immediately to Adhu Aqua. Alive." She explained responding to his reaction.

Alaric was about to respond when a knock came at the door.

He watched as she waved for him to hide. He looked around the room for anywhere to hide but it was barren. He decided to hide behind the door. She sheathed her daggers before answering the door. She opened the door slightly.

"We have to come to collect the man you are harbouring." A voice said. Familiar.

Alaric bit hard on his fingertip until it drew blood. He then began smearing the blood on the door.

"I apologise, he has escaped," She said.

"You wasted our time." The door yanked open suddenly as the woman fell to the floor. Alaric saw blood drawing from her nose. His hands started to shake. It is Diable all over again. The blood. The death. He began to hyperventilate.

A familiar large man entered the room. He did not notice Alaric behind the door. Jugz.

"You little bitch, always causing trouble. She ordered us not to kill you, but we can have some fun." Jugz said. He raised his boot to stomp on her. Alaric cast a barrier on the woman. Jugz' foot bounced off of it. Alaric released the barrier and slammed the door shut. He knew there were more. The rune he drew on the door shone a pale yellow. The woman quickly rolled away as the barrier was removed. Jugz turned around to face Alaric. His face burst with anger.

"You!" He yelled. He grabbed his sword. Alaric watched Jugz walk towards him. Jugz was unaware of what was happening behind him. The woman grabbed her daggers and swiped at Jugz' calves. Jugz fell to his knees with a shout of pain. Alaric wasted no time and kicked at Jugz' chest. Jugz groaned. Great, he is still injured. He swiped a kick at Jugz' head causing him to slump to the ground. He turned to the door that was bulging with every bang.

Not going to last long. He watched as the woman was about to pounce on Jugz. He swiftly stopped her. He then swept her off her feet as he lifted her. She protested. Alaric jumped out of the window. Glass shattered around them. He prayed that they hadn't been far from the ground. His prayers were answered as the drop was not very far.

They ended up in some sort of alleyway. The woman forced her way out of Alaric's grasp. She then motioned for him to follow. He nodded as they ran through alleys. He noticed she tied her hair up as she ran. She then pulled the hood of her cloak on. Alaric did the same with his hooded robe. She led them to a dead-end.

"We should be safe for now," She said.

Alaric sat down against a wall of a nearby building.

"Is there any place to get some food?" Alaric asked.

She didn't respond. She is terrible at communication.

"Do they normally treat you that badly?" He asked.

No response.

After a few minutes, she walked.

"Where are you going?"

"Food. You stay here. You move, I will find you and kill you," She threatened.

"Not like I know where to go." He said as she left.

Chapter 17

Ashe read the same section of the tome over and over again. Trying to decipher the cast that had been written. She had been strolling through the city. They had left the inn early and had separated. She sighed as she couldn't decipher the text. She found her way to the centre of the town. Chapman's factory was unlike anything else in the town. It was the only building that was built directly on the Gwyn River. The building stood on a large circular stone platform.

It had two bridges connected to it, presumably to be accessed from both sides of the town. The Gwyn River cut Isern in two halves. The halves had been connected via a series of bridges. Ashe had never seen architecture like this in her life. She had gone from wooden huts with the village of Diable to large stone buildings and large landscapes filled with mountains and deserts. This had been everything she wished for as a child. Priest Able would tell her stories of his journeys within the mainland but she hadn't expected to experience them herself.

"Impressive, isn't it?" A voice to her right startled her. An elderly man stood watching the factory alongside her.

She nodded. "It is unbelievable."

"Not from town, I see." "This one building is owned by King Godric himself." The old man said.

"King Godric...not Chapman?" She asked.

The old man chuckled. "Chapman just runs the damned thing. There are three of these buildings in all of Hominus. One on West Hominus and there are two others on East Hominus."

"What purpose do they serve?"

"They manufacture metal for the king."

"Why is manufacturing metal so important?"

The old man seemed surprised by her question. "Godric, the King of Metals."

Ashe was confused by the relevance of that statement. "Is there any way to access the factory?"

The old man shook his head. "They do not allow outsiders in. Only men of high nobility and blues are allowed within the factory."

"Blues?"

"The soldiers, my dear." The old man pointed at a few blue-robed soldiers that patrolled around the building. "They are probably getting a bit suspicious of us gawking at the building."

Ashe spotted a few soldiers that stared at her. She watched as the old man began walking away from the building. She followed him.

"Excuse me...um...sir. Do you perhaps know of a place where I can obtain some sentz?"

"That depends, dear. There are probably many stores around here that require an extra pair of hands but they wouldn't pay a lot I am afraid."

"Is there no way to earn sentz faster?" She asked.

"You should have mentioned you were desperate. When the light dissipates tonight, head to the northeast corner of town. You will find what you are looking for there." The man held a weird expression as he walked away.

There were still many hours until night came. She decided to continue strolling through the town, this time looking for any sign of Alaric.

Florian spent his time walking through the town aimlessly. His thoughts were a jumbled mess. He had to focus on earning sentz and getting information on Chapman, so why was he stuck thinking about Alaric's and his relationship? He felt angry and confused. He still hadn't forgiven Alaric for not telling them about the caster attack back in Diable.

This jumbled up with the whole mess at Versus caused him to question his older brother. Is he even the person he claimed to be? Florian replayed the aftermath of the Diable attack over and over again within his mind. And some aspects never made any sense to him. Alaric claimed the villagers fought back but would they even stand a chance? When he fought Jugz, it was made clear to him that a single soldier is much stronger than a simple mysur.

How had they fought back? There was another weird inconsistency. Every caster that died that day had one thing in common. A singular cut at their throats. Surely if a fight occurred there would be more than one type of injury. When he found

Alaric, he had been covered in blood but had no visible wounds. Alas, Alaric held no weapon close to him.

If he had asked Alaric himself, he was certain all he would receive would be lies. Florian had been struggling with this since they had left Versus. He couldn't trust Alaric until he had known the truth. He was ripped out of his head when he heard two voices call out to him.

"Excuse me, sir!" The voices called.

Florian turned around, two young boys stood a distance from him. They waved at him. One of the boys had been taller than the other. They looked similar, almost like brothers. Florian walked over to them and knelt so that he had been on their level.

"How can I help?" He said with a smile.

"Grandpa is looking for some help." The younger one said. They dragged Florian by the wrists. They led him to a wooden house. The house had not been built completely. The roof consisted of only a few wooden planks. The brothers led him into the house. There he saw a younger woman watching over an elderly man who lay on a bed.

"Grandpa, we found some help!" The brother's yelled.

The woman turned around to look at Florian.

"Boys, I told you to stop bothering random people." The woman said.

The brother's let go of Florian. The woman walked over to him.

"I am sorry about them. They just wanted to help their grandpa." She apologised.

"It is not a problem. Maybe I can help." Florian said.

The woman was stunned.

"I mean, as long as you don't mind me." He said.

"Let the boy help. We need all the help we can get." The old man groaned.

The woman chuckled.

"What do you need me to do?" Florian asked.

"Before that, I am Jinny. The old man is my husband's father, Tybalt. And they are my two sons, the older one is Jasper, the younger one is Jeph." The woman said.

"Who are you calling an old man!" Tybalt yelled, causing Florian to chuckle.

"I am Florian, it is nice to meet you."

Jinny led him to an area where long wooden planks were placed.

"We need someone to finish the roof. The old man, unfortunately, hurt his back while he was working." Jinny said, glancing at the wooden skeleton that was their roof.

"What happened to your husband?"

"Oh, he is a soldier. He works at the factory. He only returns late at night. We can't possibly ask him to do this for us."

"I am certainly not an expert in roof building but I will see what I can do."

Jinny went on to explain the specifics of what he had to do.

This was how Florian found himself balancing precariously on top of a house. Hammering away at the wooden planks. He watched the two brothers play, fight and make up all in a few hours of the day. It reminded him of his fights with Alaric when they had been younger. They had always fought over everything but would stop once Ashe began to cry. The thought brought a slight smile. The evening arrived and Florian had been mostly done with the roof. He climbed down the roof. Jinny was waiting for him as he climbed. She thanked him for his work and handed him five pieces of sentz. Which he hesitantly accepted.

"How about you join us for dinner?" Jinny asked.

"I couldn't possibly do that."

"What are you saying, you helped us it is only right we treat you. I am certain the boys are excited for you to join us."

Florian could not refuse and found himself eating alongside the family. The food was the best he has ever tasted. The brother's got into another argument which was stopped via a reprimand from their mother. Florian smiled.

"Do you have any siblings?" Jinny asked suddenly.

Florian nodded. "An older brother and a younger sister."

"Do you get along with them?"

"With my sister, yes. My brother...well."

Jinny chuckled. "That is usually how it goes with siblings."

"Do you have siblings, Miss Jinny?"

"Why yes, I have five sisters and we fight all the time."

Florian looked down.

"Is something wrong?" Jinny asked.

"It is nothing."

Jinny looked unconvinced.

Florian sighed. "It is just that...my brother. We were not exactly in the best of circumstances when he left."

"Did your brother pass on?" She asked solemnly.

Florian shook his head. "I am not certain."

Jinny smiled softly at him. "He is out there. And when you reunite, give him a big smile."

Florian chuckled. "Maybe."

After the meal, he headed back to the inn and booked himself a room. He did not see Thorin or Ashe. He assumed they had already been asleep since it had already been late. He went to sleep.

Thorin found herself serving drinks and meals at a tavern. She had been lucky that the particular barmaid had fallen sick. She begged the owners to allow her to help. They were sceptical since she had been a mysur. She had since spent half the day working at the tavern. The tavern was large, much larger than her grandmother's.

The tavern had been incredibly busy since early light. She wondered how these people could drink so casually while there had been mysurs suffering daily. Half of the reason she sought out this job was so that she could gain information. She thought that working within a tavern would allow her to overhear some useful gossip. This was where her luck ran out, unfortunately. She had overheard nothing useful.

Recently though, the most interesting topic that most people were talking about was that a few soldiers got attacked. No one had the specifics, they all just stated that a mysterious man attacked a soldier who was named Jugz. As night was slowly approaching, a group of soldiers entered the tavern. Thorin had been a bit hesitant to serve them but followed through regardless.

The evening went smoothly until one soldier went to speak to the owners of the tavern. The tavern suddenly went quiet. Nobody spoke and if they did they whispered. Thorin looked around but did not notice anything strange. The soldier returned after the meeting with the owners.

He nodded at the other soldiers who got up from their seats. They were headed directly towards her. Thorin reached for her blade but was quickly interrupted as a soldier from behind began to choke her. She was screaming and struggling as they dragged her out. She watched as the people within the tavern just watched on whispering amongst one another.

CHAPTER 18

Is she going to come back? Alaric thought as he sat in the alleyway. It had been way past midday as the sky was darkening. He had not seen anyone since his escape from the house. If you could call it a house. He watched as the woman turned the corner holding a loaf of bread. She broke it into two pieces and gave one half to Alaric.

"Thank you," Alaric said as he scarfed the bread down rapidly.

"Savia," The woman whispered as she bit into the bread.

Alaric gave her a questioning look.

"My name...is Savia"

Progress.

Alaric finished his bread in no time. He then turned to Savia. She was still eating her bread.

"I promised I would help you but I require you to explain your circumstances."

Savia looked indifferent.

Great, she is not going to speak.

"I...want you to...free me."

Alaric had to concentrate to hear what she said. "Free you of what?"

No response.

"I need you to cooperate if I am to help you."

"Why did you protect me earlier?" She asked.

"I just felt it was the right thing to do."

"Liar, scaev was supposed to be cruel people."

"And I said, I am not part of the scaev."

No response.

"Why are we just sitting here? I have better things to do." Alaric stood up and was ready to walk but the familiar dagger at his throat made its presence. So fast.

"First, help me, then you can do whatever you want." She said

Alaric sighed. "I am trying but you are not giving me anything."

"We wait for night," She said. Savia removed her dagger and Alaric sat back down.

Moments passed in silence.

"You have no intention of giving my pouch back."

"Can't," She whispered. "If you are not scaev....why are you to be brought to Adhu Aqua?"

"I am not certain...but Great Lord Ivo probably has something to do with it."

Savia reacted with surprise.

"It has been sixteen years since I have seen Ivo. If he is searching for me then it probably means his message got to the king." Alaric felt as if he had been talking to himself. It felt sort of...refreshing. Savia did not respond, she just sat there.

It was late when Savia finally got up. She motioned for him to follow. It had not taken them long to reach their destination. They stood in front of a large establishment. The building had not been very tall but it had been wide. It had no stand-out features, other than the two soldiers that stood guard at the large entrance. The soldiers ignored Savia instead watched him precariously. Savia walked up to the entrance and he followed. The soldiers didn't do anything but watched as they entered the building.

Alaric did not know what to expect but it certainly had not been this. The whole establishment had been lit by a series of chandeliers. The place was packed full of people. There had been a musky aroma that had been strong. Savia seemed unsurprised by the happenings around her. There had been men and women alike that seemed formally dressed, they all wore extravagant jewellery. Some had been drinking and others hadn't.

This was not what surprised Alaric though. Alongside the 'noblemen' were half-naked and fully naked women and men alike. Each one had been chained by the neck. The chain in which each nobleman/woman had a tight hold. What is this place? Alaric assumed the chained individuals were mysurs. Some mysurs were dancing for their 'owners'. Some 'owners' enjoyed their slaves.

"Why are we here?" He asked.

Savia gave no response. She led him to the back area of the establishment. There they found a stage. On the stage was a large velvet couch on which a woman sat. She had revealing silk clothing. She had possibly been in her late thirties or early forties Alaric assumed. She had been incredibly attractive. Two chained men lay on the couch alongside her. There had also been two soldiers adjacent to the couch. The woman reacted immediately as Savia entered the stage.

"My dear Savia, you have caused me quite the trouble earlier," She said. She walked up to Savia and grabbed her face sensually. Alaric noticed how uncomfortable Savia looked. This is what she meant when she asked me to free her.

Savia grabbed the pouch that dangled from her belt. My pouch.

Savia was about to give it to the woman before she got slapped across the face.

"Did I give you permission to attack the blues?" The woman asked.

"No...Lady Gwen." Savia said.

The woman tried to slap her once again but Alaric grabbed her wrist. He watched as the soldiers reacted immediately. They grabbed their swords. Lady Gwen waved them off.

"It seems you got yourself a nice plaything, Savia." Lady Gwen analysed Alaric. She licked her lips as she took her time inspecting him. Alaric hadn't felt comfortable under her stare. She had stared a moment longer below his waist.

"Who might you be, boy?" She asked.

"He is nobody," Savia responded immediately. Alaric hasn't heard her speak this loudly before. Alaric let go of Lady Gwen's wrist. She kept her eyes on him, smiling slightly. Savia gave Lady Gwen the pouch. She opened it and her eyes grew wide with bewilderment. "Well done, Savia. It seems you have hit the jackpot." Lady Gwen placed her hand on Alaric's chest. "Though I should probably have you to thank." Her hand ran down Alaric's chest and down toward his groin. Alaric flinched and stepped back causing Lady Gwen to chuckle. Lady Gwen gave Savia three pieces of sentz. Savia turned to leave the stage.

"I am not done with you quite yet, Savia." Lady Gwen called out.

Savia never made eye contact, her eyes were set firmly on the floor. Almost mysur-like.

"I would like for you to meet your new partner."

"Partner?"

"Why yes, another like you just fell into my hands." Lady Gwen along with her soldiers led Savia and Alaric toward a basement section of the establishment. There they found large man-sized cages. More naked women and men were locked up. Lady Gwen stopped at the second last cage. Alaric froze as he saw the figure in the cage.

"Alaric! Help me!" Ashe yelled when she saw him. She banged on the iron bars of the cage. Alaric ran up to her. "Alaric?" Another familiar voice called.

"I am so glad you are okay," Ashe said.

"I am fine, but you seem to be in trouble," Alaric said.

Ashe nodded. "Thorin is here too." She pointed at the cage adjacent to hers.

"And Florian?"

Ashe shrugged.

"It seems we know each other already." Lady Gwen said.

Alaric turned around. He had been irate. "Release my sister and my friend, now!" Alaric ordered.

"Oooo feisty. I like it." Lady Gwen said. Alaric walked up to her but was stopped by the soldiers.

"Losing your head now...may lead to the loss of heads," Lady Gwen said sternly, causing him to stop struggling.

Alaric looked back toward Ashe. She did not seem harmed, she had her spear with her and was not chained. He glanced at Thorin's cage. She had been chained and her clothes had been ripped revealing herself. She hadn't had her blade with her.

"Your sister came to me for work," Lady Gwen said. "I offered her the ability to work the floor but she refused. Then a wonderful idea came to me. Why don't I just make her my pet, just like Savia."

Alaric allowed himself to calm down. Do not cause a scene, think rationally.

I quite like angry Alaric. He reminds me of someone.

Shut up.

"The other struggled but it is just a matter of time before we break her in," Lady Gwen said, glancing at Thorin.

In a bizarre contrast to the mood of the room, Alaric began to laugh. Everyone looked at him with confusion.

"What is funny?" Lady Gwen asked.

"Nothing, I just connected the dots." "You are just a pawn in this town," Alaric said mockingly.

"Be careful of the way you speak to me, boy. I am Gwenllian the Queen of Isern's Underworld. Nothing happens in this town without my knowing." She seemed agitated at Alaric's comment.

Exactly the response I wanted.

"Funny, everyone I spoke to said that this town is Lord Chapman's. No one quite spoke of a Gwenllian." Alaric said.

Alaric saw the scorn on Gwenllian's face.

"What is your point, boy?"

Alaric smiled. "It is not so much a point as it is a proposition."

Gwenllian lifted her eyebrow.

"There is one thing all casters thrive for. Power. Chapman is the one who has all the power in this town. I am guessing Chapman allows you to run your 'business' with good compensation."

Gwenllian's expression did not give anything away but she let Alaric explain further.

"It would be quite a shock if Chapman was removed from his position. I am sure that will leave a big power gap, one that could be filled by someone of your stature."

Gwenllian began chuckling. "Fool, you cannot take Chapman down."

"Maybe, maybe not. But with your help, I am certain that our chances will be greater."

"And why would you assume that I will help you?"

"Sentz. You would have free access to Chapman's entire stash. The funds he receives from King Godric. As well as the sentz he scams out of Gwyn villages."

"Tempting offer but what happens if you fail?"

"You get to keep me. You've heard my name, Great Lord Ivo will pay good money for me. Or you could keep me for your pleasure."

Gwenllian walked up to him and ran her hand down his arm. "You sure know the way to a ladies heart." "When do you plan to take Chapman out?"

Alaric tried desperately not to flinch. "How about we meet here tomorrow and discuss the plan?"

"That seems reasonable. I will have your sister's head if you don't show up."

Alaric answered with a firm nod. He then turned to Ashe.

"Will you be fine staying here?" He asked.

She nodded. "Who is she?" Ashe pointed at Savia.

"She is...a friend...I guess."

"You guess?"

"Yes, it is complicated." "I will find Florian and then we will be able to get you out."

"You too, Thorin." He said loud enough for her to hear.

"You'd better." Her voice echoed slightly.

Alaric noticed Savia leaving the room, he quickly said his farewells and followed her. He felt uncomfortable walking through the main room. The smell and sounds of the room was a topic he had not been accustomed to yet. Savia looked back towards him occasionally. Once they got outside, Savia turned toward him. "Why are you following me?" She asked quietly.

"I was hoping you would let me stay with you for the night."

"So that you can kill me in my sleep?"

"If I wanted to kill you, I would have done it by now."

Savia scoffed in disbelief.

"You would be surprised by the things I have done." Alaric glanced at his hands. Why is it so much easier to talk to her?

"We all had to do hard things. You are not special," Savia said.

Alaric laughed. "My whole life was spent with people who told me how special I am. Alaric is so smart, Alaric will be like his father, Alaric will be our saviour. You are the first person to tell me otherwise."

"Good for you, I guess," Savia said emotionlessly. She began to walk. Alaric followed. She led him back to the alleyway where they had sat before. Savia sat against the wall. Alaric sat next to her.

"Pretty comfortable," Alaric said.

She eyed him, failing to see the humour. "Soldiers are waiting for me at my home. I can't return tonight."

"What do they want with you?"

Savia crossed her arms and held tight onto her arms.

Oh...

"She is going to betray you," Savia whispered.

"Gwenllian? I know. But I intend to do the same."

"She will eat you alive."

"Me maybe but not him..."

Savia raised an eyebrow but did not question further.

"You do not have time to worry about me, you'll have a more difficult part to play," Alaric said.

Savia faced him. He almost got lost in her raven black eyes.

"You will be helping us take down Chapman."

Savia shook her head.

"You want to be free, right. Then this will be the least you will have to do," Alaric said.

"Why should I trust you? Everyone in this town betrays me," Savia said softly.

Alaric sighed. "You don't. No one should trust me. It will just bring pain. I would not be shocked to find you gone in the morning."

Savia faced forward and closed her eyes. "I will choose who I will trust."

Alaric smiled softly as he closed his eyes.

You better be prepared as well.

You could ask nicely, I was the one who saved you against that masked fellow.

Chapter 19

Savia woke up as the first light from Ysgafyn's twin shone through the mountains. Savia could never sleep more than four hours each night. A side effect from growing up on the streets of Isern. Every soul that walked into Isern was a potential enemy or competition. She could not allow them to get ahead of her. She glanced to her side. Alaric laid there softly snoring. She thought about killing him many times already but there was something about him that stopped her.

She could not quite place the feeling. There had been no reason to keep him around. He would eventually betray her like everyone else. She watched how he leaned as he slept. Thoughts of the previous day passed through her mind. He had protected her against the blue and he had stopped Lady Gwen from slapping her. What is his true goal? Does he just want my body like all of the others? Why do I feel safe when I am with him? Safe...I am definitely not safe.

She stopped him from leaning too far forward. She analysed his face. She then pulled out one of her daggers. One swipe and it is all over. He confuses you. She couldn't do it. She hid her dagger again. He promised he would free her, she had seen many empty promises before.

Men that ensured her that they would whisk her away from the street life only to disappear without a trace. Leaving her alone to fend for herself. Her mother's words rang through her head. 'Savia, one day someone will come for you. Do not shy away from their love. They will give to you what I couldn't.' Many claimed they loved her over the years. None turned out to be true. She just wrote her mother off for being delusional. Alaric began shifting alongside her.

Savia swiftly stopped staring at him.

"Good morning," He said in his morning voice.

Savia nodded. "You are not...surprised...that there is...not a dagger in your chest?"

Alaric chuckled. "I think that would be an honourable way to go out." Alaric stood up and began stretching. "You know that is a strange question to ask someone who just woke up."

"You are the one who is strange." Savia stood up imitating him.

"Perhaps."

Alaric had been tall compared to Savia. Despite him towering over her, he never seemed hostile towards her. Even when they have been fighting in her home.

She was dragged out of her thoughts when he spoke. He had been looking toward the sky.

"It is probably too early to look for Florian. How about we have a spar?"

"Spar?"

Alaric nodded then stared at her. Those stupid blue eyes.

"We need to kill time and we need to sharpen our skills before the operation," He explained, cracking his fingers. "Few rules though, no casting and no causing major injuries."

"Can I use my daggers?" She asked.

"Of course."

They faced each other standing a few metres from each other. It was Alaric that moved first. He dashed forward and swung a boot at her. Slow. Savia easily dodged it. She used his body's momentum to shove his leg away from her. She aimed a tame dagger at his chest.

She hadn't expected him to reverse kick her with the same leg. His boot hit the back of her head. Alaric had withheld some power but it was still enough to daze her slightly. She had been facing the ground on all fours. He baited me. Instead of waiting to get back to her feet, she balanced herself on her arms and swung her body in an impressive manoeuvre.

Her legs swiped Alaric's out from under him. Alaric fell on his tailbone. She did not stop, with her daggers firm in her hand she charged the prone figure. He laid on his back as he caught her wrists before they reached him. She struggled to free her wrists. She put pressure on his abdomen with her knee. With an incredible display of strength, he flung her over himself. She landed painfully on her back. He kept a tight grip on her wrists. She was getting to her feet when he let go of her.

"Stop," He said. "What can we learn from that short scuffle?"

Savia shrugged.

"Let's start with you. You are incredibly fast and agile, however, you lost the moment you attempted to overpower me. You will not win most battles of strength."

Savia raised an eyebrow.

"When you knocked me down, you should've either tried to restrain my movement or aim to kill."

"You told me not to cause major injuries,"

Alaric chuckled. "True, I have said that."

"And you?" Savia asked.

Alaric thought for a bit. "I need to stop taking my foes at face value."

Savia did not understand what he meant.

"You are not going to ask me, what I meant by that?" Alaric chuckled. "Listen, I knew you were fast. Much faster than I am, therefore I tried to bait you into dodging my kick. It worked, but I never considered that you would be able to twist and swing your body like that."

Savia got tired as it seemed he wouldn't stop talking. Savia lunged at him, aiming a strike at his chest. Alaric was startled and jumped to the back, barely dodging the blow.

"You talk too much," She said.

"Why does everybody tell me that?" He said, smiling softly.

They continued their sparring until they were fatigued.

Savia walked silently behind Alaric through the streets of Isern. She knew that they were supposed to be looking for someone named Florian but she had no idea what he looked like. Why am I even going along with this? She could have spent her morning stealing as she normally has, why did she have to spar with him? She had learnt a bit of how to fight better but he was just going to betray her. There was no need to waste time. She almost bumped into Alaric's back as he froze before her. He seemed to be looking up at something. She followed his gaze and saw a man knocking a wooden plank into the roof of a building. She watched Alaric's expression darken.

"Florian!" He yelled.

The man on the roof was startled and looked toward them. The man gasped and climbed down the roof via a ladder. As he climbed down, Savia noticed the door opening revealing a woman. She seemed curious as to what was happening outside of what seemed to be her house. The man she assumed was Florian finally reached the ground. He held a big grin on his face. He dashed and hugged Alaric tightly. Alaric did not seem to reciprocate the hug. He still held a scowl.

"Alaric, you are alive!" Florian said

Savia watched as the other woman gasped a little as she heard Alaric's name. A part of her wanted to tug at Alaric's robe and tell him to get out of here. Why do I care?

Florian withdrew from his hug. "Did you find Ashe and Thorin? They'll probably be happy to see you."

Alaric's frown deepened. "What the hell are you doing?" Alaric yelled.

Florian was taken aback at his tone.

"Ashe and Thorin are captured!" "And what are you doing? Enjoying your time with these casters."

Florian was stunned.

Why does he hate casters that much?

The woman tried to get between the two men.

"I am pretty sure, Florian here did not know anything about that. He was helping us with our crisis." The woman said.

Alaric did not even look at the woman. He shoved her aside. "This is a family issue."

Florian attempted to punch Alaric. Savia watched as Alaric swiftly gestured with his hands to cast a small barrier around himself. Florian's punch hit the barrier.

Alaric shook his head. Savia assumed in disappointment.

"Where are they?" Florian asked.

"Now you are suddenly interested. Pathetic."

So he can be petty too.

Alaric turned around and began to walk. She followed closely behind him.

"Tonight, the north-east corner of town. Be there." Alaric said as he took his leave.

She watched his expression closely. He held a frown but there was something deeper there. Maybe...regret.

Nighttime came and Savia had been waiting alongside Alaric at Gwenllian's establishment. Despite it being nighttime, it hadn't gotten any colder. It had always been like this in Isern however. It had never rained or had even been windy. The warm temperatures had always been constant. People often say that Isern is the calm before the storm of Adhu Aqua. She never knew what the saying meant.

"Was I a bit too harsh?" Alaric's voice broke her out of her thoughts. She did not know how to answer his question. She was not well averse to sibling arguments.

Alaric took one look at her and chuckled. "Do not have siblings, I am guessing."

How did he know? She shook her head. Alaric then looked forward.

"Will he come?" She asked.

Alaric nodded. "He will be here. He may be a little naive but he is a much better man than I am."

Why does he always talk down to himself?

They waited for a while but just like Alaric predicted Florian arrived. He hadn't shown any angry expression on his face. Alaric and Florian glanced at each other. They hadn't said a word. Alaric entered the establishment. The establishment was as disgusting as it always had been. Savia saw Gwenllian at the back of the large room. Her eyes were fixated on Alaric.

"Alaric..." Florian whispered from behind Savia.

"I know. I will deal with it." Alaric said quietly.

Deal with what?

They met with Gwenllian at the stage they were at earlier. Like usual she had her hands all over Alaric. The sight angered her. Why did it? There was no reason to get angry by it. Gwenllian took one look at Florian and looked back at Alaric.

"You bringing me more fresh blood?" Gwenllian asked teasingly.

"He is off-limits. You will only have me." Alaric said.

Gwenllian got close to Alaric. Her body practically touched him. Savia had one hand on her daggers. "Aw, what a spoilsport. But I am fine with that. I prefer my men with a little...kick to them." Gwenllian ran a finger across Alaric's lips and walked away. They followed her to the basement level. There they met with Alaric's sister- her name had been Ashe if she recalled properly. The one they called Thorin had also been moved into Alaric's sister's cage. She wore a robe that she probably got from Alaric's sister. Savia, Alaric, Florian and Gwenllian stood on the outside of the cage. Florian said his apologies to Ashe and Thorin. Both of them had not been as angry as Alaric had.

"Can we get back to business? There are sentz to be made," Gwenllian said. She was guarded by two soldiers.

Alaric cleared his throat. "All we require is a method of getting into the building. I suppose you can handle that for us."

"Perhaps. But tell me, are all of you planning to enter the factory?" Gwenllian asked mockingly.

Alaric nodded.

"Impossible." Gwenllian scanned everyone in the room. She first pointed at Alaric and then at Ashe. "Both of you will stay here...as insurance."

Savia watched as Thorin and Florian were about to argue but stopped when Alaric raised his hand. What kind of hold does he have on people?

"That is fine. Now tell us, how do you intend to get them into the factory?"

"Weekly there arrives a shipment of iron ingots from Arstutia. The iron ingots are collected from a merchant outside of town by one of Chapman's soldiers." "From there it is simple, ambush the soldier and steal his identity and replace the ingots with two of your friends. That should get you into the factory," Gwenllian explained.

Alaric thought for a moment. Savia watched as the rest just watched him with hopeful eyes.

"Once they are in the factory, where will they be taken?" He asked.

"There is a storage unit placed somewhere in the middle floors. You are on your own from there. Chapman does not speak about his affairs very often. But there will be one certainty, I want Chapman dead." Gwenllian said in the most serious tone Savia has ever heard her.

She could swear she saw Alaric's face change a split second when Gwenllian mentioned wanting Chapman dead.

"When does the next shipment get here?" Alaric asked.

"In five days. Now if you will excuse me, I have some guests to entertain." Gwenllian left followed by her soldiers. Leaving Savia alone with Alaric and his friends. They waited until Gwenllian was out of earshot to speak.

"Why are we dealing with a snake, like her?" Thorin asked.

They turned to Alaric.

"We have no choice. She gave us a chance, we will have to take it." He said.

Florian still did not look directly at Alaric as he spoke. "We can't do it without you. We are also not strong enough. And that woman is surely going to try something."

"I can say with certainty, whether or not you take care of Chapman, she has no intention to let me go." Alaric said.

The rest looked at Alaric.

"Do not worry about it. Florian, you are strong enough and will be even more so if you figure out how to wield that sword."

Florian was about to speak but Alaric continued his speech.

"When you are in the factory, you will have to rely on stealth to take out the soldiers. You cannot face them upfront." Alaric continued to speak about their plan once they infiltrated the factory.

"Thorin and I cannot take out the entire factory by ourselves," Florian stated.

"Why'd you assume you are the only two? You have an incredibly powerful person joining you." Alaric stated as he motioned to Savia, who froze in place. She pulled her cloak's hood even tighter against her face.

"Who exactly is she? You mentioned she was a friend," Ashe said behind bars.

Friend, he considered me a friend? I tried to kill him. Savia and Alaric's eyes met. He is going to tell them I'm a thief.

"This is Savia, she is a caster. She will help us," He explained. Is that it? I never even offered to help.

Thorin gave her a scowl. Florian looked at her with indifference and Ashe beamed at her.

"I don't trust her," Thorin said.

"She will not betray us," Alaric said.

"How sure are you about that?" Thorin said.

"I just know. Let's drop this. We have to prepare for the infiltration."

Before they left, Ashe called Alaric. Savia did not need to wait for him but she felt she needed to. She watched as Ashe showed Alaric some sort of Large book. She had been pointing at a specific page. Savia watched as Alaric's eyes grew large. Ashe gave him the book. Alaric scratched at the stubble on his chin. Savia noted he often did it when he was thinking. He was pulled out of his thoughts when he noticed Savia waiting for him. Savia could swear she saw his lips curve upwards a tiny bit.

They left the basement level and headed for the exit. Gwenllian smiled at her as they left. They met with Florian at the entrance. He too seemed to be deep in thought.

"I got us rooms at the inn," Florian said as he began to walk.

"Florian, I am sorry for lashing out at you like that."

Florian stopped in his tracks. "What really happened that day?"

Alaric did not seem confused. "You figured out my story wasn't the complete truth? Unfortunately, I cannot tell you."

Florian was about to grab Alaric but Savia withdrew her daggers and in a moment she was between them. Florian stopped immediately.

"He got you under his thumb as well? Typical," Florian stated.

Am I under his thumb?

Florian turned to walk.

Alaric placed a hand on her shoulder. "I keep secrets to protect you and Ashe."

Florian stopped again. "Protect us from what?"

"Protect you from me..."

Savia wondered what he meant by that sentence.

Florian continued walking. They followed him toward the inn. Florian had enough sentz to pay for three rooms. The two men just walked into their respective rooms. This left Savia in her room. She was not accustomed to bed. She could not fall asleep. She instead took to the floor where she fell asleep peacefully.

Chapter 20

Florian found himself crouched behind some bushes. To his right had been Thorin who had still been dressed in Ashe's robe. To his left had been the woman Alaric called Savia. The past four days he watched as Alaric and Savia spar. He couldn't quite place it but it seemed she had some sort of hold on Alaric. He asked her about it but she did not answer. He was pretty sure she had not spoken a single word to him. He heard her talk silently to Alaric on a few occasions.

He had not spoken to Alaric since that night. He can't be thinking about those things now, however. They were on an important mission. They watched as a blue-robed soldier stood waiting on the road. The soldier was a large mean-looking man. If Florian had a choice he would avoid antagonising such a man. It had been late afternoon, he noticed that Thorin alongside the soldier had been getting impatient.

"The shipment should be here by now," Thorin whispered.

Florian nodded. Savia just kept her eyes on the man.

"Do you think that Gwenllian betrayed us?" He asked.

Thorin shrugged. She had her blade firmly placed in her hands. Florian still had the crimson blade on his back. He had barely made progress with using it. He now could only hold it for a few seconds. He eyed the soldier's blade. He could probably steal it. After a few moments, he could hear a quiet rumbling. A man dressed in a full suit on horseback came slowly into vision.

The horse had a wide metal container attached to it. The container had been moved by its many wheels. The soldier and the smartly dressed man spoke at first, then the soldier checked the contents of the container. He seemed pleased with what he found. They then worked together to unlatch the container from the horse. Once the container had been freed from the horse, the suited man took off on his horse.

This was the time they had to strike. Florian was frozen. He watched as Savia charged. She had been incredibly fast and silent. The large man did not hear her coming. She kept her body low to the ground and once she reached striking distance she pierced the back of the man's calf with one of her daggers. The man dropped with a scream. What am I doing? I should be moving.

When Florian got up from his prone, Thorin had already been upon the screaming man. She expertly dispatched the man. Her blade ran through the man's neck. The man stopped screaming. As Florian got closer he could feel the bile rising in his throat. It had almost been like that day. He knew he had to steel himself. They could not accomplish the mission without killing a few soldiers, not to mention Chapman. Thorin's voice brought him out of his trance.

"Let's go, we are already late," She said.

Thorin and Savia opened the container. They were met with large iron ingots. They began unpacking the container. They left Florian with a more difficult task. He had to undress the deceased man. He kept his eyes closed as much as possible. Eventually, he got the man out of his clothes. Luckily most of the blood was on the floor and only some remained on the man's clothes. Hopefully, nobody notices. The man's clothes had been a little loose on him. Not that he minded that much. Savia and Thorin got into the container.

There had only been space for them to lie tightly side by side, much to Thorin's dismay. She had openly announced her distrust of Savia. He could understand where she came from. Alaric just brought in a random person to join them. Not to mention she had been a caster. He wasn't even sure Thorin trusted them. He placed the iron ingots softly on their bodies, according to Alaric's plan. He saw Thorin's scowl at her current position. Savia kept a straight expression. He placed the lid on the container.

Okay, all you have to do is drag this container to the factory. Isern had not been far, probably a three to five-minute walk. Florian walked, pushing the container forward. It had been a bit heavy but nothing he could not have handled. As he got closer to the centre of Isern, his heart began beating out of his chest. When the factory came into sight he froze. This had not been part of the plan.

A large squadron stood at the entrance of the factory. He knocked twice on the lid of the container. Their signal for telling each other something is wrong. He kept pushing the container. A few soldiers watched him. He put up his hood. As he reached the factory, the squadron made a path for him to walk through. At the end of the path was the factory's entrance. A soldier waited for him there.

He had been quite young and seemed happy. Alongside him was an older blonde woman, she had also been dressed in blue robes. She glared at Florian. Next to her was a large cat-like animal. He recognized it. Alaric told him about it before. What was it called again? An ocelot that's right. He greeted the young soldier, trying to keep his nerve. The young soldier did not question him, instead, he just opened the container to check his contents. Florian had been tense.

After a few moments, the young soldier smiled and closed the container. He motioned that Florian should follow him. He opened the steel doors of the factory and Florian pushed the container into it. The inside of the factory had been very humid. Probably due to all the metal. A loud clang could be heard continuously. It pulsated throughout the building echoing against the wall.

The hallways had been wide. There had been a few soldiers roaming around the ground floor. They had chatted amongst each other casually. They walked past a staircase. Alaric told them to gather as much information as possible. The walls had been unbearably bare, there was no sight of any artwork. Instead in a few rooms, he noticed there were large full-sized models dressed in metal armour. The armour had blue accents. The young soldier brought him to a large cage-like container. It had been guarded by another soldier.

"Storage!" The young soldier said.

The other soldier nodded. The young soldier motioned for him to push the container into the cage. Then something happened that Florian never experienced. The cage began moving up. The young soldier seemed to be humming casually, not noticing the surprise on his face. This must be normal to them. Act natural.

"What is the deal with that large squadron outside?" Florian asked.

"They don't tell recruits like me much, but I heard that someone from Meinspir is visiting Lord Chapman."

"A large squadron for a singular person?"

"Ridiculous isn't it, but that is just how Meinspir is. Home to the elite. People like us could never understand."

The large cage jerked to a halt. The young soldier left first and then helped Florian drag the container out of the cage. They dragged the container through the long winding hallways. Florian took note of the location of the staircase. This floor had a severe lack of soldiers. Perhaps Chapman does not think anyone would be stupid enough to steal from him. They reached a room that had iron ingots packed on shelves.

"You can get back to your duties, I can unpack this," The young soldier said.

"I can help. I don't mind," Florian replied.

The young soldier shook his head and lifted the lid off of the container. Florian panicked. The young soldier packed out a few ingots before Florian got behind him. Florian held one hand over the man's mouth and he used his other arm to strangle him. The young soldier struggled. The soldier began to gesture with his hands. A phen user. Florian let go of him and kicked him.

The soldier crashed into the container causing it to jerk a little. Florian rapidly withdrew the blade that he stole.

"What the hell-" The soldier could not finish his sentence as a blade pierced his chest. Florian could see the soldier trying to speak, nothing but blood escaped his mouth. Florian withdrew the blade with shaky hands. The young soldier fell limply to the ground. Florian could not think straight. He had just taken someone's life. He began hyperventilating. The soldier probably had a family and I took him away from them. Florian had tears waiting to escape his eyes. Calls of his name broke him out of his trance. The calls came from the container. He made his way to the container. Refusing to look at the body on the ground. He lifted the iron ingots out of the container. Thorin jumped out first.

"I'd thought I would suffocate in there," Thorin said. Florian could not focus on what she said. Savia slowly exited the container as well. She had said nothing, she just looked at the body that lay there. Florian knew that the plan was just beginning but he struggled to listen.

Thorin shook his shoulder. He looked at her teary-eyed.

"Where are the stairs?" She asked quietly. This was the quietest he ever heard her speak.

"Right, left and it should be on the right," He whispered. Savia took off immediately. She was really fast. Thorin grabbed Florian and dragged him by his arm. He knew this was part of the plan. He had to head up and confront Chapman.

"Don't think about it. Ashe's life is on the line," Thorin said, dragging him to the staircase. Thorin had been wrong, Alaric would save her. He knew it. But he steeled himself regardless.

Once they reached the staircase, Savia had been long gone. He pulled himself from Thorin's grip and headed up as silent as possible.

Chapter 21

Alaric stood outside Gwenllian's establishment. He did not want to go in. He had to, for Ashe and Savia's sake. This part of town had been emptier as usual. Possibly due to it being mid-afternoon.

Are you ready?

No response. He has been quiet for a few days. Alaric had been panicking. His plan relied on him and Alaric hated that he had to rely on him. He decides to enter the establishment. The showroom in the daytime had been a different sight. There had been no or little noblemen or women.

It didn't smell as bad and it was quiet. The mysur slaves had still been shackled. They sat in silence. Alone and naked. It was a fate he wouldn't wish on his worst enemy. He was going to save them. He had to. But first, he had to get rid of her. He looked toward the stage where Gwenllian watched him. A grin on her face.

Her demeanour insisted that he had to go towards her. She was inviting him. He walked toward the stage. He had not looked at the mysur slaves, he could not. He would not jeopardise the plan. He reached the stage. Gwenllian had still been protected by her two soldiers. She smiled at him. That smile. He hated it. She wore revealing clothing like usual.

"You came?" She asked.

"We had a deal. I at least intend to keep mine," He said. It came out harsher than he intended. He had been incredibly nervous. How could he not be, his brother, friend and whatever Savia is to him are risking their lives.

"Ahh, you break my heart. Do you think I will not honour our agreement? Why, I would do anything to get my hands on some premium meat such as yourself." Her hands ran across his chest like usual.

"It is not every day I get the son of Jerial showing up at my doorstep." She said, wagging her finger in his face.

A new scent entered his senses. He began feeling drowsy.

"You knew?"

"Of course, I even met you once. You were about three years old. Still in the arms of your pitiful mother. Of course, Great Lord Jerial did not care about any of that when he chose to bed me."

Alaric was struggling to keep his eyes closed.

"You have to take responsibility for what your father created."

Those were the last words he heard before darkness engulfed him.

He felt as if he were drowning. It was a familiar feeling for him. It happened on numerous occasions. He hated it. He could see, feel, hear and smell everything but he was not in control.

I did not say you can take over yet.

Silence

Alaric knew it was pointless to struggle; there was nothing he could do. Another panic hit him. He wouldn't be able to keep his promise to Savia and the people of Nezzagwyn.

Give me back my body!

No response.

Alaric deflated. When his body regained consciousness, his body had been stripped bare. He could also feel metal restraints on both of his wrists. He had been laid upon a soft bed. He seemed to be in a private room. He felt a heat in his lower half. Gwenllian had been atop of him, wearing nothing less than he was. She had been moaning. He could see the purple of his eyes glow against her skin. He could hear his voice chanting quietly. Gwenllian seemingly did not hear it, she had been too preoccupied. A sharp pain could be felt at his wrists. His body did not seem to react to the pain. Alaric wanted to scream, but he had not been in control. The restraints around his wrists began to melt into a silvery liquid. His hands had been free. Alaric watched as his hands grabbed Gwenllian at the throat.

"Ahh, Gwenllian. It is good to see you are doing well," His voice said.

Gwenllian had been struggling against his hold. She could not overpower him.

"You not..." She struggled.

"I did not give you permission to sleep with my son," He said.

"Lord J-"

Alaric watched as Gwenllian's eyes went lifeless in his hands. His body did not let go of her body. He lifted her off of him and tossed her like a ragdoll off the bed. His body did not stop there. He got off of the bed and began stomping violently on her head.

Please stop!

Alaric listened as his body was cursing out the corpse underneath it. His foot had been moist with blood. Alaric could only watch, begging and pleading for him to stop.

The door swung open. Alaric saw Gwenllian's two soldiers enter the room. He tried to warn them but they could not hear him. His body chanted at incredible speed. The soldiers had their swords drawn. As his body finished the cast, the soldiers began to move in slow motion. They could not react to what happened next. Alaric's body moved with speed that should not be possible. In an instant, his body was upon them. Stealing one of the soldier's blades and swiftly cutting a single slice into their throats. The men dropped in regular speed. More men attempted to enter the room but with a single swipe of his hand, the door closed. They banged on the door but for some reason, they could not enter. His body searched the room for his clothes. When he had found it he swiftly got dressed. He continued to search for something. He took a few keys he found in the room.

"For you," His voice teased.

He opened the door. Soldiers immediately tried to enter. There had been dozens of soldiers. They all tried to cut him down. Alaric watched as his body dispatched every soldier with ease. He did it with a laugh as blood was smeared across his body. Screams rang through the hallway. When every soldier had been killed, Alaric finally was given control of his body. He let go of the blade. He looked at his hands, they had been covered in blood. Memories of the island returned to him. He began hyperventilating.

This is what you wanted, isn't it?

You asked me to help you.

Where is my thanks?

Alaric began throwing up violently on the floor. He had been crying.

It took a while for Alaric to regain his composure. He moved with no purpose. He eventually found himself at the showroom. The mysur slaves stared at him with horror in their eyes. Just like they should. I am a monster. He slowly made his way to the basement level. He reached Ashe's cage. She stared at his clothes that had been stained with blood. She gave him a concerned look. She spoke to him but he couldn't hear her. It was not that she had been speaking softly, his mind was constantly replaying the horrifying scene. His hands gripped the blade as he sliced the soldiers down with a smile. He tested the keys on her cage. One of the keys worked and Ashe had been freed. She ran to him and hugged him. Suddenly, the world was returned to him. His senses were no longer numb.

"I was so worried when I heard the screams," Ashe said.

Alaric tried to pry her off of him but she did not budge.

"You will get blood on you..." He said softer than he intended.

She shook her head. "I do not know what happened up there but I want to take some of your pain."

Alaric allowed her to snuggle into him. He almost teared up again.

"We need to free these people...come on, let's go. I am fine now," He said. Ashe let go of him. She still gave a concerned look.

"I promise, I am okay."

Ashe was not convinced but nodded regardless. He began to unlock the other cages. The slaves seemed reluctant to exit. Ashe began encouraging them, slowly they followed Ashe out. They returned to the showroom. Alaric had expected more soldiers to show up but none did.

Alaric and Ashe began to free the slaves restrained in the showroom. The entrance to the establishment swung open. He turned immediately to face the entrance. He cast a barrier around everyone in the room except him. This was rapidly draining his stamina. A lone figure entered the showroom. Alaric recognised the figure. He let his hands fall to his side, allowing the barriers to disappear. The woman at the front of the room had been the same woman he saw Florian with. The same woman he shoved. She reached down her shirt and revealed a Rixa amulet identical to his. She walked up to him and kneeled before him.

Scaev? Why is she bowing to me?

"Lord Alaric, there is some bad news. There is something amiss at Chapman's factory," She said.

Lord? What is going on?

Alaric did not have time to assume if the woman had been lying. If there was something wrong at Chapman's factory, that meant that his loved ones would be in danger. He would use this woman's apparent loyalty towards him. He tossed the keys to Ashe, who clumsily caught it.

"Ashe, free the rest of them but stay here. I will be back soon," he ordered.

Ashe immediately got to work. Alaric turned to the woman.

"What is your name?" He walked as he talked. The woman followed him.

"The name is Jinny, Lord Alaric."

Alaric found himself back in the dreaded hallway. Jinny whistled at the massacre.

"Impressive."

Alaric ignored her.

"Sentz, we need sentz and a lot of it. Gwenllian should have a lot."

Jinny nodded and moved past him.

After a few minutes, both he and Jinny exited the establishment with many bulging pouches of sentz.

"What is happening at the factory?" He asked.

"It is better if I show you," Jinny said as she rushed through the street.

They stopped a few streets from the factory, where he found out what the problem was.

They stared at the large squadron of soldiers blocking the entrance of the factory.

This is bad.

Want me to slaughter them?

Alaric ignored the voice in his head.

"What shall we do?" Jinny asked alongside him.

"This is bad, but there is at least a bit of good news."

Jinny glanced up at him, wanting him to elaborate.

"They are not charging into the building. This means they are still unaware of the events happening within. It won't last, however. The factory only has one exit, we will have to deal with the soldiers one way or another."

"And how do you plan to do that?"

"I have a few plans." Alaric did not want to show his hand to the mysterious woman. "Show me to a stable. We will need horses and a lot of them."

Jinny obliged by showing him through the town.

Eventually, they reached a stable. It was run by an elderly man. At first, he was stunned at the blood that covered Alaric, but he tried his best to force a smile. Walking towards the stable, Alaric felt that there was something off about the town. Some people stared at his bloody figure but there had been no sign of any soldiers. It was strange.

"Give me all your horses. I want every horse in this town," Alaric ordered.

"I-I am a-afraid we cannot d-do that, sir." The elderly man said.

Alaric and Jinny placed all the sentz pouches onto the counter.

"I will not ask again." Alaric had not meant it to sound ominous but by the terrified look of the man, he guessed he had.

The man nodded. Alaric turned to Jinny.

"Bring half the horses to Gwenllian's establishment, the other half keep it close to the factory. Try not to get caught."

She nodded. "What will you do?"

"Take care of the soldiers. Oh, and if you betray us."

"I will never think to do such a thing, Lord Alaric." Jinny bowed.

Alaric scoffed as he left the stables. He rushed back to meet with Ashe. He took one glance at the factory. Nothing seemed to change. When he arrived at the establishment, Ashe had freed every slave there. She had been talking animatedly to them. She turned as she noticed Alaric.

"We have bad news," He said.

"Are they fine? What happened? When are we leaving?" Ashe was panicked.

"Calm down. Breathe. There are more soldiers than we expected at the factory. We will have to do the thing."

Ashe's eyes went wide. Then she started shaking her head. "It is way too soon, we don't even know if it will work."

"Ashe, it is fine. It will work, it has to work or we are all dead."

The last word made Ashe freeze. Alaric followed and placed a comforting hand on her shoulder. He then turned to the slaves, who had been watching them. They seemed to look down when Alaric had been in front of them.

"From today, you all are free. Gwenllian is gone," Alaric announced.

The slaves did not look enthused.

One of the slaves spoke up in a soft voice. Alaric almost did not catch it.

"We...have nowhere to go." It was a skinny woman.

Alaric tried to muster a smile. He was sure he probably looked weird.

"Maybe not, but you will find a place."

The slaves were shocked at his response, choosing to look up at him.

"Horses will arrive here shortly, leave town only a few at a time. Be careful not to raise suspicion. Wait outside of town, later a woman named Thorin will find you and lead you to your new home." Alaric elaborated to them.

Alaric heard murmurs among the group.

"Nezzagwyn, you will find a place there. If you choose not to go. You are welcome to stay here," He said as if answering their looming question.

"Why...why are you doing this?" It was the same skinny woman.

Alaric looked at his bloodied clothing and then spoke. "It is because I know what it feels like to not have hope. And I want to give that hope to all of you. You are not here of your choosing, you have a right to leave."

The crowd seemed content with his answer. Some even gave him a soft smile. He turned to Ashe who was beaming at him.

"Come on, we have to leave," He whispered to Ashe, who nodded.

As they walked through the streets, Ashe spoke up.

"I thought you said Florian was more charismatic than you."

Alaric flushed. "He is, my speech back there was terrible."

Ashe chuckled. "It was perfect for them."

They stopped their walk when the factory came into sight.

"It is a waiting game now, let's practise," Alaric said as he grabbed the tome and paged through it.

Chapter 22

Savia stood crouched behind a wall as she eyed the incoming soldier. The clanging was especially loud on this floor. She did not pay it any mind though. The only thoughts going through her head had been Alaric's advice. He always gave her advice when they would spar. And they sparred a lot. The soldier was startled when Savia jumped out from behind the wall and in one twirling manoeuvre sliced his throat and stabbed his abdomen. The man did not have time to scream as he suddenly dropped.

Savia grabbed his body to make him fall quietly. Do not get in confrontations, surprise your targets. End it quickly with your speed and agility. Alaric's words lingered in her mind. She often wondered why he even bothered to give her advice, she could easily use it to kill him. If she actually could kill him. He won the majority of their spars. She only won a few but she couldn't take pride in it since he seemed distracted. She warned him of the bad habit but he just waved her away. A bigger issue now faced her.

She was tasked with securing the exit and freeing metalworkers if she found them. And found them she did. A group of ten men chained by the neck, stood shirtless pounding their hammers onto red hot metal. The room was wide. The heat emanated outward like an inferno. The men had been sweating profusely, none of them bothered to wipe the sweat. Their eyes were fixated on their work.

Alongside the ten metalworkers were three blues. All three held whips in their hands and seemed to be having fun lashing it out onto the workers. The three blues were her biggest problem. There was no way she could take one out without the other two noticing her. She could throw her daggers and take out maybe two but that would leave her unarmed against the remaining blue. What would he do? Savia got an idea. She dragged the corpse of the soldier she had killed earlier.

After a moment of steeling herself, she tossed the corpse into the doorway of the wide room. She could hear a commotion inside the room. She waited outside the door. She heard footsteps rapidly approaching the doorway. Once the footsteps had been close enough, she swung into the doorway with her daggers readied. Unfortunately, the first soldier was struck through the head by Savia's dagger. He had been kneeling over the corpse. The blues body went limp. The other soldiers yelled loudly.

Savia used the body as a shield as she charged the second soldier. Instead of attacking the second soldier, she tossed the corpse toward him. The man panicked and caught the body. Savia used the distraction to toss her dagger at the third soldier. The soldier tried to dodge but he was too late as the dagger pierced his right eye. Savia did not stop. She began chanting, she then placed her remaining dagger onto the ground. Large concrete spikes began forming from the ground. The spikes pierced the soldiers, leaving large holes in their bodies.

She had to catch her breath. She normally did not cast often, forgetting how exhausting it can get. The heat in the room certainly did not help. She then realised that the metalworkers had been staring at her. She did not like the attention all that much.

She went to extract her dagger from the eye of one of the soldier's corpses. Everyone in the building probably knew they were here now. Either that or horrific screams were normal here. She eyed the metal constraints on the worker's necks. There had been a large key-shaped hole.

"Where is the key?" She asked softly.

The workers looked toward one another, unsure if they could speak.

Savia did not want to wait for them to speak but thoughts of Alaric's disappointment forced her to be patient. A larger man spoke up. Savia thought he looked a bit familiar.

"Lord Chapman has the only key. But you are a caster, can't you free us yourself?" The man's voice had been gruff and hoarse. Probably from dehydration. She did not want to cast to free them, but waiting for Florian to kill Chapman would take too long. She sighed. She walked over to one of the metal workers and placed one of her daggers on the metal chain portion of his constraint, She began chanting. Her dagger shifted as tiny metal spikes formed on the dagger. The restraints were forcibly released. When she released all of them, the large man spoke again.

"Why are you doing this?"

She wanted to ignore them, once again Alaric's stupid face appeared in her thoughts.

"Just doing as I am told," She said.

The men did not seem convinced by her answer but followed her regardless.

She pointed at the whips which were first met by confusion but the large man picked one of them up.

"You want us to use it as a weapon, yes?" He asked.

Savia just nodded. Two of the other men picked up the remaining whips.

"Stay behind me. Overwhelm the enemy with our numbers. Make it quick." She was not accustomed to ordering people around.

"Who is your master?" The large man spoke up again.

First, Gwenllian flashed through her mind and then Alaric.

She shook her head. "I do not serve anyone."

The man raised his eyebrows but spoke no further.

Thorin was not having an easy time. She had not expected Florian to have such a strong reaction to killing someone. She usually would think nothing about it but at this time she needed him the most. So he had to snap out of it and soon. As they headed up the staircase, they were immediately met with a soldier heading down. Thorin panicked.

The soldier looked at Florian and smiled.

"Lord Chapman would not be happy if he found you fooling around with whores at work. But don't worry about it, my lips are sealed," The soldier said as he chuckled.

Florian next to her did not say anything. The man raised an eyebrow but as he was about to pass them, Thorin swung her blade across the man's neck. The man had not anticipated it and rolled down the stairs as he presumably bled to death. Florian turned to look at the man's body with wide eyes. Thorin dragged him by the wrist.

"There is no time for this, Florian. You need to get it together," She whispered.

He nodded. "I am...fine. Just need to calm myself."

Thorin nodded. She was not sure if he was telling her the truth but she did not have time to grill him. She was assigned to escort Florian to Chapman. She also had to find the metalworkers on the upper floors and escort them to the entrance, which Savia should have cleared out. Not that she trusted the woman would. During the time she had been locked up alongside Ashe, she could not practise with her blade.

She spent most of her time mulling over how poor she fought against the mysterious figure in the barren lands. She was not a caster, she knew that but she had been strong in her way. She always thought she could at least compete with any man when it came to fighting, at least without casting. But now that had been shattered, the mysterious man had not even used any casts but she could not even put a scratch on him.

She dragged Florian up the stairs toward the top floor. Luckily for them, they had not run into any other soldiers on the staircase. A set of double doors were the only thing they were met with on the top floor. She assumed that the doors led to Chapman's office or something like that. She turned to Florian.

"Listen, take the time you need, but once you go through those doors, there is no turning back. Whatever you choose to do...I will have to respect it but Chapman has to die tonight."

Florian did not respond to her, he just eyed the double doors.

"I will be heading back down." She gave him one tug on the wrist. He looked at her. "You can do this." She then let him go and headed back down the staircase. Thorin did not believe her own words. She would hate Florian forever if he did not go through with it. She did not want to leave the fate of her father and the other men of Nezzagwyn in his hands. But she had been forced to. With Alaric unable to be here, she would be kidding herself if she had not doubted the plan's success.

She could not afford to let her mind dwell there. She was now expected to free the workers and kick some caster-ass. Thorin had not been known for her stealth, hence it came to no one's surprise when she got spotted immediately. She cursed under her breath as she ran down a corridor. The soldiers behind her began yelling as they chased her. She expected them to cast but they did not, they just kept chasing her. She turned the corner and waited. She heard one of the soldiers speak.

"If Lord Chapman finds out there is someone in here, we are all dead." A woman soldier said.

They don't want to cause a ruckus.

Thorin swung her blade as the first soldier turned the corner. With a scream and a horrible slash across the chest, the soldier was dispatched. Thorin was about to break off in a sprint when something unexpected happened. The previous female soldier was struck down by another soldier. Thorin was stunned for a second. The soldier looked at Thorin and withdrew an amulet from his neck.

Rixa, that means...

Thorin held her blade towards the man.

"Scaev...what do you want?"

The man placed his finger on his lips, asking her to be quiet.

"We heard that you are going to take Chapman out. We have come to help." The man whispered.

"Why should I believe you?" Thorin did not attempt to lower her voice.

The man was already losing his patience. "We don't have time, there are bigger problems. We cannot leave, the entrance is blocked off."

"Lead me to the metalworkers." Thorin ignored the man's sentiment.

The man scoffed and walked past her. He mumbled something as he walked. Thorin kept her blade pointed towards him but followed after him.

The man used his disguise to fool unsuspecting soldiers and kill them. Thorin had to admit that it was an efficient method that they had stumbled on.

"How many of you are here?" Thorin asked.

The man raised an eyebrow unaware of what she meant. After a moment it clicked for him.

"I am the only one in the factory. My wife is meant to save Lord Alaric."

Lord Alaric. Did Alaric plan all this? Had they been Scaev all along?

Thorin had to quickly push those thoughts out of her head.

"If Alaric is free, then we do not have to worry about escaping. He will have a plan, or maybe the green snake will help him again."

Thorin watched the man's confusion at her mention of the green serpent.

He didn't know about Versus then.

"You put much faith into Lord Alaric. Are you perhaps the one he beds." The man looked at her suggestively.

Thorin felt like throwing up at the suggestion. "No, he is not what I like."

Before the man could speak further she asked him another question. "You do not seem to have much faith in Alaric. You do not care for your master?"

The man chuckled at her suggestion. "Lord Alaric is not my master. My master is far greater than Alaric will ever be. Lord Alaric is, however, someone important."

Thorin raised an eyebrow. "Who is your master?"

"A non-believer has no right to know." The man began laughing.

The man brought her to a room. She could hear the sound of metal hitting metal coming from the room. She peeked into it. There stood about eight metalworkers, bare-chested slaving over heated metals. There had also been two soldiers in the room. She observed the metalworkers closely. He is not here. The man alongside her had entered the room. He at first casually walked and then he began to chat to the other soldiers. Thorin watched as he suddenly got violent and began to kill the other two soldiers. Thorin saw the happy expression he showed when he murdered the men.

Dangerous. That was the only word that crossed her mind.

The metalworkers looked terrified. They shivered as the man broke their restraints. They did not move once their restraints were broken.

"Follow her!" The man yelled. The workers looked toward Thorin, who nodded. They hesitantly walked toward her.

"I...know...you." One of the workers said while looking at Thorin.

The man looked vaguely familiar.

"You...are...Thord's daughter." The worker said.

Thorin nodded at the man. "I have come to free you all."

"Still...as...reckless...as always."

Thorin gave a small smile at the man's words.

The Scaev man led them down to other rooms. There had still been no sign of him. They eventually reached one of the lower floors. Their group grew larger as they descended. She had been surprised, all the soldiers that had been on this floor laid on the ground in a pool of their blood. The little woman seemed to keep her word. Thorin looked out of one of the factory's windows. It had gotten pretty dark. They have maybe been in the building for an hour or two.

As Thorin turned a corner, she had to duck under a swinging dagger. She was about to be struck by another dagger. She did not have time to dodge. She closed her eyes awaiting her death. It never occurred.

"Thorin?"

The voice she had recognised. Her eyes shot open and behind the little woman, he stood. She ran into his arms.

"Papa!" Thorin shouted. She could not care if anybody heard her. She did not care that she had been sobbing. He was here and he was alive. That was all that mattered to her.

Her father, the man known as Thord, had been large and well built.

"What are you doing here, Thorin?" He asked while attempting to console his crying daughter.

"Saving you, what else?" Her voice came out between sobs.

"That is dangerously stupid of you." He laughed.

And how Thorin missed that laugh. It had been five whole years since she had heard it. Just before he had been taken by Chapman. Her mother tried to stop them...

Thorin broke out of her embrace.

"You turned into a beautiful woman just like her," Thord said. This caused Thorin to beam at her father.

Thorin turned to the little woman. Savia, she should remember the person who freed her father. Savia had kept a glare on the scaev man, she held her daggers in such a position as if ready to strike.

"Who is he?" Savia asked. This was the first time Thorin heard her speak. It was barely louder than a whisper.

The scaev grinned at Savia. "A caster, I thought Lord Alaric knew better than to trust such scum."

Thorin walked up to Savia and stood at her side.

"He is a scaev, he helped us," Thorin attempted to explain. "Although I hardly trust him as well."

"Did Alaric send him?" Savia asked.

"I do not think so. Unless he had been lying to me, Alaric had no idea what a scaev was before he met me." Thorin tried to explain.

Her explanation did not put Savia at ease.

"We have bigger problems than him right now. There is a squadron waiting for us when we leave." Thorin informed Savia.

Savia did not respond, this brought Thord to speak up.

"We are well aware of that. Thorin you came here with a plan right?" He asked.

"Plan for infiltration and liberation, yes. Escape plan...not so much." Thorin told her father. He brought a hand to his face.

"I wouldn't worry about it that much. If he is out there, we have to pray he is. It should all go smoothly." Thorin smiled. She tried to keep positive. It was supposed to be a happy time. She just reunited with her father.

"Who is he?" Thord asked.

"His name is Alaric, a real madman. If I'm being honest. He probably should have died twice since I knew him and both times he came out perfectly fine." Thorin could hear her good mood flow through her words. She would not have been able to speak with such freedom before.

"Seems like you have a lot of faith in this so-called madman." Her father chuckled.

Thorin shook her head. "Not me, grandma does. And so does the entire Nezzagwyn. A lot of things have happened since you were taken." Thorin turned away from her father. "We are still missing one more, then we can leave." Thorin grabbed Savia's wrist and ran towards the staircase.

The smaller woman immediately broke out of her grip but as Thorin looked back she had seen that she had still been following. They reached the top floor. The large double doors had still been shut. Thorin did not know why but her pace suddenly dropped. Instead of a mad dash, she took slow and small steps to the doors. She noticed Savia had done the same behind her. When she reached the door, she realised she had been holding her breath.

She could hear no commotion on the opposite side. What kind of monster had Chapman been? She moved her hands to the door handle and pushed the doors open. Her eyes went as wide as saucers at the sight before her. The room had been uselessly too large. Walls filled with paintings. Most paintings were of a stubby man that had a severe lack of hair, only a few strands remained.

The rest of the paintings were a portrait of a large man in a suit of armour. The man had an ugly scar across his nose. The room had been a mess. Golden furniture had been smashed into pieces, the few that remained had signs of heavy laceration. Toward the back of the room had been a large and pristine desk with a big chair. None of this had been what stunned Thorin, however.

Florian laid face down on the ground in a pool of blood. A chunk of his torso had been missing and he had been bleeding viciously. He held the crimson blade in his hand. He had not seemed to be conscious. Sitting on his knees next to Florian had been a young boy. He had short blond hair, and his face had been freckled. He was dressed in a suit as most noblemen. The boy had his eyes closed and his arms spread towards Florian's near lifeless form.

A green liquid flowed from the boy's chest towards Florian's wound. The liquid seemed to be defying gravity. The boy had been sweating profusely. There had been another body in the room. Just north to Florian's had been a body that had been cleaved in two. The body was separated diagonally across the torso. The cleave had been too clean, like the body naturally detached that way. Thorin recognised the body as the stubby man from the paintings. Thorin grabbed her blade and angrily walked toward the kneeling boy.

"What in Heinzidal's name are you doing to him?" Thorin yelled. The young boy opened his eyes and faced Thorin. His eyes were blue, shining like a crystal.

Chapter 23

Florian was lost in his mind when Thorin left him. She had said that she would respect whatever decision he made, but he was not certain how much she meant that. He stood just outside the double doors. He had his hand pulling on his collar as if the clothes he wore had been suffocating him. Does he go in? Will he leave? Will everybody be disappointed if he left? Will he end up like the young soldier?

He never understood why Alaric demanded that he be the one who has to take out Chapman. Why could he not stay with the others and then they all face Chapman together? Before Versus he had never doubted Alaric...but now he can see some cracks in Alaric's character. He knew these cracks were most probably present from the beginning but he had just been too blind to notice it. Voices broke Florian out of his mind. Two voices coming from the other side of the door. Does Chapman have more soldiers in his office? This was a dumb idea.

Florian bit his lip and tapped his foot. He brought a trembling hand onto the door handles. He remembered to breathe. If the odds are against me, I can just run away. No big deal. He slowly opened the door. He heard the voices go quiet as he opened the door. Behind a large desk along the back wall of the room, a short fat man dressed in a brown suit.

What was left of his hair looked as if they were desperately wanting to leave. Anger washed over the man's face as he stared at Florian. Across from the man sat a young boy with blond hair and blue eyes. His face had been indifferent when he looked at Florian.

"What is the meaning of your disturbance? I did not call for you!" The fat man yelled aggressively. Florian assumed the man to be Chapman. Florian closed the double doors behind him and placed a shaky hand onto the hilt of his stolen blade.

"Lord Chapman, there has been an emergency," Florian said, trying desperately to fool him. He moved closer to Chapman. He ignored the young boy. Chapman raised an eyebrow at his words but then waved him off.

"It probably has something to do with Gwenllian. Stupid whore is always up to no good." Chapman said in disgust. "I don't think I have ever seen you before. What is your name, soldier?"

Florian watched as the young boy moved from his position between Florian and Chapman.

"Florian-" He was cut short as he had to dodge a fast-moving projectile. He just barely got out of the way. He was currently on one knee leaning to his right.

"I do not care what your name is. How dare you interrupt my meeting."

Florian realised that Chapman held a whip in one hand. He glanced at the section of the floor that the whip had hit. The floor seemed damaged. He then brought his eyes to Chapman's whip. He noticed red symbols shining softly at the base of the weapon. Runes.

"You dare escape your death, maggot,"

Florian unsheathed his stolen blade and attempted to charge at Chapman. He found this to be difficult however as Chapman kept him at bay with his whip. The whip confused him. It moved as if it had a mind of its own. Chapman did not have to move his arm very much for the whip to lash out. It seemed focused on Florian. It had grazed him a few times. The areas burnt.

"Did Gwenllian send you here to kill me?" Chapman had been asking him these questions a few times already. Florian refused to answer them. Opting to focus on dodging the wild moving whip.

"You can't kill me, you can't even touch me." Chapman was laughing. Florian noticed a thin layer of sweat that was beginning to appear on Chapman. He can't keep it up all day. I can't as well. Florian assumed Chapman to not be a good caster, this was due to his body shape. Casting requires stamina as well as stria. This also meant that Florian did not want to expose himself by casting prematurely. He had to come up with an idea. He stopped trying to charge foolishly and backed up. He had been out of the range of the whip. Chapman did not chase. He remained rooted behind the large desk. He seemed content to remain there. He then turned to the young boy.

"Everard, come closer. This madman might attack you." Chapman's tone had been wildly different to the one he used to speak to Florian. It was almost endearing. The boy, Everard, did not look at Chapman; he focused on what happened across the room. Florian had made his way to the golden furniture while keeping his eyes focused on Chapman. Noticing that Chapman was distracted, he lifted a small golden stool and tossed it with all his might towards Chapman.

He had hoped that the boy would not alert Chapman. He was correct, the blond boy just watched him. The stool flew through the air. Chapman had been unaware. As the stool got close, the whip moved wildly, shattering the stool into many pieces. One of the stool's many pieces hit Everard causing him to yelp. Chapman panicked and moved away from his desk and towards Everard.

Florian used this moment to cast. The floor beneath Chapman's seemed to melt and he lost his balance. In his panic, he dropped his whip. Florian did not waste time anytime and began to charge. He tried his best to wave away the intrusive thoughts that were clouding his mind. He was before Chapman in a flash. He raised his blade with shaky hands and was about to strike.

The look on Chapman's face caused him to close his eyes. Don't look at me like that. Don't be terrified. Please. Florian brought down the blade. The blade went close to Chapman when it stopped. Florian opened his eyes. He gasped when he saw what was happening.

Chapman had been smiling at him. A cruel grin plastered on his face. His sword had been held in position by the whip that hung loosely. It had been wrapped around his blade. Chapman had not even been holding the whip. Florian tried to break the whip's hold but it was strong. Chapman began to laugh.

"Do you think you are the first to attempt to kill me?" Chapman mocked him. The whip moved his blade on its own. He tried to wrestle back control but the whip had been too strong. The whip forced him to point the blade at himself. The whip yanked viciously. Florian had let go of his blade and moved at the right time. His blade pierced through his left shoulder. Searing pain. Florian yelled as he stumbled backwards, falling onto his behind. The whip had let go of its hold on the blade. Chapman grabbed the whip and walked towards Florian, who had been breathing heavily. The rage on Chapman's face had been palpable.

"As I said you cannot touch me."

I can't do it. I am sorry. Ashe, Alaric, Thorin...I am sorry. He pulled the blade from his shoulder. He clenched his teeth. The pain had been unbearable. The blade dropped to the floor. It echoed loudly as it fell. Blood gushed from his wound. The blood reminded him of the blade on his back. The blade he could not figure out. He looked up towards Chapman. The man had been dishevelled, he had been sweating so much more than before. The whip lifted and was about to strike him. The whip did not move as fast as before. Florian rolled out of the way. He couldn't avoid the blow entirely as the whip caught a bit of his torso.

Florian screamed. He brought his right hand to the wound and kept pressure on it. Blood was already escaping between his fingers. For some reason, Chapman did not attack immediately afterwards. Florian stumbled to his feet. He took one glance at Chapman. His eyes had been bloodshot and the hand in which he held the whip had been red. Florian began to limp away. He did not head to the door instead of heading towards the golden furniture. He could not die while trying to escape, everyone will think him a coward.

He slowly weaved between the furniture, the whip lashing out at the furniture breaking a few of them into pieces while others just got a few lacerations. The whip caught him a few times, exactly on the wound on his torso. Florian screamed. His vision was getting blurred. There was nowhere to run anymore. No more furniture to hide behind. Florian turned to Chapman, who stood in the middle of the room.

Though his vision was blurred, he could see that the foul man had been smiling. Florian let go of the wound. A new wave of pain hit him. He slowly brought his right hand to the hilt of the crimson blade. He limped towards Chapman. As he got close enough, the whip hit him on the wound. Florian did not have the energy to scream. He removed the sword. His energy drained rapidly as usual. He swung the sword loosely at Chapman. He could no longer see. He had not been in range. He felt a strange wind passing through his body. As he swung he fell to the floor. He could not hear anything. As his world fell into darkness.

Chapter 24

Thorin walked up to the young boy, her blade drawn. Her face contorted in rage.

"What are you doing to him?" Thorin yelled.

The boy looked at her, at first emotionless but then something broke as his face burst into emotion. The green liquid that connected the boy's chest to Florian's wound dissipated. The boy did not seem to answer her question, instead opting to just look at her.

Thorin mumbled something before kneeling before Florian's body. Florian had been breathing, albeit slowly. She released a breath she did not know she had been holding. You did well, Florian. You'd better live long enough for us to escape. She took the crimson blade from his grasp and slid it back into the sheath. Savia stepped forward with Florian's other blade.

It had been stained with blood. Other than their moving bodies, the room had been quiet. Thorin picked up Florian and flung one of his arms over her shoulder. She, along with Savia, moved toward the exit. A voice halted them in their tracks. It was the same blond boy.

"If he doesn't get treatment he will die." The boy's tone had been proper and he spoke similarly as that of a nobleman.

Deep inside her mind, Thorin knew that his words were the truth. She just turned back to the exit and began walking, making sure Florian did not collapse under her grasp.

"I can save him!" The boy yelled.

Thorin scoffed. "Why should we trust you, little boy?"

"I am the only one who can. His wounds are too severe. He is not going to survive the next floor, never mind outside."

"If you are lying, you are dead," Thorin threatened.

The boy first grabbed the whip that had been in Chapman's clutches and then walked up to them. He gulped as he saw Savia clutch her dagger.

"Can you heal him while we walk?"

He nodded. "It will take longer, as I will have to focus."

Thorin nodded.

They walked through the building in silence. The green liquid from the boy's chest was conjured as the boy cast. They met up with the large group of metalworkers as well as the scaev. Nobody said a word as they headed to the exit. Eventually, they reached the large steel doors.

"What do we do about the soldiers outside?" Thord asked.

"We pray...we pray to whatever gods exist. Once we open these doors, it will be a rush. All metalworkers should follow me and head for the southern exit of Isern." This was the moment Thorin had waited for. She imagined this day for the past five years. It will not fail. It cannot fail. She nodded to her father who reciprocated the act. A metalworker opened the large doors. An older woman dressed in blue robes stood in front, behind her and there had been a force of one hundred soldiers. She wasted no time and drew her sword when she saw the group that stood in the doorway of the factory. Her eyes locked with the young blond boy. The other soldiers withdrew their blades.

"Lord Ever-" The woman could not finish her sentence as her body was forced to the side. Screams could be heard from the soldiers. Thorin did not know what to expect from Alaric but it certainly had not been this.

It had been well past midnight and Alaric had been getting impatient. Ashe had not been much better. She had been reading the same portion of the tome over and over. She bit her bottom lip and tapped her foot.

"Come on, let's get closer." Alaric grabbed Ashe's wrist and that seemed to break her out of her trance. He led her to the middle of the street, just a couple of paces from the squadron. People would probably assume that they are suspicious but that was the least of his worries. He even saw a few soldiers of the squadron watch them. He did not have a clear view of the door but he was waiting for a reaction, any change in the crowd was what he was looking for. He turned to Ashe who still held the tome.

"Ashe, you know the cast. Stop fretting, it is going to work."

Ashe nodded to him.

"All your fidgeting is making me nervous."

She chuckled. "Since when do you get nervous?"

Alaric gave her a small smile, realising she is back to her normal self. "All the time. I am just better at hiding it."

"You should teach me because all this stress is getting to me. And I do not want to lose my hair at eighteen."

Alaric chuckled but then stopped suddenly. "They are here."

"What?"

"Soldier on the far right turned to face the factory and he hadn't done that for the past hour." Alaric cracked his fingers. "It is showtime."

Ashe hurriedly attached the tome to her belt. Alaric stood with his back towards her. He faced the squadron, who seemed to be taking out their weapons. This has got to work.

He felt Ashe's hand on his back. She began chanting. He moved his arms. One above his head and one below. In the shape of an S. He moved with fluidity as he made a few more gestures. He could hear Ashe coming to the end of her chant. He began to kneel. Ashe followed him, keeping her hand firmly on his back.

He placed his hands on the ground to end the cast. Please work. His pleading worked as he felt most of his energy drain from his body. The factory had been placed in the centre of the Gwyn River. The water from the right-hand side of the factory had decreased immensely. The ground far below could be seen. The water on the left side of the factory increased. The water did not flow into the town, instead, it grew higher into the sky as if some invisible force blocked the water from breaking into the town. A large tidal wave moved around the factory from left to right.

Washing away the soldiers that stood on the platform. The water continued into the sky, looking like a tornado of water swirling around the factory. He could hear the screams of the soldiers that were washed away by the powerful current. After a few moments, the water tornado dissipated. As the cast ended,

Alaric could feel his energy slowly coming back. The path was clear. He could see figures from within the factory.

"Run!" He yelled at the top of his lungs.

Two things happened at once. Somewhere from his right, Jinny came running along with the stablehand. They were followed by a few dozen horses. Alaric assumed that she saw their cast by the look on her face. In front of him, she saw the small group running towards him, he could make out Thorin struggling. Somebody had been slumped over her shoulders.

He stumbled to his feet, he then proceeded to help Ashe to her feet as well. She seemed exhausted.

"It worked..." Her voice was soft. She was smiling softly.

Alaric nodded. "Celebrate later. We need to head out."

"Where to?"

"The mountains behind Isern, then from there to Adhu Aqua."

Jinny made her way before him.

"That was quite the feat, Lord Alaric. But it seems to have left you in a poor state," She said mockingly.

Alaric scoffed. "This is no big deal." He knew he was sweating and breathing heavily.

The first of the metalworkers arrived in front of Alaric who was now positioned in front of the horse army.

"I believe Thorin has told you what must be done. Take a horse and run towards the exit. Outside of Isern, there should be another group waiting for you there." Alaric said. At first, the men seemed unsure but then got onto the horses. Two men sat on a horse at a time. Regular civilians had come out of their homes to watch the commotion. As Thorin walked closer, the situation became clear to him. Florian had been unconscious.

Thorin held his arm so that he did not fall over. Florian had been bloody. Too much blood. He should not be alive in that state. A strange green liquid seemed to be connected to Florian's torso. Alaric followed the line of green liquid and found that it was connected to the chest of a young boy who followed behind Thorin. Savia had been walking behind Thorin as well, she kept her eyes on the boy.

Alaric looked toward Thorin. He recognized the look on her face. It was a look he was sure reflected off of his face. Guilt. He had not known what happened in the factory but from the look on her face, he was sure that it had not been her fault. She finally reached him.

"Alaric, I am so-"

"You know what you have to do. Lead these people to Nezzagwyn." He cut her off.

"But..."

Alaric moved Florian's body off of Thorin's shoulder and onto his own.

"This is what you came here for. This is what I promised to the people of Nezzagwyn. Bring them home, Thorin. And tell Miss Thea I will come to visit soon." Alaric gave her the best smile he could muster.

Thorin bit her lip and nodded at him. She placed her hand on his shoulder.

"Thank you, Alaric. For everything you have done." She said as she passed him.

The metalworkers led by Thorin left towards their goal. The horses galloped towards the outskirts of Isern.

Alaric faced the young boy who stood closer now. "You are going to be riding with us, boy."

"Are you the one who cast the giant wave?" The boy asked.

"Perhaps."

Alaric did not have to answer the question because the boy's eyes told him everything he needed to know. The boy was terrified of him.

Alaric turned to Ashe who watched the exchange carefully.

"Take Florian and the boy to the base of the mountain behind Isern. I will meet you there."

Ashe smiled at him. "Go get her."

Alaric nearly choked at her words but then wordlessly jogged away. He was running through the streets of Isern. A place he had only stayed in for a week, but these streets he had come to know. He knew where he was headed. A place that should be unconventional to stay at but where he knew she was. And she was there. She sat with her back against the wall in the familiar alleyway.

She looked up at him when he had arrived. The shock was written on her face.

"What are you doing? We must leave." He said.

"Why?" Her voice was soft, like usual.

"You asked for freedom and I had promised you I would give it to you."

Savia did not answer.

"If you are worried about Gwenllian...I took care of her. She will never bother you again." "Leave with us or go your own way, you are free to do what you want."

Savia went quiet again. He was about to leave when he heard her voice.

"Where are you headed?"

"Meinspir. That is our destination."

Alaric watched as her eyes lit up when she heard the city's name. She silently got to her feet.

"I will go with you."

"Great, we have to hurry. We don't have much time."

He ran through the streets of Isern once again but this time he had been flanked with his companion. Alaric did not understand his attraction towards Savia, he had just assumed since she had been a beautiful woman that he had been attracted to her looks. He had never felt this way over anyone before. All he wanted to do was protect her. Even if he knew that she is well equipped to protect herself.

CHAPTER 25

As she had been standing next to her horse, in front of her had been tall mountains. Not as tall as Versus. If anything these mountains had been dwarves compared to Versus. Behind her had been the town of Isern. The tall building in the middle makes certain that you would never miss it. Florian had been laying on the floor. He was breathing softly.

The young boy who said that his name was Everard had also been on the floor, resting as he said. They spoke a little on the way to the mountain base. He had said that he was a healer from Meinspir, that he was in Isern to try and heal Chapman from an incurable disease.

She was not certain she believed the boy but she had no reason to not trust him as well. And it seemed that he was responsible for keeping Florian alive. That was all she wished for. She was speechless when she saw the state he had been in. She wished that she had been the one that had been sent to the factory instead.

She knew Alaric would have never allowed her to go. She was cut from her thoughts when she heard a horse gallop towards them. She tightened her grip on her spear. She heard Everard shuffle on the floor. Once she saw the figures on top of the horse, she smiled.

Alaric rode in front and Savia had a tight hold on him. She looked terrified. The look on Savia's face made Ashe chuckle. The horse stopped in front of them. Alaric got off first and helped Savia down. Now that Savia had been back on the ground her expression went neutral. Ashe walked up to her.

"Not accustomed to riding horses?" Ashe asked.

Ashe expected Savia not to answer.

"No."

Ashe's eyes went wide when she heard her voice. She almost jumped and hugged the woman but she chose not to. She realised the woman would probably not like that. Instead, she smiled at Savia. To her surprise, the woman gave her a small smirk.

"Do not worry, I was the same way when I rode the first time."

This time Savia did not respond. Ashe did not mind it. She had made precious progress.

"My name is Ashe, I am Alaric's little sister."

Savia was silent before she spoke. "Savia."

"Nice to meet you Savia. And thank you for taking care of Alaric. I know he can be stubborn."

Savia looked at her dumbfounded. Savia mumbled something but Ashe could not hear it. She asked for Savia to repeat it but she never did. Ashe's concentration turned to Alaric who walked up to Everard.

"Stand up, boy. We have no time to rest." Alaric grabbed Florian and hoisted him over his shoulders.

"I am no boy, my name is Everard."

Alaric just glanced at him. "Whatever you say, boy." "Heal while we climb."

Everard had a sour expression.

"You know what I do?"

Alaric did not turn to face him, instead, he began to walk up the narrow pathway of the mountain. The green liquid formed from Everard's chest once again.

"Desano, a small group of casters that reside in Meinspir. The rarest type of casting available in all of Hominus. You can heal most illnesses. The amount of Desano that exists is a mere one in ten million," Alaric spoke with no emotion. The rest of the group followed behind him. She was exhausted but kept moving. Her eyes were getting progressively heavier as they climbed.

Alaric seemed to notice this. "We will rest, once we are further away from Isern."

Ashe nodded at him.

"How did you create that tidal wave?" Everard asked.

Ashe half expected Alaric not to answer him because of his attitude towards Everard earlier. So, when he responded it slightly shocked her.

"It was a simple enhance cast mixed with a barrier cast using the river as the material."

Ashe watched as the cogs in Everard's head turned.

"But on that level, it should be impossible... I have heard of casters working in tandem to create a mixture of casts but..." "I refuse to believe that was all you did."

Alaric held a slight smirk. "Maybe we had some help from a god."

Everard raised an eyebrow. "God? Like the ones, Ysgafyn folk believe in? How did you channel their power?"

Ashe giggled. Alaric did not answer any of the boy's questions after that.

They reached a flat section of the mountain trail and Alaric told them to rest here. Once Ashe's body relaxed, sleep took over immediately.

Ashe woke up to a low growl. A large cat-like animal stood before her. It was about to pounce on her. Ashe lifted her arms to protect herself. The animal did not reach her. It bounced off of the barrier that surrounded her. She immediately scrambled to grab her spear when a voice yelled out.

"Stand down, Yago!" It was Everard. At the sound of his voice, the cat immediately relaxed. Everard walked up to the cat and rubbed its fur. The cat seemed to be enjoying it and leaned further into Everard's touch. She looked around and noticed Alaric as well as Savia was ready to fight.

"Everybody can relax. This is my companion, Yago. He has been with me ever since I was a child." Everard explained.

"And what is keeping the ocelot from attacking us, boy?" Alaric asked.

The cat growled as Alaric spoke.

"Yago won't attack unless I tell him to."

Alaric raised an eyebrow at Everard but spoke no further. Instead, he turned to Ashe.

"Are you okay?"

"I am a bit startled but I feel good."

Everard walked up to her and was followed by the ocelot.

"I apologise for the rude awakening, Lady Ashe. Yago can be a bit protective of me sometimes."

Ashe waved him off. "It is fine, Everard. If anything Alaric is a bit protective of me too."

The boy chuckled. "I guess they are quite similar, Alaric and Yago." The ocelot growled as he said it causing her to hold back a laugh. She did notice how Everard did not add an honorific to Alaric's name when he had called both her and Savia 'Lady'.

She glanced at Alaric who was speaking to Savia. Savia had been nodding at him. Alaric picked up Florian, who had more colour to his cheeks and had been bleeding less, up from off the ground. He then turned to Ashe. "It is time to go. If the ocelot caught up to us, who knows who might be following us."

Ashe nodded as they began their trek further up the mountain.

Godric had grown more and more frustrated over the past months. He rubbed viciously at the scar over his nose. There had been no news regarding Jerial. Not of his existence or his actions. Just a stupid letter they have received from a merchant claiming that Jerial threatened him. He had called to meet this senile merchant just for him to say that Jerial had been a young man. He knew that the merchant had been spewing lies.

So he had him executed for his insolence. Jerial had to be as old as he was, and he definitely would not be wasting his time in a poor village such as Nezzagwyn. He spent all his time focused on finding Jerial. It had slowed his progress at invading Ysgafyn. He did not care about the invasion, Jerial had been the bigger threat, a threat that could potentially bring ruin to his kingdom.

Godric thought back to the day of the King's Rite, a day where he stood victorious over his competitors and now council of

Great Lords. Part of him always felt as if his victory had been a fluke. His ascension to the throne had been built on lies. All because of one man. Jerial the Merciless. He had not taken the Rite seriously.

The most powerful caster to live on Hominus since Heinzidal had given up the throne and given it to Godric. The thought infuriated him. All that he had left Godric with was this nasty scar. Then the bastard went to die alone in his castle. Godric had sent assassin's and tried to poison Jerial many times but he always evaded the attempts.

Godric had long since stopped the assassination attempts and then Jerial just dropped dead. It was suspicious. Godric did not sleep for months. His greatest enemy and the strongest caster of his generation just dropped dead. A loud knock broke Godric out of his thoughts.

"Your majesty. I have come with news. May I enter?" The voice was muffled.

"You may enter Dalton," Godric said.

The iron doors opened up to reveal his loyal servant. Dalton had been at his side before he ascended to the throne when he was still a Great Lord. They have been through a lot together. He trusted this man with his life. Dalton walked until he was before the throne and knelt before Godric. Godric noticed that the doors were not closed behind Dalton as they usually are. He could see the stress on the man's face.

"Bad news, I assume?"

Dalton slowly nodded before he spoke. "We have received a letter from Betisa."

Godric raised an eyebrow. "She should be in Isern by now."

Dalton nodded. "I am afraid they were attacked, Your Majesty."

Godric leaned forward.

"They are not certain if the attack was directed at them. Chapman has been killed as well as all his men. And I am afraid Lord Everard is missing."

Godric assumed Dalton thought he was going to react badly but he just sat back.

"Tell me more about the attack."

"An unknown caster of immense skill summoned a large tidal wave and wiped out Betisa's whole squad. Betisa would like to add that it had caught them off guard."

Godric smiled and then began laughing. "This is what we are looking for. This unknown caster has to be him. He went to take out Chapman because he wanted to stop my metal factory. Everard's presence was just a bonus for him."

"What shall we do, your majesty?"

"Send word to Great Lord Ivo, he shall personally go to Isern and search for any sign that Jerial is or was there. And when Betisa returns, have her executed. The Zidal Empire has no use for weak casters such as herself."

"And what of Lord Everard?"

"We shall do nothing about Everard. It is unfortunate but he chose his death."

Dalton hesitantly nodded. As Dalton walked back to the entrance, a spear flew through the air. Piercing Dalton through the chest. His body fell limply to the ground. Godric instantly moved off the throne. He held his arms in front of him with his hands stretched out. His palms facing toward the ground.

The red runes on his gauntlets shone as the metal floor twisted as if made of liquid and two blades were formed. The blades had been made entirely from metal and floated into his grip. Two blue-robed soldiers entered the room each wielding a blade of their own. They tried to charge Godric but he was faster.

His armoured boots slid against the metal floor as he glided across the room. It looked as if he had been on skates. He was fast. Much faster than a normal man. The two soldiers could not react in time as their heads fell off of their bodies. Godric dropped the blood-stained blades onto the floor and the floor absorbed the blades, leaving only a blood puddle behind.

Who is foolish enough to assassinate me?

Chapter 26

It was near the summit of the mountain that Florian finally woke up. They had been hiking for a few days. No one seemed to be following them, Alaric permitted them to slow their pace a little. Throughout the few days, Florian had been getting progressively better. The bleeding had completely stopped and the hole in his torso closed up. It left a bad scar, however. Ashe stood hovering over Florian along with Alaric and Everard when his eyes began fluttering open.

Savia had been further back checking their surroundings. Florian coughed roughly as he woke up. She carefully lifted his head and began pouring water into his mouth. They had acquired the water when they found the Gwyn River's source. With Florian's thirst quenched, he began to look at them.

"I...am...sorry...I...couldn't...beat...him." Florian's voice came just a little higher than a whisper. His voice had been hoarse.

"Shhhhh...don't speak." Ashe calmly caresses him on the head.

"And you are wrong, you beat Chapman. You did a wonderful job." Alaric smiled at him.

Florian's eyes widened at his remark.

Everard nodded. "You sliced him right in two."

Florian broke eye contact and looked downwards.

Alaric bent and ruffled Florian's curly hair. "It is okay, we are safe right now. You should just focus on healing."

Florian nodded.

Alaric and Everard walked away towards Savia. She stayed with Florian. She moved behind him and placed his head on her legs. She looked out at the now darkened landscape they found themselves in. Mountains blocked their vision on both sides, blocking them from seeing the horizon. Alaric had said Adhu Aqua would be on the other side of the mountain.

"I...shouldn't...have...been...able...to..hit...Chapman...from...t hat...distance." "How...am...I...not...dead."

"I wasn't there but I will try to explain." Ashe motioned for him to look at Everard.

"He was there when you fought Chapman, right?"

Florian nodded.

"He is also the one that kept you alive. He has some sort of healing capability. I think Alaric called it Desano."

"Why?"

Ashe shrugged. "We didn't ask." Ashe pointed at the crimson blade that had laid next to Florian. "That blade was the reason you beat Chapman. Apparently, that blade is part of Heinzidal's Arsenal."

Ashe could sense Florian's confusion.

"It is one of twenty legendary weapons that Heinzidal owned. Each requires a large amount of stria and stamina to even wield.

Most of them are kept by the Zidal Empire but a few of them are still missing. This one included."

Florian had a confused look on his face. Ashe chuckled.

"At least that is what I was told."

Ashe filled Florian in on the happenings of the past few days. At some point, Florian fell asleep and she followed quickly after him.

The next morning the group began their trek once again. Alaric carried Flroian on his back. If he had been struggling he did not mention it. A few hours into their trek they reached the summit. The view from the summit had been breathtaking. All that effort climbing the mountain seemed to disappear when she laid her eyes on the stunning visual.

The Great City of Adhu Aqua could be seen from the summit. It defied any expectations Ashe had. Isern had been a speck of dust compared to Adhu Aqua. Ashe had always thought Isern had been large, especially compared to what she knew about in Diable Island and Nezzagwyn.

Adhu Aqua was a real city about one hundred times larger than Isern. Even being this far from the city she could see that the entire city had been made of tall buildings with slanted roofs. It looked as if it would take an entire day and then some to cross the city by foot. The entire city had been inside a huge wall. She assumed they could only see beyond the wall because they had been on top of the mountain.

Closer to them had been cultivated fields that looked like patterns that had been drawn onto the ground. Of all the buildings within the city walls, there had been one building that made the rest look like dwarves. It was the furthest north and looked like a castle from the fairy tales that Alaric read to her when they were younger.

Behind the castle was the sole reason she had been speechless. At first glance, she assumed it was a void. It was a lake. The small movement made certain of that fact. It stretched further than she could see. There had been dark clouds covering the sky above Adhu Aqua and heavy rain poured down onto the city.

"The Great City of Adhu Aqua. A beautiful sight." Everard said while standing next to her.

She instead turned to Alaric. "This is your home? Why would you ever want to leave?"

He did not respond, instead, he had a very sad expression. She looked towards Savia who noticed his expression as well.

Everard did not notice as he asked questions. "You are from Adhu Aqua!" He asked with wide eyes.

Alaric nodded.

"That means you are a nobleman like me. You did not seem to be a nobleman when we met."

Alaric glared at Everard. "You are correct, I am a nobleman. Something far nobler than you will ever be, boy."

Everard just scoffed. Ashe chuckled slightly. They had been hostile towards one another the entire journey to the summit.

Ashe tapped Alaric on the arm. He turned towards her.

"Why don't you tell us a little about Adhu Aqua while we make our way towards the city," Ashe asked.

Alaric sighed. It had clearly been a topic he wanted to avoid.

"Fine. Though I did not live there very long." Alaric said as he began their descent.

"Adhu Aqua, the great city or whatever they call it nowadays, had a much simpler name before. It was called The City of Still Waters. Not a good name hence the change to Adhu Aqua." Ashe listened closely to him as he spoke. She had never enjoyed his lectures before but this seemed to be a topic that she would like.

"Adhu Aqua is the name given to the large lake that is situated on the northern end of the city. The city is responsible for the food cultivation and production in the Zidal Empire therefore is not known as one of the strongest cities such as Arstutia or Impestra."

"All in all it is a pretty miserable city."

Ashe raised an eyebrow. Alaric turned to her.

"It never stops raining and the people all think they are smarter than the next."

Ashe's eyes widened at the former statement. "It never stops raining? Like the desolate lands?"

Alaric nodded. Everard spoke up after that. "Every Great City has a sort of...defect. A weird weather condition. It has been studied by many scholars but they all come to one conclusion. That the cause of these heavy weather abnormalities was due to a large concentration of stria being cramped in one place. Whether that is true or not remains to be seen."

"That is crazy. I want to visit other great cities," Ashe said.

Alaric had a small smirk on his face. "After we reach Meinspir, you can travel as much as you like."

Ashe knew that Alaric was trying to get her to be happy but she did not like the way he excluded himself from the prospect of travelling.

"Okay."

As nightfall approached and the group made camp, Alaric asked to speak to Florian and Ashe specifically. Savia and Everard understood and made themselves scarce.

Alaric sat next to Florian, who was lying on the ground, and opposite Ashe who was sitting crossed legs.

Florian had been quiet ever since he woke up. She caught him glancing a few times at the whip that Everard carried with him.

"Why'd you want to talk to us?" Florian's voice broke her out of her thoughts.

Alaric sighed. "I think it is pretty clear that Priest Able is a member of the scaev."

This was a topic Ashe did not want to think about. The man who raised them is some sort of madman who worships nixum.

She refused to believe it, she will not believe it.

"Then why'd the scaev within Isern help us?" Alaric spoke as if he could read her mind.

Ashe bit on her lip.

"What are you talking about?" Florian asked.

"That woman that you helped in Isern, she was a scaev. She helped us evacuate." Alaric explained.

"Woman...Jinny?"

Alaric nodded. "She seemed keen to help us as well."

"Wrong." Ashe's claim made Alaric shift in his seat.

"She was keen to help you and only you. She called you 'lord'. And she did not acknowledge me at all." Ashe explained further.

Florian turned his head to look at Alaric.

"You are right, this probably means they know about me." Alaric placed a hand on his chest before continuing. "Priest Able is keeping tabs on us by using his scaev connections. He wants to make certain we get to Meinspir at all costs."

"Should we still go?" Florian asked.

Alaric nodded. "Yes, but not for the reason he wants us to. He is probably scheming and that envelope he gave us is the key. And I assume it has nothing to do with breaking the oppression of the mysurs."

"Then why still go to Meinspir?" At this point, Florian and Alaric had been talking to each other. Her mind was still taken by the fact that their guardian had been a bad person.

"To kill King Godric," Alaric announced. Florian jerked up and Ashe sat with wide eyes.

"Wait a minute...you can't be serious...you have truly gone mad. There is no way to do such a thing." This was the most Florian spoke in days.

"Relax, I know. No matter how impossible it seems right now, it is something we have to do. I vowed to protect the people of Nezzagwyn and how things are now, the mysurs will never be free. There will always be another Chapman." Florian flinched at the mention of the name.

"That is why one of you two will need to take the throne and free the mysurs. This can only happen once the current King is dead. Once the King is dead, according to the law of the Zidal Empire, A King's Rite will have to take place. A vicious battle of the throne where the best casters fight until the last to remain standing becomes the king."

"The best...casters. We are not anywhere close to that." Florian whispered.

"I know, but you will leave them with no choice. Once you arrive at Meinspir you will know what to do."

Ashe snapped and began yelling. "Why are you excluding yourself? Why only us two? You are going to be there as well!"

Alaric moved quickly to her side and placed a hand on her shoulder. He spoke low and ominously.

"I am not going to make it past Adhu Aqua."

Chapter 27

They looked like ants before the ridiculously large metal gate that stood before them. Florian could walk and stand on his own. He no longer needed to be carried. He regained most of his strength a few days ago when they had been making their way down the mountain. His torso and left shoulder still felt a bit weird but all in all, he felt as if he had been back to normal. Well, as normal as he could be.

His mind had still been riddled with questions. At the forefront was Alaric's declaration a few days ago. He and Ashe begged Alaric to explain but he just ignored them. He could tell that Ashe was hurt by his words. And then there was Alaric's insane plan of assassinating the king.

A plan that he would not be a part of. Florian did not know what to feel. One part of him wanted to be angry at Alaric and he had been angry for the longest time. He had been angry ever since Alaric protected them at Diable Island. The other part of him was sad for Alaric. He had been his brother for as long as he could remember.

He couldn't let Alaric die, there is still so much he wanted to know and only Alaric could tell them. Florian had a feeling that everything would get revealed in the city that they were just a few steps away from entering. He stood at the front of their small group.

Ashe stood next to him, she had the same expression she carried for the past few days. Her eyebrows were furrowed. Close behind them walked Everard and further back Savia walked alongside Alaric. Both of them had their hoods up. The soldiers that had been manning the gate looked at them suspiciously. He was about to walk through the gates when the soldiers stopped him. This caused Yago to growl at the soldiers.

"Sorry sir, I cannot allow unauthorised figures into the city without proper identification," one soldier said.

Alaric walked up to where Florian stood. He pulled his hood down.

The soldier looked at him.

"Excuse us, but you will have to let us through," Alaric instructed.

"We don't have to do anything!" Another soldier exclaimed with his hand placed firmly on his sheathed blade.

Alaric chuckled, enhancing the soldier's unease.

"You cannot kick us out when you have been looking for me this entire time."

The men did not speak, instead waited for Alaric to explain.

"Send a message to Great Lord Ivo. Alaric, the man he has been searching for is on his doorstep."

Florian thought he heard one of the soldiers gasp. This was another reason to be angry at Alaric. He never shared his plans with the rest of the group. This had been the first time Florian had heard that people were looking for him.

"Um...Lord Alaric. You are still alive. I am afraid Great Lord Ivo is not currently within the city. But I have orders to escort you to the castle." The soldier that threatened them at first said.

"Do so then. We are fatigued from our travels."

The soldiers seemed to hesitate but immediately got to work.

"We will have a carriage ready for you shortly." The soldiers yelled.

After the soldiers were out of earshot, Alaric turned to the group.

"We will be safe, no one will try anything as long as you are with me," Alaric said.

"You said you were a nobleman but you never said you were someone of such great importance. To be personally escorted to Great Lord Ivo's castle. Who are you? His secret lovechild or something?" Everard questioned.

"Wouldn't you like to know, boy?"

Everard scoffed.

"Regardless, we just have to wait in this city for Ivo to return, then you four can be on your way to Meinspir."

Florian looked toward Ashe. Her scowl grew deeper.

"On a first-name basis with a Great Lord. Is there something I am missing here?"

Everard's question was met with a glare from Alaric.

"Do not act as if you are not hiding things from us, boy."

Yago growled at Alaric mirroring Everard's glare.

The carriage arriving broke the building tension.

Florian dragged Ashe into the carriage. It had been spacious inside and the cushions had been comfortable. Unlike the rocks, they have been sleeping on within the mountains. Next to enter the carriage was Everard who helped Yago. Savia entered next and finally Alaric. Once everyone was settled in, the carriage began to move into the city. The carriage had been pulled by two armoured horses which were controlled by a soldier.

The streets bustled with people, all of them wore luxury garments. Men were dressed in suits and the women in dresses. Everyone held an instrument that blocked the rain from ruining their clothes. He also noticed that despite all the rain the streets were mostly clear of puddles. All the water flowed on the slanted roads into small slits alongside the road. The soldier who drove the carriage spoke up.

"Impressive isn't it? I assume it is the first time you are visiting our city. It hasn't always been like this y'know. Adhu Aqua was always flooded with water y'know. That's til our previous Great Lord developed our anti-flood system, y'know."

Florian wondered how many times the man could say 'y'know' in a singular sentence. But no matter how he looked at it, the city was incredibly impressive. Tall buildings, immaculate streets and people that seemed to be wealthy if their clothing said anything. The driver gave credit to the previous Great Lord, which was not going to go well for Alaric. He glanced at Alaric and there it was, he had been scowling. Florian continued to sightsee. He was not fond of new places as Ashe was but he could respect when something was incredible, and this city was nothing short of it. A few people glanced at their carriage but most ignored them. The people seemed happy.

"Y'know being from outta town, you musta heard the stereotypes of us Aquians, y'know."

"Stereotypes?" Florian asked.

The driver chuckled. "Y'know how they say, the people of Adhu Aqua act as if they know it all, have it all and spend it all. Y'know."

Florian did not know what the man was explaining. Alaric explained further.

"Other than Meinspir, Adhu Aqua is the most affluent of the Great Cities. Everyone who lives here has a lot of sentz. Due to that and the great business education that is taught within the city, the people here get a bad reputation. While most are the fault of the Aquians, some are just unfair comments."

"What kind of comments?"

"They think we think that we are better than them, smarter than them and more elite than them. But as I said, the Aquians do not do themselves favours."

The driver chuckled at Alaric's last comment. "Damn straight we don't."

"There is also another reason that most hate Aquians... This city has a reputation for producing some of the most powerful casters in the history of Hominus. Many kings from the past such as King Balthander came from Adhu Aqua. Naturally, this makes the other cities quite jealous. Especially, Cognizance" Alaric explained.

"Doesn't help that they are our neighbours y'know. Damn Coggies think that the frozen palace got anything on our city, damn crazy they are y'know." The driver was cackling at that point.

Ashe leaned to whisper something to Alaric. Ashe's scowl got deeper at Alaric's response. Florian assumed that she did not like the answer.

The light in the sky was dimming as the carriage finally stopped before the castle. It had been a long journey to the castle. The ride was not quiet however, the driver who was named Ballack kept talking and explaining things about the city. He went through the different power struggles and even the best places to eat.

Much like everything else in this city, the castle made them look tiny. The entire castle had been made of stone, the roofs were spiked upwards like all the other buildings. It towered over the rest of the city. It had even been built on an elevated plane. Green banners broke the grey of the stone.

There were large gardens that sat out in front of the castle. They had been currently tended to by dishevelled looking people. Unlike the citizens, they had been wearing rags. It suddenly clicked with him that they were mysurs. Of course, there would still be those that were getting taken advantage of.

A soldier dressed in armour met them in front of the castle. His armour shone in the fleeting light. His armour had green accents. He had sharp blue eyes and kept his hair trimmed short. His face had been hardened and his jawline was strong. Florian could tell that the man had been glaring at Alaric.

"Lord Alaric, you have been missing for sixteen years. I'd have never assumed you would show up, you must have heard Great Lord Ivo's call." The soldier said.

Florian could tell from the man's tone that he did not seem happy.

"Your Great Lord called for me, it is well mannered to do as he says. You do not simply disobey a Great Lord." Alaric said.

The soldier turned to walk towards the castle, their group followed close behind.

"Col Gregory, second commander of 'The Eyes'. I shall oversee your stay until Great Lord Ivo returns."

"Alaric Burchard, son of-"

"Son of previous Great Lord Jerial Burchard, there is no one in this city that doesn't know who you are." Col interrupted.

Florian heard Everard gasp.

"I guess, I thought you all thought me dead," Alaric claimed.

"Most do, Great Lord Ivo however never stopped searching for you. Where have you been all this time?" Col glanced at them.

"I have been around. Only heard of the call recently. Figured I would make a turn."

Col scoffed at Alaric's remarks.

The rest of the walk was done in complete silence. They stopped before the large wooden doors that were manned by two soldiers. At Col's presence, the soldiers gave him a salute and opened the doors. The small group entered.

"The place has not changed since Great Lord Ivo's ascension. He ordered that every room remained the same. He was very particular about that."

Florian stared at the infrastructure within the castle. Beautiful was an understatement. The floor was covered in rolled out carpet, paintings covered the walls and the vast amounts of ornaments were streaked in gold and silver. There had been many soldiers patrolling the hallways of the castle.

They all saluted Col and glanced at the small group following him. Mysurs could be seen cleaning at various locations in the castle. He looked toward Ashe, her eyes sparkled as she scanned every nook and cranny of the castle. It hadn't settled in that this was Alaric's home before he was at Diable.

This was way more luxurious than anything he had ever seen in his lifetime. Col led them to a room that had a long table that was surrounded by chairs. Mysurs came from a different room carrying large platters of food and began to place them on the large table. The mysurs bowed at Col once the food was placed. He did not miss the look of disgust on Col's face as he nodded to the mysurs.

"Never understood why but Great Lord Ivo always had a soft spot for the powerless," Col said.

Florian frowned.

"I understand why, but that is only something Ivo can tell you about," Alaric said.

"Eat up here and afterwards I will have some of my men escort you to your rooms," Col ordered. "Lord Alaric, do not assume you know anything about Great Lord Ivo. You know nothing about this city, not when you abandoned it. The Heir of Adhu Aqua abandoned its people when tragedy befell the city." Col turned to walk away.

Alaric laughed. Everyone in the room looked at him. "You know nothing. None of you does. Not what's about to happen nor what happened sixteen years ago."

Col stopped at the door, he didn't turn to look at Alaric.

"I was just five, a scared kid. That no one bothered to check on. I was held up like an idol, their hero's only son. But no one truly cared about me. Do not speak when you know nothing, Commander."

Col left after Alaric's admission.

Florian had never heard any of this before. He wondered how long Alaric bottled all his problems. No one spoke until Alaric's next words. "Let's eat."

The food was delicious, fantastic, any superlative that could describe the bliss that the food brought. After surviving on dried fruit and nuts for days, this was a great change. There was a wide variety of meats, vegetables, fruits and bread. Ashe, Florian and Savia were stuffing their faces while Alaric and Everard ate more calmly.

"Is it true?" Everard asked.

"Yes, Jerial Burchard is my father," Alaric stated.

Alaric placed down his cutlery and looked at them.

"Leave at first light, this city will not be safe for you four," Alaric warned.

Florian looked at Ashe who met his eyes. They had not said a word.

"No."

It had been Savia who spoke. Florian had not heard her speak so loudly before. It seemed as if Alaric was surprised at her as well, his eyes had been wide and his lips were parted.

"Do not be st-" Alaric was interrupted.

"I will drag your lifeless body from this city if I have to, but you will be with us when we leave for Meinspir," Savia said.

Ashe laughed first, then Florian.

"You plan to die here, fine. Just do not expect me to idly follow your death wishes." Savia continued.

Alaric sighed. "Do what you want."

They began to eat once again.

Chapter 28

Jerial woke up from his bed with a grin. Col had shown them to probably the worst rooms in all of the castle. Desperately cramped. Jerial hopped on his feet. He made his way to the curtained window. He pushed the curtains aside to glance outside. The sky had been darkened by clouds. Rain is still pouring. This had been home.

He looked at his reflection in the window. It had been purple due to the light that emanated from his eyes. He always felt strange looking at this body. It had reminded him of when he was younger but something was different, that stupid woman did not fail to leave her mark. Jerial moved from the window and towards the door. He swung the door open and walked through.

The corridor was slightly lit by torches that hung on the walls. He quickly slipped into the room that was next to the one he slept in. In the room sleeping softly was the one they called Florian. A stupid boy, one who did not deserve to live if he was being honest. He had always wondered why his son kept a fool like him around, especially when their relationship had been frayed.

Jerial was not here to kill him; however, he was here for something of great importance. Lying next to the bed, still sheathed, had been the Blade of Heinzidal. An artefact that he had been looking for for years and one that he had reluctantly been forced to leave behind when he had raided Versus.

He already had a few of Heinzidal's legendary arsenal, hidden deep within this castle. He had never used them, the blade was the one he had always truly wanted. Swordplay had been his favourite thing growing up, even going as far as becoming one of the greatest swordsmen to grace the land. He grabbed the sheathed blade and silently exited the room. He immediately unsheathed the blade. He felt the blade tug slightly on his stria and stamina reserves.

He thought back at how the stupid Florian kid could not regulate his reserves when he held the blade. He expected the blade to pull even more but his plan seemed to work. He had two stria reserves now, his own and from the Rixa amulet that hung from his chest. Jerial walked through the corridor twirling the blade in his left hand as he walked. He knew this castle like the back of his hand. He finally made his way to the much larger part of the castle. Two soldiers approached him.

"Lord Alaric, I am afraid we have orders for you to remain in your room." The soldier was barely finished when his throat was carefully slit. The soldier dropped lifeless onto the floor. The other soldier was about to pull out his sword when the crimson blade was at his throat. Purple eyes met brown terrified eyes.

"I am not Alaric. I am Great Lord Jerial and I have returned to take back what was once mine. Will you join me, soldier?" Jerial kept his voice low. The soldier shook his head. Jerial wasted no time dispatching him as well. This continued as panic ran through the castle. Nobody seemed keen to join his side, so he had to punish them. Here he stood beyond a few corpses. Their blood painted the floor crimson. He heard the sound of footsteps behind him and he turned around. Standing behind him crouched with two daggers firmly in her hands was the woman his son called Savia. She kept her gaze on him.

"Who are you?" She asked, her tone tainted with anger.

Jerial smiled at her. "What do you mean? I am Alaric."

"Liar."

Jerial gave her a hearty laugh. "You are a smart one. I see why he took such a liking towards you. What was it that gave me away, other than my eyes?"

"Your aura." Savia's knuckles whitened around the hilt of her daggers.

"My aura? What in Heinzidal's name are you talking about?" Jerial asked.

"You are threatening, he is comforting."

Jerial gave another laugh. "I see, that was always a part I could never beat out of him. His mother's fault, you see, taught him compassion. Unnecessary things really." "But you are right, my name is Jerial, that stupid fool's father."

He saw Savia's eyebrows tilt upwards.

"Dead?"

Jerial shook his head. "I never died, I lived within him this entire time. I just decided to take control."

"Give him back!"

Jerial's laugh was cut short as spikes made of hardened blood came directly towards him. He poured more stria into the crimson blade and swung it casually through the air. The corridor suddenly became windy as a gust of wind pulsed from his blade. The gust tore through the blood spikes sending specks of crimson dust through the air. The gust stopped before Savia. He noticed Savia was about to dash at him, he quickly chanted a basic cast. The stone floor moved up and covered Savia's legs keeping her rooted in place. Savia tried to break out by stabbing it with her daggers. He cast again this time the stone crossed her hands successfully petrifying them. Savia kept struggling. He knew it was fruitless. He walked up to her, pulled her hood down and grabbed her hair. Forcing her to look up at him.

"You are not like the others back there, you have the talent to be strong. My foolish son sees it as well. Join me and I can teach you how to become strong."

She spat at him. He slapped her with the back of his hand. Harder than he meant to because it had drawn blood from her nose.

"You know he can see, hear, feel everything I do while I control his body. He is stuck helplessly watching me slaughter all these men. Do not make him watch as I kill you and his siblings slowly while I laugh away."

"I will kill you!"

"Kill me? If I die he dies. Be careful what you wish for." With those words, he let go of her hair and continued further into the castle.

He was then met with a small group of armoured soldiers who were led by a familiar man.

"Second commander Col Gregory, what pleasant surprises are you bringing me?" Jerial asked.

The commander was glaring, his hand firmly on his broadsword.

"What is the meaning of this Lord Alaric? We bring you to your home and you massacre your people?" If his voice was thinly veiled with dissatisfaction earlier it is now full-blown rage that escaped his lips.

"You have got it wrong, commander, I am not Alaric. He is gone, I am Great Lord Jerial Burchard. I am sure you are familiar with the name?"

"You must have gone insane!"

Jerial rolled his eyes. He poured more stria into his blade and swung it toward the left side of Col. The wind tore through the armoured soldiers that stood on the left side of Col. There was no time to scream as their bodies were sliced in two by the gust of wind. Col could only stare wide-eyed as half of his squad was dispatched with ease.

"You see the power I wield. No one in this city can come close to my power. Why not join me and I can take my place as the rightful ruler. With you at my side."

Jerial saw how Col's hands shook.

"Stand down men!" Col ordered. Some men were reluctant to put their swords away.

"Now! Failure to do so will be considered treason and you will be executed!" He ordered. The men listened.

Jerial walked up to the commander and placed a hand on his shoulder, ignoring the flinch that followed. Col had been a head shorter than him, he leaned into the commander's ear.

"You will make a fine right-hand man. First Commander Gregory." He whispered.

The commander smiled.

"Yes, Great Lord Jerial. We are at your service!" Col saluted him. Jerial turned to the halved group of soldiers.

"I have a task for all of you. Gather the corpses and take their heads off. Any soldier who does not show allegiance to me, Great Lord Jerial, is to be shown the heads of their comrades. If they are still not compliant, you have to take their life. If you fail to do so, all your heads will be added to the pile."

The soldiers stared at him wide-eyed.

"You heard the Great Lord, now get to work!" Col ordered alongside him.

The soldiers were frozen at first but with a casual wave of his crimson blade, the soldiers got to work.

"Commander Gregory, there is a young woman a few hallways back. I want you to escort her to the dungeon. You might have some trouble getting rid of my cast but I am sure a talented caster like you can disenchant it easily."

"Yes, sir. And what of Alaric's friends?"

"Leave them, they are harmless." Col began to walk away. "Oh, and another thing, you should be careful about the way you speak about my son. He may be foolish but he still outranks you."

Col nodded. "Yes, sir."

CHAPTER 29

Ashe was awoken by a voice that appeared inside her head.

People of Adhu Aqua. My people. I, Great Lord Jerial, have returned to take my place as the ruler of these lands.

Ashe jumped out of the bed at the sound of his name. She opened the door to see that it was guarded by two soldiers. Ashe tried to struggle past them but they stopped her.

"Let go of me!" She yelled.

"We have orders to escort you to the Great Lord after he is done with his announcement. Please wait in your room." One of the guards said.

Ashe stopped struggling and returned to her bed.

Do not be alarmed. You thought me dead but my death was just a ruse. King Godric attempted to assassinate me but I was much smarter you see. For on my deathbed I created a new cast. Giving up my physical body and transferring it into my son. Now, here I live in Alaric Burchard's body. I may be in his body but I have kept my strength. This is because my son and I are of one mind, we both have the same goal. To bring glory and honour to Adhu Aqua. We have spent sixteen years training our body and with the advice of Ivo, we have returned. Now rejoice, my Aquians for I have returned.

Ashe could hear people yelling in praise throughout the castle. It caused an uneasy feeling to appear in her gut. She was certain that the voice she heard in her head was lying.

Do not be alarmed by the barrier that our talented Phen casters are putting up around the city. This is just to protect us against the wrath of the Meinspir army that are surely going to try and invade. You have no reason to fear because I will protect each and every one of you. Our city will not be ravaged by those savages.

More cheers rang through the castle.

The speech in her head went on for a while before the voice inside her head cut out. The door opened and one of the guards entered.

"The Great Lord will see you now."

Ashe went to grab her spear when the guard spoke again.

"No weapons."

Ashe reluctantly let go of her spear and allowed the two guards to escort her. They led her to the highest floor. There were barely any guards on this floor. She found herself looking at the paintings on the wall. Most of them were of a chiselled man that looked quite similar to Alaric, perhaps just more hardened. Instead of Alaric's blue eyes, he had light brown eyes.

He was dressed in thin black armour. He kept a black robe under his armour that shot out the bottom of his chest piece. The paintings were portraying him to look like a hero. One painting caught her eye. It was of the same Alaric looking man but next to him stood a beautiful woman in a white dress that contrasted the black armour the man wore. Her eyes were painted blue and she held a baby in her arms.

She was dragged in front of a large door. Col stood in front of the door glaring at her. He did not say anything. A few moments later, two guards escorting Florian arrived. At his arrival, Col opened the door. It revealed an empty throne that sat against the wall opposite the door. The throne was made of some sort of blackened metal.

The rest of the room was bare except for a table that was oddly placed on the right side of the room. There was a balcony on the left side of the room and it forced light into the darkroom. Col walked into the centre of the room, Ashe and Florian followed. The guards stayed outside. A figure emerged from the balcony. A familiar figure.

Dressed in the black armour she had seen in the painting. The only difference was the crimson blade that was strapped to his back. He was damp from the rain. His short hair stuck to his forehead and his armour had been shining in a metallic gleam. It was Alaric, it looked just like him except for the eyes. His eyes shone a bright purple instead of the usual blue. Alaric had been smiling at him. A devilish smile that she had never seen on his face before.

"Alaric, what is the meaning of this?" Florian asked.

"You will not speak to the Great Lord in such a manner!" Col exclaimed.

He was quickly silenced as Alaric raised his hand.

"You may take your leave now, commander," Alaric ordered.

Col hesitated but turned to leave.

"I believe you have heard my speech this morning?" Alaric walked towards the throne and sat down. Florian and Ashe walked closer.

"What is happening, Alaric?" She asked.

Alaric glared at her. "Alaric is no longer in control. You shall call me, Great Lord Jerial."

Ashe's eyes widened. Florian began laughing next to her.

"What is so amusing, boy?" Jerial asked.

"Nothing, it is just slowly making more sense," Florian said. "You killed those casters on Diable Island." "You caused his weird actions. I always thought he knew more than a regular person should."

At the accusations, Jerial chuckled. "Diable Island, the damned place I hated living there but it was a forced venture. But yes, I killed those casters. At first, I forced my son to watch the soldiers rip the villagers into pieces, then I used these hands, not his hands, to strike down the rest."

"Sorry, Alaric. I was being pretty terrible to you weren't I?"

Ashe couldn't keep up with so many revelations. "Where is Alaric?" She pleaded.

"You are looking at him, his body at least." Jerial pointed at his chest. "His soul however is somewhere in here fighting desperately for control. Poor thing really believed that I couldn't take control whenever I needed to."

Ashe did not realise that she was crying. "Give him back!"

"I'm afraid I cannot do so. I have plans to fulfil. I don't expect to give him control ever again."

Florian walked up to him, his fists balled in anger. Jerial snapped his fingers and Florian stopped dead in his tracks.

Florian had been holding his head. His face showed that he was in pain. Ashe rushed to Florian's side.

"I can kill you with a flick of my wrist. Do not try anything stupid." "I called you here to be polite and tell you that you are no longer welcome in my castle. Leave Adhu Aqua, this place has no use for you."

"Where are the others? Everard? Savia?" Ashe asked.

"The boy escaped early in the morning. The beautiful lady too. A real sneaky one that girl is."

"You will not get away with this." Ashe cried.

"Do not tempt me, girl. The only reason you are let go is because I have a little sympathy for my boy. I could break him by killing you but where is the fun in that, I love watching him struggle." Jerial laughed.

Florian seemed to recover and grabbed her wrist.

"Let's go," Florian whispered.

"But-" She tried to fight it but he dragged her out of the room.

"There is nothing we can do. We have to recuperate and then strategize. That is what Alaric would want us to do." Ashe noticed that he had been crying too.

They were led back to their rooms.

Ivo was a bit frustrated. He was sent a personal request for him to visit Isern and search for any evidence that his previous master had been there. His master had been dead for sixteen years. A man whose remains still exist in Adhu Aqua. After hearing nothing about his revived master for six months, he had assumed that the intel the king got had been false.

He wondered why the king sent him to Isern specifically until he arrived in the small town. He usually left this land to be governed by a man known as Chapman. A good friend of King Godric, that was enough for Ivo to steer clear of him. Isern had become chaotic. Chapman had been dead and so had most within the metal factory. There had been a weird massacre in a building on the northeast edge of town.

A building that Ivo assumed to be a brothel for the weird smells he found there. The town had been in a power struggle. Many people fought for control of the town, at the forefront was a timid stablehand who had more sentz than one in his position should have. The soldiers did not know how to handle it. That's when they looked to Great Lord Ivo to solve it. Ivo had become a Great Lord at nineteen, a feat that no one had ever done before.

A feat that was only possible because he had been the only pupil of the greatest Ilium caster of his generation, Great Lord Jerial. A hero that had great intellect. His inventions had changed Adhu Aqua for the better. Many noblemen from all over Hominus sought his wisdom. He was not eager to share, however, usually kicking them out.

The only thing greater than his intellect was his combat capability. He was a hero for stopping the biggest civil war the Zidal Empire had ever faced. Impestra had been unhappy with the compensation they received for their imports, so they marched their army to Arstutia to send the army through the Eastern teleporter.

Only to get wiped out by Great Lord Jerial and the Adhu Aqua army. It came out later that they had been hired by the Great Lord of Arstutia at the time. Regardless, his deed at the time was written in legend. The man who had defeated the strongest army in all of the Zidal Empire. Ivo had seen his strength up close. He had been given a part of that immense strength. He had been a cruel master, especially to his son. Ivo sighed.

"Are you okay, Master Ivo?" The voice next to him said.

"Just thinking, Cressela."

Cressela was his second in command. First Commander of 'The Eyes', a group of the strongest casters in Adhu Aqua. The name is ironic because he was blind. He was particularly fond of Cressela, she had been by his side ever since he was put in his position. She had gained quite a reputation for her stoicism. She had been a beautiful woman, before he became blind. Blind was a strong word, he could see just not in the way a regular person could.

The familiar protective aura that he saw her now was very disappointing, he wondered if she was still beautiful as before. They had been wedded for a few years, a secret only known to a few despite the many rumours of their relationship. Ivo sat at Chapman's desk while Cressela was looking through parchments and explaining them to him. It had mostly been documenting merchant trades from villages around the Gwyn River and a few trades made to Meinspir.

Nothing special. A few did catch his eye however, Chapman made strange deals with a woman known as Gwenllian. The documents did not go into much detail on what they had been dealing with, however. They had asked around about the event that occurred a few days, the only lead they got was that a group of black-robed adventurers cast a huge tidal wave to take out all the soldiers in front of the factory. A huge tidal wave...Ivo understood why it might intrigue the king, a strong caster and so close to Adhu Aqua. All things led to Jerial.

"What are we going to do, Master?"

Ivo sighed. "We will go back home. I will order the Hughes family to take control of this town and send a small group of soldiers to at least keep it stable. It is clear that he is not here."

"Very well." Ivo heard the chair move to his right. Cressela grabbed his forearm and he stood up as well.

"We will find him," Cressela said.

"Which one?" Ivo chuckled.

"Lord Alaric, of course."

"You know me well." His smile turned into a scowl. "Do you think I am cruel to wish that my former master is dead?"

Cressela went quiet before answering. "I do not think you are cruel. You have told me the stories."

"But he had given me everything. All that I have is because of him." Ivo countered.

"That may be true but one's good deeds do not necessarily outweigh the bad."

Ivo chuckled at her comment. "You will never let me win, would you?"

"Not as long as I am by your side."

Ivo pouted, causing his beloved to chuckle.

He allowed Cressela to lead him out of the factory. Outside the factory, he heard a familiar man speak.

"Heinzidal's balls! This town stinks!" A man spoke.

Ivo chuckled. Drustan Drucker was the fifth commander of 'The Eyes'. He was quite young when they recruited him but he had shown great potential. Despite not knowing what he looked like, Ivo found his rash tone and humour amusing. Much to the chagrin of Cressela.

"Would you not speak such profanities before the Great Lord, Commander Drucker," Cressela stated sternly.

"I will once the Great Lord tells me to, O Great Protector."

This happened on occasion, the two commanders always seemed to get on each other's nerves. After a few moments of bickering, Ivo stepped forward and put a stop to it.

"Commander Drucker, we shall be heading back to Adhu Aqua. Gather the men." Ivo ordered.

"Finally, I would not have survived another day in this place."

He heard Cressela sigh next to him and he gave her a little nudge.

Chapter 30

Savia sat in silence. The room had been dark. The only sound that could be heard came from water droplets falling from the ceiling. A couple hit Savia on the head. She sat curled up in a ball in the corner of her cell. The cell was small and metal bars kept her from escaping. They had dragged her far underground and pushed her into this cell. She hadn't seen anybody since.

She pulled her cloak tight. She refused to cry. Her mother had been a fool, telling her someone will whisk her away. Someone will free her and love her. All of it had been rubbish. She trusted for once, thinking it will be different this time, only for everything to fall apart again. She wouldn't cry. Was she wrong? He did keep up his end of the bargain, he freed her. He did not force her to follow him.

That was her own will. Maybe he had manipulated me into thinking that. She shook her head. He wouldn't do that. Why did her mind do this to her? She was torn. She thought she should hate him but she couldn't bring herself to. She thought back to their time together in Isern. He had told her a few cryptic things back then. Why didn't I realise? He had been suffering back then. She felt stupid.

She now realised why he felt safe to her. He had been the same as her. Someone who needed saving. Someone who wanted to be free from the burden of their parents. And he had set her free. I forced him to. That was beside the point. Things were finally becoming clear to her now. She had a goal to accomplish. She had to free him now. It was time to do something for him. With her resolve steeled she found new energy. There was still a major issue. She was stuck in this cell and nothing she tried worked.

The metal bars were too strong for her to break and for some reason, she couldn't cast in the cell. She spent most of her time trying to chip away at the stone wall behind her with her dagger. She stopped when she heard footsteps echoing nearby. She took her place back in the corner of the cell. The footsteps stopped as a figure stopped before her cell. It was a man dressed in armour that had green accents.

Similarly to the commander that dragged her here. She immediately glared at the visitor. He was a tall man with olive skin. He had no hair on his head and had black expressionless eyes. He had not said a word. He moved and put on an intricately designed ring that engulfed two of his armoured fingers. He then put his other hand on one of the metal bars.

The hand that held the metal bar shone red and the entire bar began to liquidy. Savia noted the steam that emanated from his hand. He melted another metal bar. There was now enough space for Savia to slip out. The man seemed to realise this and stepped aside. Savia did not move a muscle.

"Are you not going to escape?" The man's voice was deep.

Savia grabbed her daggers. The man in turn shook his head and then sighed.

"I am not here to pick a fight. I am Orvyn Burchard, third no second commander of 'The Eyes'. I am here to ensure you safely escape and join your friends."

"Burchard...You are lying."

"I should have expected this." Orvyn shook his head. "The Burchard family has a long history here in Adhu Aqua. One I will not get into here, just know I have no loyalty to Lord Jerial. I am but a distant relative."

"Why should I believe you?" Savia said angrily.

"You need not believe me because it is the truth. But tell me what do you plan to do here in the dungeon. Starve and rot with the others or are you going to find your friends and do something productive?"

Savia hated that the man was correct. She did not have time to waste. She needed to figure out how to save Alaric. She put her daggers away. For only the second time in her short life, she was allowing someone else to help her. She stepped out of the cell. Orvyn nodded at her. He walked behind her as he navigated her through the dungeon. There were only a few soldiers that they had come across. Orvyn told them that Jerial had requested to see her. Orvyn led her to the back of the castle. The huge void-like lake stood before them in all its glory.

"We do not have much time," Orvyn said as he picked up the pace. He led her to the edge of the lake where a small boat stood. Orvyn handed her two oars. "Head east until the eastern wall is in sight. You will be in the market district. Ask for directions toward the Drucker House. You shall meet your friends there."

Savia did not have time to thank him as he was already on his way toward the castle. Savia hopped into the boat and began rowing.

Everard was running through the streets of Adhu Aqua alongside his pet ocelot, Yago. He only had one goal and that was to get out of the city. That goal was shortly extinguished when a pale yellow barrier formed around the entire city. Everard stopped in the middle of the street. He could hear people complaining as they walked around him. He was drenched in the storms of Adhu Aqua. He did not know why he had been scared.

Great Lord Jerial had passed on before he had even been born. A man that had no right to terrify him. But he heard the tales of that man. A man that was dangerously too smart for his own good. A man that stopped at nothing to get what he wanted. A hero to some and a menace to others. He remembered the joy the people of the capital spoke with when explaining his death.

The thorn in Meinspir's side had passed away. That was all they had said. How they had been wrong. Everard had been trembling. His presence was surely the catalyst for change in the Zidal Empire. A terrifying thought. Everard had left his room early in the morning only to be met with a horrifying image. Men with slit throats had laid out on the floor.

Their blood staining the carpets. Other soldiers had been decapitating the already lifeless bodies. Everard knew he had to escape the castle. So he ran, not looking back at the soldiers who called out to him. That's how he found himself here. With the announcement that was spoken inside his head complete, he knew that he messed up. He got involved with the wrong people.

He just tried to help. He couldn't watch and do nothing when he saw Florian dying in Chapman's office. They seemed at first glance like kind people, who would've thought he was travelling with one of the greatest casters. The big tidal wave made sense now, Alaric had help he was able to do it with the power of his father. I have to get out of here.

Florian sat alongside his sister in a spacious room. They were in one of the highrise buildings close to the eastern wall of Adhu Aqua. They had a good view of the city. He noticed Ashe had been looking out of the windows the entire time. The door to their room opened, he immediately turned his attention to the figure who entered. The man that escorted them here.

"Y'know I was surprised when Commander Orvyn asked me to escort you here, y'know." "Y'know Commander Orvyn does not speak much but he seemed in a weird mood, so I like had to help him y'know."

"Commander Orvyn?" Florian asked. "And where is here?"

Ballack nodded. "Forgot you are new to the city y'know. Commander Orvyn is the third commander of 'The Eyes'. Y'know the group of really, really strong casters y'know. A big, big deal he is y'know." "And you are in the main house of the Drucker family y'know. Also known as my house. Y'know my brother is a commander of The Eyes. Compared to him I am just a no-name y'know. That was why I was surprised when Commander Orvyn approached me, y'know."

The bombardment of information was giving Florian a slight headache. He was still struggling to recover from Jerial's attack earlier.

"Slow down, sir. I can hardly keep up." Florian said.

Ballack chuckled.

"What were Commander Orvyn's intentions?"

"Y'know he said that the Drucker family should keep you three hidden until he arrives y'know."

"Three? We are the only two here."

Ballack shrugged. "Y'know he said he was freeing a lady from the dungeon and she will arrive here shortly."

That must be Savia.

"And the boy?"

Ballack had been puzzled. "Boy? Y'know the commander did not mention a boy. He said there were only three of you, y'know."

Where in the world is Everard?

Florian glanced at Ashe who had still been looking out of the window. He followed her stare and noticed she had been looking at the castle this entire time. He placed a reassuring hand on her shoulder.

"Y'know what a crazy announcement earlier. Great Lord Jerial's resurrection has got the old heads excited y'know. I mean I get it but something is off about the whole situation y'know. Like something stinks, y'know."

"Y'know it is time for me to get you two some food. I'll be back later, y'know."

Florian nodded as the man made his way out. Ashe turned to him.

"What are we going to do?" She whispered.

"My idea might not be as good as Alaric's but I do have an idea." He did not wait for her to question him before he explained. "We have to use Commander Orvyn. We do not know if he is helping us or trying to kill us but as long as we are alive we have to use what we can." "Ballack said that Orvyn freed Savia from the dungeon. Which means Jerial had lied to us about her escaping. Orvyn went against direct orders by freeing her. Which means we might have an ally in one of the strongest casters in the city."

"But how are we going to separate Alaric from his father?" Ashe asked.

"I don't know...but we will find a way I am certain. Let's just wait for Savia."

"I am worried about her." Ashe continued. "Alaric seemed to be all she had. Did you not see how she looked at him? She adores him and now that was taken away from her."

Florian shook his head. "He is not gone just yet. He is fighting in there, I know it. Savia knows it as well.

It was late that night when Savia joined them with a determined look in her eyes.

CHAPTER 31

"Something is wrong," Cressela said. He sat behind her on the horse.

"I can feel it, there is an energy surrounding my city," Ivo said.

"More like a Phen barrier," Cressela replied.

What is happening?

"I hope the families are not causing issues again," Drustan stated behind them.

"Even if that sort of event occurred, I did not give permission to erect a barrier. There is something bigger going on." Ivo said.

"It couldn't be the same group of adventurers who attacked Isern, could it?" Drustan asked.

Cressela scoffed. "There is a big difference between Isern and Adhu Aqua. Those adventurers wouldn't have been able to set foot into the city."

"You got a point there, O Great Protector."

Cressela scoffed at the nickname.

"Let's make haste, we cannot waste any more time!" Ivo ordered.

"You heard the Great Lord!" Cressela yelled.

"Yes, Commander!" The soldiers exclaimed as the small squadron picked up their pace.

Ivo felt his horse pull to a stop. He had assumed they reached one of the gates to the city. Another reason he was certain of this fact was that he felt a familiar aura in front of them.

"Commander Gregory, it is not common that you are so eager to meet us," Ivo said.

"I was made aware of your arrival and thought it would be kind to welcome you back." Col retorted.

"How thoughtful." Cressela retorted.

While Cressela's relationship with Commander Drustan had been playful, her relationship with Commander Col had been hostile. Nothing he ever did could smooth it out. Cressela helped him get off of the horse. He steadily made his way to face Commander Gregory.

"While that seemed pleasant, you must be aware that it raises some suspicion." He said.

"I am well aware of that."

"Have you lost your honour, Commander Gregory? To whom are you speaking?" Cressela asked.

Ivo heard the man chuckle.

"Why is there a barrier around my city, Commander?" Ivo asked sternly.

"Just precautions, it seems that Meinspir is plotting an attack against us."

Ivo was taken aback by the news. He and the king were on good terms. Why would they attack?

"These are matters that we should discuss within private quarters. But still, you had no orders to erect a barrier." Ivo said.

Ivo turned back to where he assumed his horse was.

"There is more news, a man named Alaric is currently being held within the castle. He mentioned that he knows you." Col stated.

What happened when I was away?

Ivo struggled to hold back a smile. He felt Cressela's hand on his shoulder.

"Do not get your hopes up yet," Cressela whispered.

Ivo nodded as she helped him onto the horse.

The soldiers began to move but they were halted as Commander Col raised his hand.

"What is it now, Commander?" Cressela asked in a rude tone.

"I am afraid I have orders to only allow the two commanders and the Great Lord within the city walls," Col said.

"Orders from who?" Ivo asked.

"The Great Lord."

"Great Lord, The Gr-" Cressela was interrupted by Ivo.

"Very well, let us meet the Great Lord."

Col led Ivo, Cressela and Drustan through the barrier and the gates.

The streets of Adhu Aqua were more packed than usual. He tried to greet as many of the citizens as he rode.

"The people are too happy, you wouldn't assume they are the ones being trapped within the city," Cressela whispered.

"Someone must've reassured them somehow." Ivo kept his voice low.

"Commander Gregory?"

"No, he may be a high ranking commander but he has done nothing to win the trust of the people. It has to be someone significant."

"I knew the commander was ambitious but this is taking it too far, giving control of the city to another person."

"The person must have been good at convincing him."

"What of Alaric? He is a known figure among the aquians."

"Yes but most of the population is not fond of him for what he has done."

"He had done nothing, he was just a five-year-old kid." Cressela scowled.

"We understand that. And he couldn't convince the commander because..."

"He is a mysur, right?"

Ivo nodded.

Ivo knew that Cressela had been avoiding one name, the only person it could've been. Especially with the latest events in Isern.

They rode the rest of the way in silence.

He assumed it had been nighttime when they arrived at the castle. He could tell from the lack of aura he felt from the sky. He could normally feel the faint presence of Ysgafyn's twin. As the four entered the castle, servants arrived to dry them off.

Seems regular enough.

"Where shall we meet the Great Lord?" Ivo asked.

"In the throne room, of course. He had been waiting all day for your arrival." Col said.

Col led, Cressela walked in front of Ivo and Drustan took the rear. The loudmouthed man had been surprisingly quiet throughout the whole day.

"Is something wrong, Commander Drucker?" Ivo asked.

"It is the city, it feels...off. I don't know, maybe I am off." The young commander answered.

Ivo chuckled. "You are correct, the city is off. Keep a hold of those instincts, Commander Drucker."

"Will do, sir."

As they reached the highest floor of the castle their pace slowed. Ivo hated this floor, it was a reminder of his failures. Failure to protect Lady Argenta. Failure to protect Alaric. He never did any business within the throne room. He asked the servants to keep everything the same. He wondered if the paintings were still on the wall.

They reached the room and Col opened the door. Ivo was suddenly met with three new auras. Auras that were familiar to him. Without even feeling the aura in the middle before, He knew who it was. That intense aura was always only going to be one man.

Ivo was led further into the room.

"He turned his head to the left.

"Commander Orvyn."

He then turned his head to the right.

"Commander Hughes."

And then he faced the man in the middle.

"Master Jerial."

The man in the middle spoke. "You do not seem surprised to see me, Ivo" His voice sounded different.

"I have been made aware of your resurrection. I was surprised by it since I was the one who buried your remains. But now I am less surprised and more concerned." "Forgive me Master but you sound different than what I remembered."

His master laughed. "And you look blinder. I understand your concerns and we have much to discuss. Let's first discuss our similarities."

"You and Great Lord Ivo are nothing alike!" Cressela scoffed.

"Calm down Commander Beckett," Ivo ordered. Cressela went quiet.

"What similarities do you assume we have?" Ivo asked.

"We have both performed the creation ritual." Jerial seemed to be coming closer. Ivo felt Cressela move to stand in front of him.

"To create a cast one must sacrifice a part of yourself that is equivalent to the strength of the cast you want to create." Jerial continued. "You gave up your natural eyesight for something much greater. I have done something similar."

"What have you done?"

"I gave up my natural body for a new younger one. A cast that allows me to hop from one body to the next."

Ivo realised the meaning behind the words and clenched his fists.

"What have you done with Alaric? You would kill his mother and now him too?" Emotion had been raging in Ivo's voice.

Jerial laughed. "Did I kill Alaric? No, he still exists. Would you like to speak with him?"

Ivo nodded.

Jerial's aura changed and was replaced with a new aura. One he had never seen before. If Jerial's aura had been intense and threatening, the new aura was similar to Cressela's. It had been protective and calm. Alaric should not have an aura, he is a mysur.

"Ivo, get out of here. Leave Adhu Aqua-" It had been the same voice that emanated from his master earlier but this one spoke with more desperation.

"Al, I am sorry I couldn't save you," Ivo said.

The intense aura returned and Ivo knew that his master took control once again.

"That fool is really thinking about others while he is trapped." Jerial laughed. "And you apologising, quite humorous."

"Why?" Ivo asked.

"Simple, I needed a means to hide from the empire. At least for a few years as I formulated my plan. And immortality was just a bonus."

"You would sacrifice your son's life for a plan?"

The next word threw Ivo over the edge.

"Yes."

Ivo walked forward furiously. Col blocked him from Jerial. He heard the withdrawal of Col's broadsword.

"Commander Gregory put away your blade. It is not appropriate in front of our guests." Jerial's voice called out.

Ivo assumed Col listened due to the fact that he moved off to the side.

"Before things get rowdy, I called you here to make a proposition," Jerial said.

Ivo did not ask questions, he merely listened. He did not trust that he would be able to hide his anger. He noticed Cressela walking towards him and Drustan followed her.

Jerial noticed his silence and continued to speak. "Join me again as my right-hand man!"

Col attempted to interrupt but Jerial spoke over him.

"Join me and we can rule together once again. Just like the old days."

"And if I refuse?" Ivo asked.

"I will simply have to execute you. But I am a fair man, I will give you a day to make a decision. You can flee if you'd like but then I would spend my days executing each one of the Beckett family until you decide to return."

Ivo felt Cressela's aura flare at the revelation.

"I understand-" That is when Ivo noticed a small aura flaring next to his master's face.

"Drustan! No!" He yelled.

Jerial had given Ivo his ultimatum when he noticed a strange circle in the corner of his eye. He jerked his torso back just in time to see an arm brush past his face. He heard Ivo yell. He quickly gripped the floating arm. He looked towards where Ivo stood and noticed the young man to his side had only one arm. The other arm had been halved and attached to a red circle similar to the circle that the arm that attacked him came from.

"Spatial casts. Quite rare indeed. A Sio caster as a commander in Adhu Aqua, even more rare." He stated. Jerial's hand that had been gripped suddenly reddened. Steam emanated from his grip. He watched as the young man cried in pain. Jerial then released his grip. Ivo looked at the man with concern.

"You almost caught me off guard, young man. You seem to be quite talented. How about you join my ranks?" He asked.

"No thank you, I don't like to be ruled over by a dead man." The young man said.

Jerial laughed.

"Great Lord, should we punish them for their insolence?" A voice to his left said.

Jerial eyed the man. Commander Hughes. He was quite the irritation to Jerial. He had been a rather steadfast man who just spoke of his honour and justice. He was easily manipulated but he was rather boring.

"Commander Hughes, Commander Gregory withdraw your weapons. They have done nothing to warrant punishment." He said. He then turned to Commander Orvyn. "Orvyn, you should join them. You have been actively trying to undermine me."

Orvyn's eyes widened for a second before he nodded and joined Ivo's side.

Jerial looked towards Ivo who had been glaring at him.

"Choose wisely, Ivo." He mocked.

Ivo nodded at him.

Jerial smirked. His armoured boots shone green as he moved much faster than a regular person was able to. He planned to stop before Ivo but Commander Beckett forced herself before Ivo. Her gauntlet had a yellow glow and a large pale yellow shield protected her and Ivo. She was angry. Ivo placed his hand on her shoulder.

"You have some great subordinates, Ivo. They are willing to die for you."

Ivo scoffed. "Two days, give us at least two days."

"Not that it makes much difference but yes. Anything for my favourite pupil." Jerial smirked.

CHAPTER 32

It had been their third day staying with the Drucker family and Ashe still could not get herself to sleep. The family had been very welcoming towards them. Fed them and gave them each their own large room. There had been a few reasons why she couldn't sleep. First and foremost it had been Alaric.

She was worried out of her mind. To have no control over your own body must be terrible but to have no control and watch someone else commit atrocities using your body must be even worse. The second was their plan to free Alaric from his father's clutches or their lack of plan. Planning had never been their strong suit, they left that up to Alaric. Now they had to blindly place their trust in a commander who for all they know could have them killed.

And said commander hasn't even shown up to meet them yet. Well, that was not true, Savia did mention she had met him. And the last thing that plagued her mind was Everard. While she was not close to the boy, the fact that he had been missing for three days is alarming.

He did not seem to be someone who acted rashly...not true since he helped us. Ashe sighed into her pillow. Too much had happened for her to truly process everything. A rapid knock on her door had her scrambling out of her bed. She desperately wished it would be Alaric and that he would be back to normal. On the other side of the door had been Florian.

"We have been summoned," Florian said.

"By whom?"

"Great Lord Ivo."

"Then what are we waiting for, let's go." She hastily said as she pushed past Florian.

"Hold on a moment." Florian grabbed her forearm. "We should be careful, we do not know what he wants from us. He may be working for Jerial."

Ashe wriggled her way out of his grasp. "All the more reason to not keep him waiting." "Go on, lead the way."

Florian led her through the building to a large room that seemed to be a dining area. There was one large table with chairs all around it. There had already been five people sitting around the table. Savia had already been seated, she sat close to the exit far away from the other guests.

The man sitting at the end of the table intrigued her the most, his eyes seemed to be burnt shut but that did not stop the feeling she got from him. He knew her every movement. Next to the man with the burnt eyes sat a woman who seemed to be furious. She had short blond hair not too dissimilar to Ashe's.

She had a hard-edge to her look that Ashe could not pinpoint. On the other side to the seemingly blind man sat a man that was probably the oldest in the room. He had been bald and had a few wrinkles on his face. Closer to Ashe and Florian sat a young-looking man, he had looked somewhat familiar. All the new faces dressed the same way, they each had silver armour with green accents.

"Y'know you finally arrived, thought I had to search for you y'know," Ballack said as he walked up behind them. He closed the door behind the two leaving himself on the outside. The room was silent. Florian motioned for them to take a seat. They hadn't sat next to Savia choosing rather to sit closer to the armoured individuals.

"Now that everyone is present, we shall begin to introduce ourselves." The blind man started. "As you probably assumed, I am Great Lord Ivo. Well, it seems I have been dethroned." He went further to introduce his comrades. Once he was done, Florian spoke up. "My name is Florian, this is my sister, Ashe and that is Savia." Ashe attempted to keep a smile on her face. She noticed that the Great Lord had been smiling softly at them.

"Commander Orvyn had informed me that you three arrived in Adhu Aqua alongside Alaric. First, I would like to apologise for the truly terrible first impression of the city. And secondly, I would like to know how you all came to know Alaric." Ivo stated.

Before Florian could explain, she spoke. "He is my older brother. Please save him!" She knew it was a long shot but she had to try. Florian's hand found hers underneath the table.

Ivo nodded at her. "Trust me, I will do everything in my power to save him. But I need information. Now, from what I know Alaric's mother has...passed on and his father is well...you know. Therefore it is impossible for him to have blood relatives."

Ashe allowed Florian to explain the rest. He explained their upbringing on Diable Island, the sudden massacre of their village, their journey and restoration of Nezzagwyn, their rescue attempt at Versus and finally their operation to take down Chapman.

Throughout the entire story, most of the commanders kept their silence except for the one they had called 'Commander Drucker'. He had been making comments throughout and seemed impressed by their journey. Commander Beckett had to scold him for him to finally calm down.

"That was quite the journey. If not for the dire circumstances I might have detained you three on the spot." Ashe scowled at Ivo's comment.

"The man who raised you, you called him 'Priest Able'. He most probably abducted you from your parents just as he abducted Alaric." Ivo continued.

"That cannot be true he fed us, taught us and took care of us for years," Ashe said.

"I understand your position Lady Ashe but I am afraid it is the truth. Able Cornexia has been the most sought after man within the Zidal Empire for years. We believe him to be the leader of the Scaev." Ivo explained.

Can't be true. Everyone is lying. They have to be. Ashe had been trembling.

"If you have been living with Scaev it explains why Alaric has the ability to cast but enough about that. Can you tell me about Alaric?" Ashe assumed Ivo changed the topic because he could sense the downward spiral of the mood.

She couldn't speak, she hoped Florian could but he hadn't answered the question as well.

"He is strange," Savia said. She hadn't been looking at anyone; she kept her eyes focused on the wall that was opposite to her. Ashe heard Ivo chuckle.

"In what way Lady Savia?" Ivo asked.

"I cannot figure him out. He acts like he is the most knowledgeable person in the room at all times and it infuriates me. It infuriates me because he is probably right. His disregard for himself is the worst thing, he seems to want to protect everyone besides himself. He also never speaks about his problems, always saying rather cryptic things. And lastly, he is the strongest person I know. He is nothing like his father."

Ashe was impressed, Savia had never spoken that much before. Her knowledge of Alaric also impressed Ashe, she hadn't known him long but she was accurate. Ashe smiled.

"Sounds like he has become a remarkable young man." Ashe noticed the slight emotion Ivo's face showcased. He seemed happy, even emotional. He must care for Alaric.

"Tell me, Lady Savia. What is your relationship with Alaric?" He asked.

Ashe stared at Savia, who did not seem fazed by the question.

"He saved me from my hardships. That is all. I plan to do the same for him." Savia answered.

The answer seemed to satisfy Ivo who nodded.

"You all are probably curious about Alaric's history with the city and my relationship with him."

"Yes, we are. Alaric would never tell us anything." Florian said.

"Very well, I shall explain." Ashe heard Ivo sigh before he continued. "Due to Adhu Aqua being a large city, it was separated into five districts. Each district is run by a powerful family. Burchard, Beckett, Hughes, Drucker and Gregory are the five families."

"Why is this important to Alaric's story?" Florian interrupted.

"This is important to grasp the story." Ivo simply said. "The Great Lord is always chosen from one of these families. The strongest caster. That is until my rein."

"You are not part of the five families?" Ashe asked.

Ivo shook his head. "No, I was born into a lesser family. Jerial had already been the Great Lord once I had been ten. Jerial had been the head of the Burchard family as well, however, he was a bit rebellious. He summoned me to the castle once I had turned eleven, asking me to become his pupil due to my talent as a caster. My family rejoiced and encouraged me to accept. That was how I found myself training under Jerial."

"He was a cruel master, he beat me and scolded me but I dealt with it as I felt myself growing stronger. I thought he could not get any worse but then came the messenger from the Burchard family. They called for his marriage. Claiming he had to marry a woman from the other four families. Jerial did not take this news lightly. He was not a man of romance. Then he devised a plan. This was how I met Lady Argenta, Alaric's mother. She had been a mysur servant within the castle. Despite his cruel nature, Jerial seemingly had a soft spot for mysurs. He married her in secrecy and announced his marriage to his family. He kept the fact that she had been a mysur a secret, he claimed she had been from one of the lesser families. The only ones to know the truth were his commanders and me. Lady Argenta was a kind woman, despite her new position of power she treated us no different. She treated my wounds when Jerial got too violent within the training sessions."

"The Burchard family had been furious with Jerial's decision and tried to assassinate Lady Argenta on many occasions. Jerial's power was unrivalled however and kept her safe. I had thought Jerial had grown closer to Lady Argenta but those were foolish thoughts at the time. When I was fourteen, Alaric had been born. The city rejoiced as if it was the second coming of Heinzidal. They thought the boy born from Jerial would exceed his father."

"But they did not know he had been a mysur," Ashe said.

"Correct. Lady Argenta had been protective of Al, only allowing myself and Jerial to see him. I had grown quite fond of the boy during that time. Once Al could walk and speak he made his first public appearance with his father. He was paraded around the city. People already called him 'The Future Great Lord'. Alaric had been intellectual at a young age choosing rather to read and study with his mother than practising swordsmanship with his father. Lady Argenta tried her best to protect him from his father, but there were times when Alaric could not escape his father's training. It was cruel, Al had just been a toddler and Jerial had..."

Ivo did not have to continue, Ashe understood.

"Lady Argenta had been furious, I had never seen her that distraught in my life. That was when Jerial started to target her. All I could do was comfort Al through it all."

"One night when Al was five, Adhu Aqua had been attacked. Scaev, who appeared seemingly from thin air, was murdering the citizens. Jerial had ordered me along with the rest of his commanders to resolve the fight. At that point, I had already made my name as the second strongest caster in the city. I should have realised Jerial's odd actions. He had been someone who loved battle, a man that was forged on the battlefield. For him not to join the battle should have been questioned. That night as I returned to the castle, I found Lady Argenta had been killed. A dagger had been placed through her chest. Alongside her had been my master's body. He had no wounds but all the colour from his body was gone. He had turned into a husk. But finally, one person was missing from the castle. Little five-year-old Alaric had not been seen ever again."

"And the aquians blamed Alaric?" Ashe asked. There had been venom in her words.

"The people were looking to blame someone for the deaths of their loved ones. His sudden disappearance was the perfect excuse. I am not trying to defend the people, I am just asking for you to understand them." "With the loss of the Great Lord, the city was desperately looking for a new leader. What I hadn't known at the time was that Jerial had adopted me, causing me to be a member of the Burchard family. This had made me eligible for the position as I was the strongest caster in the city at the time as well. The tragic death of Great Lord Jerial and his wife Lady Argenta and the disappearance of their son Alaric became the catalyst for my ascension to Great Lord at nineteen years old. I had never felt like I deserved it and I had continuously searched for Alaric for the past sixteen years. I had not suspected him to turn up on my doorstep."

"If you truly cared for him, you would've found him," Savia said. Ashe saw the scowl on her face.

"Being the Great Lord there had been many-" Commander Beckett had tried to interrupt but Ivo waved her off.

"You are correct, I should have tried harder. That is the cold truth that I have to bear. That brings us to the current situatio n...but it seems the night has already gone too long. We should continue our discussion in the morning." The commanders got up from their seats and left the room. Savia was about to leave when Ashe's words halted her.

"Thank you, Savia."

"I haven't done anything yet." Her voice went back to the whisper.

"Your words meant a lot. I'm sure Alaric would've appreciated it."

"He'd better." Savia left the room. Ashe and Florian left shortly after.

Chapter 33

The following day the group found themselves seated at the same table. Cressela listened as Ivo explained the ultimatum he had received the previous day from Jerial to the newcomers. She never thought her hatred towards Jerial would get stronger. She had already hated him from the stories Ivo told her. The man spoke as if he had no consideration towards life. The man threatened to kill her family. The man uses his child for his gain. A truly despicable man. Ivo's speech broke her out of her thoughts.

"I will say this simply, we cannot hope to beat Jerial in a fight. He is the strongest Ilium caster to walk the land. He is a master swordsman and from what you have told me, he has obtained The Blade of Heinzidal."

"Why are we considering fighting? We just need to extract him from Alaric's body." Florian said.

Cressela watched how the two siblings had been much more relaxed and cooperative this morning as compared to the previous night. The other woman however, she could not get a read on.

"And how do you intend to do that?" Cressela asked.

Florian hadn't been able to answer.

"There is a method, however, it will require us to have a scuffle with him. Therefore we all should understand what he is capable of." Ivo waited for the rest to accept his words before he continued. "Amongst all of his casts, there are two specific obstacles we will have to overcome." Ivo lifted one finger. "Jerial specialises in incitatio. It is a special cast. He is the only one that was capable of performing it. He never taught it to anyone else as well."

"What does the cast do?" Ashe asked.

"It gives him the ability to accelerate or decelerate himself or the things around him. A frightening advantage for the ill-prepared. It has its disadvantages. He cannot affect anything that he cannot see." Ivo explained.

She thought back to the castle where she had barely blocked Jerial from Ivo. His speed was terrifying.

"Why not keep him occupied, he would not have time to cast," Florian said.

"Runic armour, ya goof," Drustan said.

She saw the confused looks on the siblings' faces.

The commanders showed their palms, while Cressela showcased her forearm. The runes that were placed there were grey. They only shine once a cast has been made.

She was not surprised by the lack of knowledge the youngsters showcased towards the armour. They had been sheltered their whole life on an island, with no awareness of the outside world.

"Brilliant inventions from the phen artisans in Arstutia. A piece of equipment that allows the ability to cast on a whim via runes. Each armour is specifically made for the wearer of said armour. It takes quite a long amount of time to manufacture therefore not everyone has access to such armour. Usually only reserved for Great Lords and their commanders." Commander Orvyn explained.

"That is correct. Occupying Jerial is not the worst idea, in a sense, we will be doing that." Ivo held up two fingers." The second issue is the blade he wields. Getting hit by that sword once will mean death. Jerial has two sources of stria which will make it easier for him to control. But that may be his weakness as well."

Ashe's face lit up as she realised what Ivo meant. "He does not have the same stamina that he would've had if he had been in his own body. Alaric has improved over the last six months however he is still not the most athletic at least compared to the rest of us," She said.

Ivo smiled. "That was something that I could not have been certain about. Thanks for clarifying Lady Ashe."

The young woman beamed at the Great Lord. Her enthusiasm rubbed off on Cressela who couldn't help but smile as well.

"That does not solve the problem of the blade being dangerous," Florian said.

"That is where I enter the fray," Cressela announced. "I am the only one at the table who can withstand a strike from that blade."

Ivo nodded. "But I would rather you not put yourself in unnecessary danger."

"This has been a snoozefest, can we just get to the plan already?" Drustan asked.

Cressela glared at the man.

Ivo chuckled. "Yes, let's get to the plan. The day following tomorrow, my commanders and I shall meet with Jerial at the entrance to the castle. Commander Orvyn and Commander Drucker will ensure they separate Commander Gregory and Commander Hughes from Great Lord Jerial. I, alongside Commander Beckett, shall face Jerial and try to hold him off."

"And the rest of us?" Florian asked.

"You three have the most important part. You will sneak into the castle and steal 'The Seal of Habbeo' from within the treasury." Ivo did not wait for questions to proceed with his explanation. "An artefact created by a previous king of the Zidal Empire known as King Habbeo. It is said to be able to seal catastrophe-level nixum. Whether it will work on Jerial is a gamble I am willing to take. He doesn't know that we have this artefact due to the recency of our discovery."

"It doesn't have to take all three of us to steal one artefact. I can stay and fight alongside you." Florian stated.

"I cannot have you die. How will I be able to look Alaric in the eyes ever again?" Ivo asked.

Florian did not look Ivo in the eyes.

"The castle will be filled with soldiers, therefore you three will have to be careful. I will explain the layout of the castle." Ivo went on to explain the intricate design of the castle and the best method to ensure the plan was foolproof.

Everard sat in a dark alley. He had been cold, wet and his stomach was in pain. He ignored the pain as he read the letter he wrote. He turned to Yago who had been sitting at his side.

"I will find a way to destroy the barrier. Once I have, deliver this letter to my father."

Everard placed the slightly damp parchment in the ocelot's mouth. Yago ran out of the alley, leaving Everard on his own. How did this happen to me? All I had asked for was to follow my dreams. Why couldn't you just give it to me?

"Hey, kid? What are you doing?" A voice called to his side.

Everard got to his feet to take a look at the soldier. "Take me to the walls."

"You must be the insane kid that was rumoured to walk the streets. Get some help before I report you to one of the commanders." The soldier said.

Everard walked closer to the soldier. "Take me to the walls." A whip wrapped itself around the soldier's neck. The soldier tried to yank the whip off to no avail.

"Take me to the walls!" Everard instructed a final time.

The soldier gave a weak nod. The whip around his neck loosened and curled around Everards left hand.

Jerial knew Ivo had a plan. It had come as no surprise to him when a letter arrived from Ivo. Ivo wants to make his decision in front of the castle, at first light. Jerial smiled. He would allow Ivo to perform whatever show he had planned. He was excited by the potential of something happening that he could not predict. He called Commander Gregory to the throne room.

"Lord Jerial? You have asked for me." Col said.

"Commander Gregory, send out a message to all soldiers within the city. There shall be no soldiers in active duty on the day we meet Ivo. They are ordered to not do anything regardless of what happens within the city. They are to stay away from the castle as well," Jerial ordered.

"May I ask why?" Col asked.

"No, you may not. Commander Gregory, you are dismissed."

Col reluctantly took his leave.

You better not disappoint me, Ivo.

CHAPTER 34

The rain this morning seemed no different compared to a regular day in the city. The rain had been different to Drustan. He hated the rain usually but this rain excited him. It was not common that there would be commotion within the city. This meant that while he had fulfilled his dream of becoming a Commander, he had become bored by the lack of work.

The Zidal Empire was supposedly at peace, Drustan would never get another chance to feel alive. He stood next to the only man that had his respect. Great Lord Ivo, the man that had given him a chance. A sio caster acting as commander is not rare unless you live in Adhu Aqua. A defect from Jerial's reign, ilium casters had been greatly favoured. It hadn't helped as Ilium casters were as common as flies.

Ivo had been speaking to Jerial. He would be lying if he said he was listening. He had barely listened to Ivo's story about growing up in the city and this kid called Alaric. He did not care all that much. What he did care about was the smug look on what was to be his opponent's face.

Commander Col Gregory, a nasty man. While they served together, they had never got along. Col had been too focused on making a name for himself and pushing himself to the limit. Drustan had been the antithesis, he had been happy with his position and happy to go on one day at a time. He knew Col had never liked since the first day he stepped foot into the castle.

Hell, no one seemed to like him. They claimed he was too lackadaisical and never respected the hierarchy. They had not been wrong. The one he was eager to fight had been Jerial. His arm still tingles from Jerial's attack. He was not going to ruin Ivo's plan, however. He had never seen the Great Lord this eager to fight and it exhilarated him. Getting tired of the preamble, Drustan decided to take action.

His right gauntlet shone with a light red glow and his forearm down to his hand had disappeared through a portal. His arm reappeared close to Col's face as he punched the commander. Col fell backwards. He was about to reconnect his arm when a gust of wind had been travelling towards him. I messed up. Spatial casts had been a special subclass of Sio types but it had a big weakness, it forced the caster to remain stationary or he risked his disembodiment.

The gust of wind was about to hit him when Commander Beckett intercepted it with her large shield. Her arm had glowed a pale yellow.

"Thanks, O Great Protector."

"Are you stupid? You could've gotten killed!" Cressela scolded.

Commander Beckett was usually strict with him but not in a bad way. They have always been on relatively good terms. He knew he irritated her. The look on her face shocked him. She had been terrified. She was sweating more than usual. How strong was that attack? He shook his head.

He just barely noticed Col running up to him. Col had his broadsword in his hand. Col's legs had a green glow. Drustan knew what to expect. He had sparred with Commander Gregory, Hughes and Orvyn. They usually used this cast. Col jumped into the air at a strange angle. His body found a foothold in midair and he jumped again towards Drustan.

He leaned back just barely avoiding Col's strike. Col's sword struck the ground. Drustan placed his left foot on the blade. He began chanting as he withdrew a throwing knife from his belt and tossed it into the sky. The knife flew through a portal. Instead of attacking Col let go of his sword and ran to the side.

This caused his throwing knife to have a new target, Drustan himself. He cursed as his right leg shone red. A stone spike shot up from before Drustan's foot and knocked the throwing knife off-course. He did not notice Col's strike until it was too late. Col swung his fist through Drustan's face. Drustan let out another curse as he was slumped to the ground.

Col let out a nasty laugh as he towered over Drustan.

"Always using tricks trying to catch your opponents off-guard. I never enjoyed your fighting style." Col said.

"You would normally not dodge, I guess Daddy Jerial taught you well." Drustan taunted.

He wanted Col to get angry, and it had been successful. Col immediately grabbed his sword. Col was about to strike when Drustan used his trump card. His entire armour glowed red as he fell through a portal. He had never put his entire body through a portal before, he did not know what to expect.

It certainly was not this. It was bright, the sky had been blue and white dots were sprinkled over the sky. He noticed a large white pillar before the scene disappeared. He tumbled out of a portal and his body bumped into an object. His armour went back to the original colour. He had his back against Col's who had stumbled forward.

Drustan reached over his head and found Col's neck. He gripped tightly on Col's neck and began lifting him. It was awkward, Col had been struggling and to lift someone over your head was not an easy task. He cast a stone spike in front of him. He lifted Col all the way and the stone spike pierced Col's torso.

It was quick, as soon as his body was struck by the spike it had been done. Commander Col Gregory had been killed. The only emotion Drustan felt was relief. He had been confident before the battle, that confidence was erased during the fight. He had been exhausted but he had one more task to fulfil. He had to help Ivo fight Jerial. He was about to move towards the fight when Jerial's face was in front of him. Jerial had one hand on Drustan's abdomen and one around his neck.

"Well done, taking care of that fool. I should thank you but no matter how irritable he was, he was still my subordinate." Jerial said.

Drustan's torso began heating up. The pain was unbearable. His body had been on fire. All he could do was scream.

Jerial's smile was the last thing he saw as darkness engulfed his entire being.

Chapter 35

Savia, Florian and Ashe sat in a small boat as they rowed across the giant lake. Ivo informed them to use the same route Savia had when she had escaped the dungeon. The journey was silent bar the sound of the water and the rain. No one dared to say a word, no one dared to look each other in the eye. Mornings were strange in Adhu Aqua, the city made no sound.

No animals, no people. This day was even stranger as the barrier that surrounded the city seemed to disappear. Ivo warned them that they could not worry about that currently as they all had a bigger task ahead of them. They embarked before first light, they desperately had to get the seal to avoid casualties.

That was not true for Savia, she desperately had to get the seal to save Alaric. Ivo had told them that the treasury was found on the second-highest of the left wing of the castle and that the Seal of Habbeo will be inside a golden chest with green accents. The trio arrived at their destination.

They allowed her to lead the way. She hastily found the entrance that Orvyn had shown her. As she entered the familiar dungeon, she gripped her daggers. She noticed that Ashe had held her spear a little bit tighter and Florian had his hand on the hilt of his blade. She stuck close to the wall as she navigated them out of the dungeon. There had been no soldiers. They entered the lowest above ground level of the castle. The atmosphere felt different. Savia frowned. Ashe seemed to pick up on her change of emotion. "What is wrong?" She asked.

Savia did not answer.

"The castle is different. It is too quiet. We have not seen a single soldier yet." Florian stated.

Savia nodded.

"Is that not a good thing?" Ashe asked.

"It is either we are incredibly lucky or they know we are here and are planning to ambush us," Florian answered.

Savia headed forward. She peeked into a few rooms. There was not a single soul on the first floor of the castle. She heard a faint scream. It seemed to originate from the outside of the castle. By the looks on their faces, Ashe and Florian heard it too. She immediately headed for the stairs, not bothering to check the other floors, she made her way to the second-highest floor. There was not enough time to worry about a potential ambush. She turned around to her comrades. "Go help Ivo."

"What no- " Florian tried to argue.

"I am fine on my own. I am a thief, I am accustomed to stealing. If there is an ambush waiting for us, it is better if I get caught alone. It means the game is not over yet. Please, this ordeal is done if Jerial kills the others." Savia explained.

Florian frowned, Ashe grabbed his wrist and began descending the stairs.

Savia began sneaking to the left side of the floor. There had been no one on this floor either. She had expected that there would be soldiers guarding the treasury but there had been none. She found the inconspicuous door to the treasury. There had been a slight issue. The door had been slightly ajar. She tightened her grip on her daggers as she took a peek inside. The room was large. Shelves lined the walls and various objects had been placed along the shelves.

There had been podiums with glass cases placed atop. There must have been hundreds of different artefacts, weapons, books and whatever the Great Lord deemed was important enough to store. Along the right side of the shelves, stood a figure clad in all black. Savia could not see a face. She scanned the room for any other enemies but found none. Alaric's teachings played in her head once again.

You will not win a battle of strength. Try to restrain movement and aim for the kill. Savia wouldn't cast, she did not want to accidentally destroy anything in the room. She quietly slipped into the room. The figure did not notice her yet. She sneakily made her way behind the figure. She would aim for the neck. She raised her dagger to strike when a gloved hand caught her wrist. A swift kick to the stomach and another to the chin had her stumbling backwards.

The figure turned to her. Its face had been completely covered by a mask. The mask was black as well and did not seem to have an opening to see through. How does he see? It did not continue its assault, turning its focus back to the shelves. It seemed to be searching for something. Savia chose to charge again. It attempted another kick, she anticipated it and dodged.

She grabbed its collar attempting a throw toward the ground, An athletic masterpiece occurred. The figure caught itself by placing its hands on the ground. It placed its boots under her arms and tossed her across the room. Savia landed on her back, it had been painful. She could not give up now, he was counting on her.

She stumbled to her feet to see the figure analysing the shelves once again. She took off her cloak, it left her in a sleeveless shirt that had been buttoned to her neck. She could taste blood between her teeth. She let her hair loose. She then tossed her discarded cloak into the figure, who hadn't anticipated it.

She used the moment of distraction to close the distance between them. She lowered her body to the ground and kicked its feet out from under it. It made no sound as it hit the floor. As Alaric instructed, she wasted no time and stabbed it in the torso. She was about to stab it with her other dagger when a fist met the right side of her torso. The punch was powerful. Much more than a regular punch. It resulted in her being flung across the room and crashing into the shelves. The pain was enough for her to blackout.

Savia did not know how much time had passed when she woke up. Her entire body was in pain. She recognized her daggers. They were strangely placed alongside her. In front of her had been a golden box with green accents. Her memories flooded back as she hurriedly looked around the room. Her cloak had been on the floor but other than that there was no one else in the room. She grabbed the golden box and opened it.

Within the box was a golden cuff bracelet that gave off a strange glow. She knew it was what she was looking for from the description she received from Ivo. She quickly closed the box and grabbed her daggers. She had no time. She had to get to him. She limped out of the room. Every movement caused her body to ache. It took a lot of willpower to reach the castle gates. After many stumbles, she had finally made it. The scene before her caused her to freeze. It had been horrifying.

Chapter 36

As she had been quite a distance in front of Florian. She had always been faster than him. She skipped two stars at a time as she made her way to the castle gates. It took a while to reach the entrance. The castle, like everything she experienced in the city, was huge. Her first impressions of the city had been positive but as she stayed longer she realised she hated the city. It had only brought her torment. She was eager to get out of the city.

Her eyes widened at what she found at the castle gates. Far to her left Commander Orvyn had been slumped to the ground; his neck seemed to be bleeding profusely. Next to Commander Orvyn was a man who she did not recognize. He had been dressed in the same armour like the other commanders. His face had seemingly melted off of his head. It was a terrifying scene.

The man had been lifeless, unlike Commander Orvyn who seemed to be slightly breathing. Far to her right, she noted that Commander Col Gregory had been pierced through the torso by a large stone spike. Close to him had been Commander Drustan

Drucker whose abdomen was leaking blood. Both had not been conscious.

The closest person to her had been Commander Cressela Beckett who had one knee on the ground. She was panting heavily. She had a cut above her eye that forced her to close it. She had a mace in one of her hands. She was staring ahead of her, not noticing Ashe's presence. Ahead of Cressela stood Ivo.

He had no visible injuries and he had not seemed as exhausted as Cressela. He had a light sheen of sweat on his skin. He held a strange-looking sword in his left hand. It had been made of black metal. It had been shorter than regular swords but its shape was what made it special. It had been narrow at the base but increased in width at the tip of the blade, it was angled upwards as well. A few paces away from Ivo stood Jerial.

The man who had stolen her older brother away from her. He had his back facing her. He held a squirming figure in his right hand. She moved to get a better look. She wished she hadn't. Jerial had been choking Everard. Everard's feet had been dangling off the ground as he struggled against Jerial's hold.

His whip had been unnaturally squirming on the ground as well. She had to do something. She aimed the tip of her spear to line up with Jerial's thigh. She chanted quietly as her spear shot forward, growing in length. She had not expected Jerial to anticipate the attack. Her spear struck.

Florian caught up to Ashe at a horrible moment. He watched as her spear extended and struck Everard through the chest. Jerial avoided the attack by using Everard as a shield. Everard immediately began coughing up blood. Ashe had been frozen.

Florian shook her shoulder vigorously for her to finally break her trance. She recalled her spear.

The blade of her spear had been painted crimson. Jerial dropped Everard, who crashed like a ragdoll on the ground. In a split second, Jerial was in front of both of them. He readied a strike with his blade when a green rope twisted around his wrist and yanked him backwards. Florian noted that the green rope originated from Ivo's right hand. Jerial was dragged along his back for a short moment before the rope snapped. Jerial got back to his feet.

"Seems like this has become quite the party. But aren't we missing one?" He asked mockingly.

More green rope shot out of Ivo's hand, the rope wrapped itself tightly around Jerial. Florian chose to use the opening to charge Jerial with his blade. As soon as the ropes attached to Jerial his entire armour shone a pale green and the rope snapped. He lifted his right hand towards Florian.

Nothing had changed was what Florian thought. His mind felt regular but it had been his body that was affected. He was moving incredibly slow. The rain around him came down at a regular pace. He saw a smirk appear on his brother's face as he flicked the crimson blade. A gust of wind came rushing towards him. At the last second, Cressela leapt in front of Florian. Her pale yellow shield blocked the attack. Florian felt his motor functions returning to regular speed. He had almost crashed into Cressela. Jerial had been suddenly in front of her. She cast another shield.

"How long are we going to do this?" Jerial punched at the shield with his right hand. The shield shattered. Another punch caused Cressela to crash backwards into Florian.

"Commander Beckett, you cannot block everything. A veteran such as yourself should-" Jerial was cut off by an attack made by Ivo. Cressela rolled away causing Florian to be free.

"Did you get the seal?" She asked.

"Savia should be bringing it," Florian answered. "She should be here by now."

"I do not think we can last much longer. He is a monster." Cressela got to her feet and headed towards the fight. He glanced over at Ashe who sat on her knees. She had been crying, she occasionally rubbed the tears away with her hands. Her eyes were transfixed on Everard's body.

She was in no state to fight. Florian heard someone call his name but it had already been too late. He felt something placed at the back of his hand. His face was forced onto the ground. His face burned as his head was pounded over and over into the ground. His face had been a bloodied mess until finally, he lost consciousness. The last voice he had heard had been Alaric's laugh.

Chapter 37

To say that Ivo was confident would be truly and utterly false. He had no idea how this was going to play out. He had spent every waking moment thinking about how to fight this fight. His 'eyes' made casts useless against him. His master will be forced to fight him physically. Despite years of training, he was certain that Jerial had still been better than him at sword fighting.

Ivo brought his dao blade, it was his favourite weapon and got one custom made from Arstutia. There was another problem with fighting his master. He did not want to hurt Alaric. He would be forced to hold back. You just have to stall. Ivo walked alongside Cressela, Drustan and Orvyn. The journey to the castle gates had been a silent one. At the castle gate stood Jerial, to his sides were Commander Gregory and Commander Hughes. Ivo stopped causing the rest of his group to stop.

"Have you made your decision, Ivo?" Jerial asked.

"Yes, I have. However, I am not sure you will like it." Ivo retorted.

"I am certain I would enjoy whatever you decided on."

"Is that so?"

"You have always been intriguing, Ivo. You ever wondered why I took you in all those years ago?"

Ivo shrugged.

"You had the potential to become even stronger than me. A frightening concept to most but to me...it had excited me. Alas, you have wasted my time. You could not get rid of your guilt. That can change if you choose to stand once again by my side."

Ivo was about to respond when he sensed the stria build up close to Commander Gregory. Too soon Drustan. He did not have time to scold him as Jerial already attacked. Ivo saw Cressela's aura block the attack. Commander Hughes' aura flared but he was intercepted as Commander Orvyn attacked. Ivo gave up his natural eyesight for something he had thought was much better. The ability to sense stria was useful.

It allowed him to avoid casts that were meant to harm him. Everyone's stria had a different feel, Ivo called it aura. It was also how he could tell people apart. This ability granted Ivo the nickname 'The Eyes'. Due to him seemingly having the ability to see while being blind. Ivo unsheathed his blade and rushed Jerial. He could tell the moment Jerial was about to cast by the flare of his aura.

Ivo's boots went green as he cast step, an ilium cast that allowed the user to make platforms out of air. He hopped into the air and changed direction, narrowly avoiding Jerial's cast. Ivo used the chance to aim a strike at his master. Auras were shaped like a silhouette therefore he could accurately aim his strikes. He aimed to strike the knee however his blade was stopped by something he couldn't sense. Ivo predicted it was

Jerial's sword by the way his aura's hand was positioned. Once Jerial's hand began flaring, Ivo immediately backed away.

"I understand how your new eyes work now, Ivo. It seems fighting you would be more of a pain than a challenge." Jerial said.

"Have you lost your touch, master? You reacted a little late to my strike."

Jerial scoffed. "Still growing accustomed to my new set of bones, you see."

Ivo watched as Jerial's aura flared and he jumped to the side. No cast was made, instead, his master turned to Cressela. He tricked me. Jerial accelerated towards Cressela, who could only manage to block. One attack went through her guard and caught her above the eye.

The cut had been shallow due to her dodging at the last moment. Ivo held out a hand and a green roped emerged from his palm. It moved towards Jerial but he had been too fast. Jerial was on Commander Drucker in no time. The commander's armour could not withstand the heat that emanated from Jerial's palm. Ivo could just watch as his commander and friend screamed in pain. Drustan was tossed to the floor. His aura faded slowly.

"Have I lost my touch? Certainly not," His master said.

Jerial had not looked as exhausted as Ivo hoped. Jerial accelerated towards him, instead of dodging he relied on his reflexes to parry the attack away with his blade. He parried a few more attacks when Cressela interrupted their duel. She swung her mace towards Jerial who could not get away in time. His master fell to one knee clutching his side. Cressela was going for another blow, she aimed for his head. Can't allow that. Ivo blocked her mace with his blade. Jerial's aura flared and he disappeared. A scream to his left. Jerial held Orvyn by the neck, with a sudden flare the usually stoic commander had been screaming. Another comrade fell.

"He is too strong, Ivo. We need to kill him." Cressela pleaded. We can't. I can't.

"Just focus on defending me." Ivo retorted.

He watched as Cressela's aura changed, her silhouette gaining a shield on her left arm.

Jerial did not accelerate towards them, he walked slowly. He is affected by the overuse of stria.

Thus began the dance of blades. Ivo did not need to parry or block attacks, Cressela blocked any attacks Jerial threw at them. Ivo could not hit Jerial who was dodging and parrying his blows masterfully. It was a stalemate. Ivo knew his time was running out, Cressela did not have an infinite supply of stamina to keep up. Ivo was given a reprieve when a boy approached the scene.

"Jerial the Merciless! You will die by my hands!" The boy yelled out. Ivo felt as if he had seen the boy's aura before but he could not quite place it. In the boy's hand had been a whip-like aura that seemed to be moving wildly. Ivo could not stop Jerial as he accelerated towards the boy. He stopped in front of the boy. The boy raised his hand to attack with the whip but nothing occurred. The whip would not touch Jerial.

His master laughed as he grabbed the boy by the throat. He couldn't hear the words Jerial whispered to the boy. The boy dropped the whip and it began squirming on the ground. A familiar aura could be sensed but he did not pay it any mind. Jerial turned around suddenly. A spear shot past Ivo's vision and pierced the boy through the chest. The boy's aura was flaring instead of fading. Jerial tossed the boy to the ground. Ivo turned to see the auras of Ashe and Florian. Jerial's aura flared and Ivo acted immediately as he yanked Jerial away with his rope.

After Florian fell, despair hit Ivo. He had been the only one left. After Jerial's latest attack Cressela could barely stand. She would be useless in the fight. All the possible options Ivo could take had been going through his mind. He only had one option. Survive, hope for a miracle. He stood face to face with his master, both had their blades drawn. The rain seemed to have become heavier as the battle continued.

"Just like old times," Jerial said.

"Just like old times." Ivo echoed.

Sword fights had become more difficult with the loss of his eyesight. He had to predict his opponents moves by their subtle movements. It was how he kept himself alive against Jerial. His master attacked continuously and vigorously. Each blow more powerful than the next. He caught Ivo on the cheek and on his arm. Ivo did not hold back as well between parries; he reciprocated the intense energy. Still he could not land a definite blow on his master. The fight continued as their blades met each other between the falling drops of rain.

Ivo was exhausted, he could tell his master was too. Jerial aimed his blade at Ivo's chest. Ivo moved his blade to intercept. Jerial's aura suddenly flared. A sword had been attached to his silhouette. He could not react in time. His blade broke and a blade pierced his chest. It was over. He felt Jerial's aura changed.

Alaric felt empty. He could no longer struggle anymore. He watched as his body dispatched everyone who opposed him. He saw the terror in Ashe's eyes as he used Everard to shield himself against the attack. It broke his heart. He watched himself pound Florian's head into the ground repeatedly. Blood pooled around his brother's broken face. At the end it had only been him and Ivo. He could feel his father's emotions. He had been elated. Ivo fought gallantly but it had not been enough. Wind wrapped around the crimson blade as it shattered Ivo's blade and pierced his chest.

Jerial relinquished control.

Blood poured from Ivo's mouth. There had been blood on his own hands. Ivo smiled softly at him. Alaric heard someone screaming, it sounded like Cressela. Ivo pushed the blade further into his chest until his body had reached the base. Alaric had been sobbing. He could not formulate any words. Ivo placed his arms around him in an attempt at a hug.

"I...am...sorry...I...couldn't save...you...Al." Was Ivo's final words as his body went limp.

Alaric felt his father trying to regain control, he knew he couldn't stop it. In his torment he never heard the figure that approached him. He felt a sudden tightness around his wrist.

He had been drowning one again. It was a familiar scene but this time there had been two of them. He had been alongside his father. His father smiled at him. A deep growl turned Alaric's attention away from Jerial.

Three large red eyes stared at them. Its pupils had been shaped like slits. Alaric could faintly see black tendrils through the dark water coming towards him. Alaric did not try to get away. He was going to allow the tendrils to take him away. Instead, he got pushed away, Jerial intercepted the black tendrils and got pulled towards the large eyes. Alaric's last sight had been his father smiling at him.

EPILOGUE

A she stared at the ceiling of her room. She had not left the room since the battle. Seven days had passed. She hadn't received any injuries, not physical ones at least. She couldn't bring herself to go to Great Lord Ivo's burial. The day after the battle news spread throughout Adhu Aqua. it mentioned every detail of the battle and of the severe losses.

Commander Beckett had been given the role of temporary Great Lord. After the battle, she was brought back to the Drucker family house. The family fed her and allowed her to stay for as long as necessary. Ballack Drucker arrived every day to give her updates on the health of her siblings and friends.

She was made aware of Alaric who had slept for three days. He had not said a word to anyone. Florian was still alive, his face however required many treatments which the Drucker family was happy to provide. He should make a full recovery. Savia suffered a few injuries but none was particularly severe. Everard was the last person she wanted to think about. They told her it was a miracle that he had still been alive.

He kept himself alive with a healing cast. He could not heal himself completely, all he could do was not allow himself to die. Ballack mentioned that he requires another means of healing that could not be found in Adhu Aqua. Commander Drucker and Commander Orvyn had not regained consciousness, they suffered severe wounds to the abdomen and neck respectively.

There was a knock on Ashe's door. She slowly rolled out of the bed and walked over to the door. She knew who to expect. As she predicted Ballack stood outside her door. He had a smile on his face as usual. It seemed nothing could faze Ballack.

"Y'know, you have been summoned to the castle. Great Lord Cressela's orders, y'know."

She was about to speak when he spoke again.

"It is urgent." His tone had been serious for a second but he went back to smiling.

Ashe nodded. She grabbed her robe and spear and followed Ballack. He led her to a carriage. Savia, Alaric and Florian had already been there. Savia seemed the same to Ashe. She wore her cloak with the hood pulled tight, she stood close to Alaric.

She also kept her eyes focused on him. Alaric wore his sleeveless robe as well. His eyes were back to their regular colour but he seemed distant. He had a bracelet attached to his wrist that had a purple glow. The Seal of Habbeo. Florian's face had been wrapped up, his eyes found hers as she arrived.

He had the crimson blade strapped to his back. They all wordlessly entered the carriage. Their journey was silent. The entrance to the castle had been pristine. There had been no signs of the battle that took place there. They were brought into the castle and escorted to the top floor.

The first time Ashe walked through these halls they had been decorated with carpet and paintings. This time the walls were barren, the carpet gone. Every step echoed through the halls. They reached the throne room and entered. Cressela Beckett sat on the throne. The only injury the woman showcased was the scar above her eye. They stood before her in a line.

"Before I get to business there is something I would like to inform you upon." She started. "Commander Drucker, Commander Orvyn as well as the Everard boy will be transferred to Meinspir. There they will be getting treatment from the Desano." Noting the lack of response she continued. "Onto the reason I summoned you here today. I was placed in charge as Great Lord of Adhu Aqua and as such I have a responsibility to protect my citizens and ensure their future. It is because of this that I ask of you four to respect my wishes." She paused for a bit.

"Lord Alaric Burchard"

"Lord Florian Cornexia"

"Lady Ashe Cornexia"

"And Lady Savia."

"You are hereby exiled from Adhu Aqua." Cressela's words did not contain any malice. Ashe could tell it was a difficult decision but it was one that had to be made. The citizens were aware of Alaric and they were rightly afraid.

"Any objections?" Cressela asked.

No one spoke a word.

"Then you are dismissed."

Ashe turned towards the exit.

"Before you leave, Lord Alaric, may I have a word with you?"

Alaric turned back to Cressela as the rest left the room.

They had waited for Alaric outside of the throne room. After a few moments, Alaric joined them.

Florian broke the silence. "Where shall we go next?"

Alaric did not make eye contact with anybody and spoke. "Cognizance."

Godric sat on his throne as Dalton's replacement entered the room. He was a middle-aged man with long brown hair cut weirdly. The sides were bare but the top had been long enough to sit below his shoulders. The man's hair was combed backwards.

"We have received a letter from Lord Everard, Your Majesty." His steward said.

Godric raised an eyebrow.

"Shall I read it aloud, Your Majesty?"

"No, Anselm. Hand it over so I can read it." Godric responded.

Anselm did as he was told and handed the letter to him. Anselm then left the room. He waited for his steward to leave before he opened the letter.

Dear Father

I have escaped the attack at Isern. I am now travelling alongside four other casters. I am safe but I do not know for how much longer. There is one caster of particular intrigue. His name is Alaric Burchard and he seems to be the son of Jerial the Merciless. What intrigues me even more is that Jerial seems to be living within Alaric. We are currently in Adhu Aqua. I encourage you to send your army, I know of your wish to eradicate Jerial. There is another problem, I obtained a whip from Lord

www.ingramcontent.com/pod-product-compliance
Lightning Source LLC
Chambersburg PA
CBHW070432170726
48291CB00002B/464

* 9 7 8 1 9 4 4 2 5 3 1 8 9 *

Chapman but it makes me feel strangely. I am scared, Father. I hope you arrive soon.

Love

Everard Adalbert

Godric folded the letter and called for Anselm once again.

"You have summoned me, Your Majesty?"

"Call all Meinspir soldiers, we are marching towards Adhu Aqua. Tell them to prepare for war. We leave at first light." Godric ordered with a smile. Jerial, I finally have my opportunity. You will not escape death this time.

Anslem nodded and left the room.

It has been too long. The Zidal Empire will change forever.

The arduous journey has just begun.